PRAISE FOR
The Runaway McBride

"A charming romance . . . Thornton displays her usual deft touch,
effortlessly combining delightful characters with an intriguing
mystery!"   —*Shirlee Busbee, New York Times bestselling author*

"A fantastic new series. *The Runaway McBride* has everything a reader wants and so much more . . . Ms. Thornton has
a one-of-a-kind historical romance full of action, passion,
mystery, and suspense that will have readers running back for
more. I was mesmerized by *The Runaway McBride*."
                                    —*Fallen Angel Reviews*

AND FOR ELIZABETH THORNTON AND HER NOVELS

"A writer of extraordinary brilliance."   —*Romantic Times*

"An Elizabeth Thornton historical always provides a powerful, entertaining, nonstop reading experience."
                                    —*Midwest Book Review*

"An unforgettable tale."   —*Booklist*

"As multilayered as a wedding cake and just as delectable."
                                    —*Publishers Weekly*

"Exhilarating Regency romantic suspense."
                                    —*The Best Reviews*

Berkley Sensation Titles by Elizabeth Thornton

THE RUNAWAY MCBRIDE
THE SCOT AND I
A BEWITCHING BRIDE

A Bewitching Bride

Elizabeth Thornton

BERKLEY SENSATION, NEW YORK

THE BERKLEY PUBLISHING GROUP
Published by the Penguin Group
Penguin Group (USA) Inc.
375 Hudson Street, New York, New York 10014, USA

Penguin Group (Canada), 90 Eglinton Avenue East, Suite 700, Toronto, Ontario M4P 2Y3, Canada
(a division of Pearson Penguin Canada Inc.)
Penguin Books Ltd., 80 Strand, London WC2R 0RL, England
Penguin Group Ireland, 25 St. Stephen's Green, Dublin 2, Ireland (a division of Penguin Books Ltd.)
Penguin Group (Australia), 250 Camberwell Road, Camberwell, Victoria 3124, Australia
(a division of Pearson Australia Group Pty. Ltd.)
Penguin Books India Pvt. Ltd., 11 Community Centre, Panchsheel Park, New Delhi—110 017, India
Penguin Group (NZ), 67 Apollo Drive, Rosedale, North Shore 0632, New Zealand
(a division of Pearson New Zealand Ltd.)
Penguin Books (South Africa) (Pty.) Ltd., 24 Sturdee Avenue, Rosebank, Johannesburg 2196,
South Africa

Penguin Books Ltd., Registered Offices: 80 Strand, London WC2R 0RL, England

This is a work of fiction. Names, characters, places, and incidents either are the product of the author's imagination or are used fictitiously, and any resemblance to actual persons, living or dead, business establishments, events, or locales is entirely coincidental. The publisher does not have any control over and does not assume any responsibility for author or third-party websites or their content.

A BEWITCHING BRIDE

A Berkley Sensation Book / published by arrangement with the author

PRINTING HISTORY
Berkley Sensation mass-market edition / November 2010

Copyright © 2010 by Mary George.
Cover art by Aleta Rafton.
Cover design by George Long.

ISBN: 978-0-425-23780-9

BERKLEY® SENSATION
Berkley Sensation Books are published by The Berkley Publishing Group,
a division of Penguin Group (USA) Inc.,
375 Hudson Street, New York, New York 10014.
BERKLEY® SENSATION and the "B" design are trademarks of Penguin Group (USA) Inc.

PRINTED IN THE UNITED STATES OF AMERICA

10 9 8 7 6 5 4 3 2 1

A
Bewitching
Bride

One

Gavin Hepburn stood at the edge of the dance floor and took a small sip of champagne as he watched, with some amusement, the rowdy antics of the wedding guests who were going through the motions of a Scottish reel. They were celebrating the marriage of Juliet Cardno to Henry Steele, the man who had been courting her for the last six months. Henry was the proprietor of the hotel on the outskirts of Ballater in the Highlands of Scotland, where the reception was being held. Most of the guests were from Aberdeen or Edinburgh, and some from as far afield as London. Not all the rooms were taken, but one guest had been assigned a cottage some way from the hotel, on the edge of the moor, to accommodate his inseparable companion, his dog, Macduff. Dogs were not allowed inside the hotel. Gavin was the guest who owned the dog.

It was late in the evening, and fiddlers were sawing their instruments as if they were foresters felling trees in a race against time. The dancers on the ballroom floor—most of the gentlemen in kilts and the ladies with tartan sashes—were twirling their partners in a wild dervish and letting out ear-piercing shrieks as the spirit moved them.

The shrieks put Gavin in mind of Macduff, who could howl like a banshee when the spirit moved *him*. It was just as well that they'd been banished to an estate cottage. It was no hardship. The cottage was primitive but not uncomfortable and was within easy walking distance of the main building. Besides, he needed a rest from the rigors of the social whirl. That was another reason he'd returned to the Highlands and, in particular, to this stretch on the river Dee. When the queen was not residing in her castle in Balmoral, Deeside became a quiet backwater, as it had been before the royal family made it famous. It was also the land of his birth.

Here, he hoped to do a little introspection as he tramped over the windswept moors and climbed the lower ranges. But something else was at work in him. He possessed the gift of second sight, and though he could not see the future clearly, he knew that in this moment in time, he was exactly where he was supposed to be. He was about to embark on something that was extremely dangerous. He didn't know what, but he knew that before long, he would be given a sign.

His gaze traveled that vast interior, formerly the great hall of a hunting lodge that had once belonged to the dukes of Fife. It was massive in comparison to his own comfortable lodge that nestled on the other side of the river but built in the same mold. Antlers and stag heads abounded, as did paintings of hunting scenes. He wondered how long it would take Juliet to change everything to suit her own taste.

He considered himself a lucky man. It might have

been he who had drifted into marriage with Juliet. It would have been the wrong thing to do. She deserved better than a man who could not offer her his whole heart. Besides, he had no desire to be made over, and he was sure that in another twelve months, the happy groom would hardly know himself.

His gaze shifted to take in the guests, but he ignored the lures that many a lass cast in his direction. He knew better than to trifle with the daughters of the local gentry. Should he be so unwise, their fathers or brothers might well lead him to the altar with a gun in his back.

One young woman caught his eye, not because she was a beauty or had presence, but because she seemed to be the odd one out in this crush of guests. *Arresting* was the word that came to mind. He didn't recognize the lady, but he recognized the cut of her gown. Only a first-class designer could have fashioned such an exquisite work of art. It was simplicity itself, a gray silk with a white lacy bodice. The House of Worth, he thought, or perhaps a competitor. He'd paid for many such gowns in his time.

As though she felt his gaze, the girl turned her head and looked directly into his eyes. He felt a buzz pass through his brain. For a moment or two, he was completely disoriented. Words formed inside his head: *Are you the one?* Is this what had brought him back to the Highlands? Was this slip of a girl the key to his visions? *Are you the one?* he silently demanded. After a moment, she seemed to come to herself and dragged her eyes away.

"Will," Gavin said, addressing the gentleman standing beside him, "who is that young woman in the gray dress, the one standing just inside the entrance doors?"

Will Rankin looked in the direction Gavin had indicated. "That's Kate Cameron, Iain Cameron's daughter

and Juliet's friend. She and Juliet went to school together."
He shook his head. "They're an odd lot, the Camerons;
unconventional is what I mean. Kate is the youngest, but
you'd never know it when they're all together. She's the
sensible one."

"You seem to know the family well."

"No, not really, apart from Kate. She and some other
girls did volunteer work at the Aberdeen clinic as part
of a school project, but she is the only one who has kept
up with my clinic since she left school. She has a way
with outcasts and misfits, so I'm always happy to see
her." He raised his voice. "I can hardly hear myself
think for the din. Let's find a quiet nook where we can
converse like civilized people."

They wandered into the hallway and found a nook
beneath—what else?—a magnificent mounted head of a
stag. A roving waiter was at their table before they had
settled into their leather chairs. They relinquished their
champagne glasses and ordered whiskey, but only if it
was single malt and had been distilled on Speyside. It
had. This was, after all, a first-class hotel.

Gavin could not tear his mind from the girl in the
gray dress. *Was she the one?* The words flowed and
ebbed inside his head. He needed more than one look
from those intense brown eyes before he was convinced.

Will clapped Gavin on the shoulder. "I think," Will
said, "that Kate Cameron has made quite an impression
on you. Do you know what I think, Gavin?"

"No, and I don't want to know."

Will laughed. "I think it's time you came out of
mourning and began to live again. I will say this. You
put on a good show. But Alice has been gone five years
now. You can't live in the past." The smile left his face.
"But leave Kate alone. She's not for the likes of you. I'm
telling you this for your own good. She has cousins who

would break your arms and legs if you were to hurt their little chick. Then there's Dalziel."

Gavin avoided the reference to Alice and picked up on the reference to Dalziel. "Your man of business? Does he have a proprietary interest in Miss Cameron as well?"

"He doesn't confide in me, but I know that his intentions are honorable—not like some I could name."

Gavin was amused. "Good God, Will! You make me sound like an out-and-out Lothario. I'm not a hunter, just the opposite. It's women who lay traps and snares to catch me."

"Just remember her cousins should you ever be tempted to let her catch you."

Gavin lounged in his chair, stretched out his legs, and studied his friend. Will Rankin was a big man, easily above six feet, and built like a Highlander who was in training for the Braemar Games. Ruddy cheeks, red hair, and his ease in wearing the kilt reinforced that impression. Nothing seemed to disturb Will's zest for life, though he'd seen his share of tragedy. He was the director of a clinic in Aberdeen that ministered to paupers and misfits and owned another clinic in Braemar for long-term patients. However, Will wasn't interested only in healing sick bodies. He was also interested in healing minds and was one of those new doctors called *psychiaters*. His patients loved him, but he was scorned by the rank and file in his own profession.

Gavin did not scorn his friend's obsession for probing the minds of those afflicted with mental illness. There were times in his own life, such as now, when he wondered whether *he* was a little touched in the brain. If he was, it was his granny's doing. Lady Valeria McEcheran had been a fully fledged witch who, on her deathbed, had passed her formidable gifts to her three grandsons, but Gavin had never been a true believer. There were episodes he could not explain, but nothing like the visions that had plagued his dreams in the last month.

Like a true connoisseur, Will swirled a mouthful of whiskey before swallowing it. "I was hoping," he said, "that you and Juliet would make a match of it. What went wrong?"

"Nothing went wrong." Gavin gave a careless shrug. "I'm fond of Juliet—more than fond—but we've known each other forever. I look upon her as a sister."

Will grunted and was silent.

A moment went by, then another. Finally, Gavin said, "I'm sure that you didn't invite me out here just to pass the time of day. What is it, Will? What's troubling you?"

Will looked away. "It's probably nothing at all. I don't want to open a Pandora's box when all I have are suspicions but no solid evidence."

Gavin straightened in his chair. "Evidence of what?"

Will began to look uncomfortable. "I shouldn't have said anything. I don't want to draw attention to my clinic or have my patients' names splashed in all the papers. They have suffered enough."

When Will was silent, Gavin said, "You can't stop there. At least tell me what kind of crime we're talking about."

"Murder," replied Will bluntly, and he exhaled a long breath. "Three people connected to my clinic have died in mysterious circumstances in the last month. If it was murder, I think I may know who the killer is. I'll be on the train tomorrow for Aberdeen. There's someone there I want to speak to before I go any further with this."

When Gavin tried to speak, Will cut across his words. "That's all I'm prepared to tell you for the moment. Gavin, I can't make unfounded accusations."

Impatience gave Gavin's voice a sharp edge. "Then why drag me out here and refuse to confide in me?"

Will gave a short, mirthless laugh. "Damned if I know, except that I feel better, knowing that you are aware that I'm afraid for the welfare of my patients. Look," he went on, interrupting Gavin yet again, "I'll know more in a day or two, and when I do, I'll tell you everything. All right?"

And more than that he would not say.

The reception began to wind down when the bride and groom left the ballroom to take the carriage that would convey them on the first step of their honeymoon. They weren't going far that first night, only to the bride's home on the other side of the Ballater Bridge. The mother of the bride was to stay on at the hotel to give the young couple a little time to themselves.

There were no sentimental tears from Mrs. Cardno. "At long last," she said, raising her voice above the babble of well-wishers, "I've finally managed to launch my daughter. I feel like spreading my wings, embarking on an adventure or," she poked Kate in the ribs, "perhaps I shall take a lover. There's not much mischief a woman can get up to when her grown daughter is always looking over her shoulder."

"Mother!" Juliet scolded, and she rolled her eyes. In an undertone to Kate, she said, "You know that she doesn't mean it."

"Who says I don't mean it? If you'd known me in my prime, Juliet, you wouldn't be so complacent." To Kate, Mrs. Cardno added, "Listen to the words of someone who has seen a bit of the world, my dear. Time is precious. Make the most of it."

Kate nodded and smiled. She liked Juliet and her

mother enormously, in spite of Mrs. Cardno's outrageous tongue. In her mind's eye, she saw them as clear and refreshing as a mountain spring. Her own family was more like dragon fire. In her memory, she had never attended a Cameron wedding where a brawl had not broken out.

Juliet's voice dropped to a whisper. "Remember what I told you about my cousin Gavin. Well, he's not my cousin exactly, but near enough as makes no difference. He has a roving eye, but he has had his eye fixed on you all evening."

Kate remembered Gavin Hepburn very well. She and her friends were all enthralled with him when they were gawking schoolgirls. He, of course, was an older man and didn't notice their existence. Oddly enough, there had been a moment there, when she'd thought that he posed some kind of threat to her. The hair on the back of her neck had risen alarmingly. She had the instincts of a creature of the wild and could sense danger a mile off, but when she'd looked into his eyes, the prickling sensation at the back of her neck had stopped. She still didn't know who or what had caused it.

Juliet wasn't finished yet. "Don't be taken in by his looks or his charm. He's not interested in marriage."

"Sounds as though we're made for each other," Kate quipped.

"Just be on your guard. Don't say you haven't been warned."

Juliet's sisterly advice ended in a screech when her groom swooped down and carried her off to the waiting carriage. A light snow had begun to fall, and everyone hurried inside. The fiddlers started up again, and more sets formed for the next country dance. Kate spent the following hour renewing old friendships with girls she'd gone to school with but who had not been raised in the

Highlands. They were Lowlanders from Aberdeen and were enthralled with the handsome young men in their kilts whose soft accents and gentlemanly manners put them in a class by themselves.

It was all good fun, because most of the girls in her crowd, with the exception of Sally Anderson and herself, were married, and some of them had children. This was not how they had planned their lives when they were a close-knit fellowship of girls on the brink of womanhood. They'd all met when they had attended a newly opened progressive girls' school in Aberdeen. They'd seen how their mothers spent their days, cutting flowers in the hothouse, attending frequent tea parties with other ladies, and doing charity work to fill the long hours, and they'd wanted none of it.

Universities, at least some of them, were allowing women to take their entrance examinations. Things were changing. They could be anything they wanted: scholars, doctors, lawyers, explorers . . .

Their fathers, sadly, were not as progressive as the school they'd sent their daughters to, and it took a great deal of money to send a child to university. She and her friends had no money of their own, so here they were, several years later, following in the footsteps of all the women who had gone before them.

She was already regarded as an old maid. An old maid by choice, she reminded herself firmly. She had made up her mind to it a long time ago. So why was she so restless? Mrs. Cardno's careless words echoed inside her head. *"Time is precious. Make the most of it."* So what did the future hold for a girl like her? She was still dwelling on that thought when she came face-to-face with the subject of Juliet's dire warnings.

Juliet had not exaggerated Mr. Hepburn's appeal. He looked like a character who had stepped out of one of the gothic novels she used to read as a girl. He could not be the hero, because the hero always had blond hair and was a vapid sort of creature who waited in the wings to save the heroine in the nick of time. Mr. Hepburn looked like the kind of man who would lead a girl into trouble, like the dastardly villain who had base designs on the heroine's virtue. As a girl, it was the dastardly villain who had captured her imagination, and she had always wondered what those base designs might entail.

"It's Miss Cameron, is it not?" the villain said. "I'm Gavin Hepburn, Juliet's friend. I can't think why we haven't met before."

"I rarely come into Ballater," she replied, "and from what Juliet has told me, I understand it's the same for you. You live in London, don't you, and come here for the fishing season?"

"I'm a rolling stone, I suppose, footloose and fancy-free. But the fishing on Deeside is one pleasure I never miss. It's not just the fishing. It's Deeside in springtime. There is nowhere else I'd rather be."

Her first impression of Gavin Hepburn began to fray around the edges. There was more to him than his reputation suggested. He loved Deeside. She knew exactly how he felt. But Juliet knew him better than she did, and where there was smoke there was bound to be fire. He was a dangerous man because he saw every woman as a challenge.

Balderdash! She was the predator here. If Mr. Hepburn knew what was going through her mind, he would take to his heels.

She made a jest of her reply. "You're a rolling stone, and I'm a stay-at-home. Maybe that's why our paths have never crossed."

People were passing them and going around them to get to the stairs, forcing them to move closer.

Gavin said, "We have another mutual friend, Will Rankin."

"Dr. Rankin?" She could feel her smile begin to waver. He was too close, too perceptive.

"He tells me," Gavin went on, "that you've visited him at his clinic in Aberdeen and have taken an interest in his patients in Braemar."

She felt her neck stiffen with tension. Why was he asking about the clinics? As naturally as she could manage, she said, "The clinic in Braemar is not far from my home. I do visit there, not that I'm much help. The patients get so few visits, you see. Any friendly face is welcome." She didn't like this turn in the conversation and put an end to it by holding out her hand. "I'm very happy to have met you, Mr. Hepburn. Perhaps I shall see you at breakfast."

He startled her by clasping her hand when the custom was for a gentleman to touch a lady's fingers. She was very glad that she was wearing gloves and hoped he hadn't noticed that her hand had developed a tremor, not because she was attracted to him, but because he was asking too many questions.

Having ended the conversation, she picked up her skirts and hurried up the stairs. Gavin watched her for a few moments, then pulled up his collar and left the house. Macduff, he knew, would be having a great time exploring every nook and cranny of his new hunting ground.

Once outside, he put his fingers to his lips and emitted a shrill whistle. No sign of Macduff. He tried again. A moment later, a huge sheepdog bounded out of the gloom and hurled itself at Gavin's feet. The dog stared up at Gavin and began to whine.

"What is it, boy? This isn't like you."

Gavin sank down and ran his fingers over Macduff's

heavy coat. "No scratches or limbs broken," he said. "What is it, Macduff? Why do you whine?"

Macduff stopped whining and gazed steadfastly up at Gavin.

Gavin straightened. "Come!" he commanded and immediately struck out along the path that led uphill to the edge of the moor where his cottage was situated.

The snow was falling thickly now, which wasn't unusual for this time of year. It wouldn't last. In a day or two, it would turn to slush. With a little luck, however, it might turn into a full-blown blizzard. That would cut Ballater off from the rest of the world and give him time to get to know Miss Cameron better.

As he trudged up the hill, he sifted through all the little flags that had caught his interest.

Are you the one? That wasn't a little flag. It was more like a firework bursting into flame inside his head. Could he trust his psychic power after neglecting it for so long? The real question was, now that it had found him, would it leave him alone?

Then there were Will and his clinics. Will had suspicions but no solid evidence to bring a murderer to justice. Miss Cameron was connected to the clinics, too. Will had spoken of her so naturally, so warmly, that Gavin was convinced that she was not Will's suspect. According to Will, she had a way with outcasts and misfits. Will, his clinics, a murderer, Miss Cameron—how were they connected?

It took him a good ten minutes to reach the cottage. He opened the door to allow Macduff to enter, but Macduff was not there. Gavin whistled; he cursed and shouted Macduff's name, all to no avail. Macduff, evidently, had found something more exciting than this lonely cottage on the moor.

When he entered the cottage, he had to push the door

shut. A wind was getting up. He could hear it whistling in the chimney stack and rattling the windowpanes. Outside, snow was piling up on the windowsills.

There was one small flag he had overlooked. For reasons beyond his comprehension, Miss Kate Cameron had caught his interest, not only as a magnet that attracted his psychic powers but also as an intriguing female in her own right.

The thought brought Alice to mind. Her vibrant beauty had stopped his heart when he'd first caught sight of her riding in Hyde Park. Her vibrant looks were matched by a vibrant personality. Naturally, she attracted men like moths to a flame. He hadn't even tried to infiltrate her group of admirers, knowing that he didn't stand a chance. All that changed when they found themselves sitting side by side at some pretentious musicale in Lady Tinsdale's music room in her house in Mayfair. They'd caught each other's eye and had both started to laugh. It had gotten so bad, they'd had to excuse themselves and leave the room. And from that night on, they had become inseparable.

Alice was a daredevil and had found her perfect complement in him, or rather, he suppressed his misgivings because Alice did not take correction easily. Her guardian was indifferent to her comings and goings and allowed her free rein. And he had indulged her, too, giving in to her every whim. If Alice wanted to attend a risqué masked ball, he readily agreed to be her escort. Curricle races, bathing in the sea, climbing the peaks in Derbyshire—Alice was up for anything, and so was he.

Everything changed the day they went sailing on her guardian's yacht. They were the only two guests. It began to be borne in on him that there was more to it than a pleasant afternoon of sailing. Alice had set the scene with meticulous care—a picnic lunch on deck and champagne to go with it. She was obviously anticipating a proposal of marriage, and he didn't know why he couldn't say the words.

He remembered the sun was shining; there wasn't a cloud in the sky, and the waves that lapped the side of the yacht were gentle and unthreatening. He had tried to imagine life with Alice for the next five, ten years, and the prospect gave him pause. Alice and her temper tantrums? Alice and her odd fits of unbridled jealousy over trifles? Alice and her steely determination to get her own way?

But those were the quirks of character that made her such an exciting companion. He didn't want to lose her. He just wanted to make sure that they knew their own minds. Or so he had told himself.

He had taken her hands in his and said seriously but gently, "Let's not rush things. Let's get to know each other better before we take that irrevocable step. I'm not thinking so much of myself but of you. I'm a boring fellow. What if you tire of me in another month?"

Would he ever forget what happened next? She had jumped to her feet and, before his startled eyes, stripped down to her underthings. "I'm going for a swim," she said, cold as ice. "When I get back, I want you gone—out of my sight and out of my life, you fainthearted bastard." Then she had climbed onto the rail and jumped into the water.

It was the last time he saw her alive.

He tensed for the guilt that never failed to grip him when he thought of the accident that had claimed Alice's life. It was there, simmering below the surface, but tempered now by the passage of time. He couldn't blame Alice for being Alice. He blamed himself for being blind to her faults.

Kate Cameron did not possess Alice's fire. All the

same, there was a restrained sensuality about her that he found oddly appealing. But that was only a first impression. When he looked into her grave brown eyes, he sensed . . . not fragility. She was anything but fragile. *Lonely* was the word he wanted.

So much introspection was making his head ache. He shrugged out of his clothes and climbed into bed. *Are you the one?* The words became a litany as he drifted into sleep.

Two

The snowfall during the night caused quite a stir at the Deeside Hotel. The trains weren't running, carriages couldn't navigate the slippery slopes, and the only way to get about was to walk. Before the storm hit, canny travelers had changed their plans, and now the hotel was filled to capacity with paying guests. There weren't enough servants to see to the influx, and dinner had been a prolonged affair.

A long, boring affair, Gavin thought. He was searching the crush of people for a sign of Miss Cameron. He'd seen her enter the dining room with a group of young women, young marrieds by the sound of them, but somehow she and her friends had slipped away unseen.

"We shall just have to make up our minds to the fact that we may be marooned here for the next day or two," joked Mr. Massey, one of the paying guests. He beamed benignly at the group of card players who sat around several tables in the dining room. Now that dinner was over, and there was nowhere for guests to go, they had turned the dining room into a parlor to accommodate everyone.

"It's no hardship for me," Mr. Massey went on. "I'm retired. My time is my own, and I like nothing better than to pass the time in pleasant company."

He was a big, silver-haired man, on the heavy side, and spoke with an Edinburgh accent. His fellow card players might have forgiven the gentleman's origins had he not been winning every hand.

He'd told the company that he'd hoped to take the train to Braemar to look up relatives with whom he'd lost touch over the years, and had had the shock of his life when the stationmaster told him that the train went only as far as Ballater.

"He told me," said Mr. Massey, frowning down at his cards, "that I'd have to hire a carriage to take me the rest of the way. That seems strange to me. Why does the line stop here? It's only what—another few miles to Braemar?"

"Eighteen miles, according to the desk clerk," his wife answered. She was the opposite of her husband, thin to the point of scrawny, and the lines on her face were not laugh lines. She was ensconced in a chair by the fire and occasionally glanced over at the card table where her son, Massey junior, was also engaged in a game of cards. It was the younger Massey who was footing the bill for this ill-fated holiday in the Highlands. Without looking up, Mrs. Massey said, "The train stops at Ballater at the queen's pleasure." Her voice was subdued and respectful.

Someone added provocatively, "Her Majesty doesn't want visitors gawking out of train windows as they pass her estate. God only knows what frolics our royals get up to that would shock lesser mortals such as ourselves. At any rate, the queen always gets her way, so the natives of Braemar make do with horses and carriages."

Mrs. Massey bristled and glared at the speaker.

Her husband laughed.

The squire and his lady, Gavin thought. One was the salt of the earth, though a trifle uncouth, and the other was a cut above him, or so she liked to think. He was sitting close to the fire, too, pretending to read a book, but that was only a device to indulge his favorite pastime: people watching. He kept looking at the entrance, hoping that Kate Cameron would put in an appearance. They'd done no more than exchange a few inconsequential words the other night, and he was determined to pick up the conversation where it had left off. It was imperative that he discover whether or not she was the one he'd been called to save.

Something whisper-soft touched the nape of his neck, and he smoothed it away with his hand, an involuntary movement that he was barely aware of, but all his senses were on the alert. Something in this room was out of kilter. What was it?

Will Rankin joined him, and Gavin moved over on his comfortable sofa to make room for his friend.

"You'll have to look to your laurels, old sod," Rankin said in an undertone. "Young Thomas has cut you out with the girls."

Gavin's gaze flicked to the object of Rankin's aside. It was true. Thomas Steele, the groom's younger brother, was the center of female attention. He stifled a yawn.

Needling his friend, the doctor went on, "He's young, handsome, charming, and comes into a tidy fortune when he comes of age. He's also a true Highlander. What more could a woman want?"

"A man?" Gavin replied without much interest. "Young Steele is only a boy."

Will smiled and nodded at the lady on the other side of the blazing fire, Mrs. Massey, who had looked up with a question in her eyes. "You must be very proud of your son, Mrs. Massey," said Will, raising his voice. "I was telling my friend that he has taken over at the helm of his late uncle's—um—publishing firm, has he not?"

Mrs. Massey's stern demeanor dissolved in a simpering smile. Her flat chest puffed out. "Gordon deserves his success," she said. "He was always a hard worker." Her fond gaze moved to her son. "His uncle relied heavily on his judgment."

Gavin hardly spared Gordon Massey a glance. He was more interested in his friend's problems. "So, Will," he said, "you missed your train this morning?"

"No trains running, I'm afraid."

"What about the problem you mentioned? What will you do now?"

"There's nothing much I can do until the trains are running again." He shrugged. "I wish that you would forget I ever mentioned it. The more I think about it, the more bizarre it seems. Accidents do happen, and I'm coming to believe that's all they were, accidents."

Gavin might have said more, but his friend was borne away by the young widow McCrae to make up a four at her card table. No sooner had his friend vacated his place on the sofa, when it was taken by Mr. Fox, another of the hotel's paying guests. Gavin swallowed a sigh. He'd had the misfortune to sit beside Mr. Fox at dinner, and he'd heard enough about the former headmaster's views on the younger generation to last him a lifetime.

Mr. Fox said solemnly, "I could not help but see, Mr. Hepburn, that you and that doctor fellow had a lot to say to each other."

"We've been friends for a long time," Gavin allowed. He didn't like the tone of Mr. Fox's remarks. In fact, he didn't like anything about Mr. Fox, from his highly polished boots to his too-tight neckcloth.

"He's a psychiater, I believe?"

"He's a doctor," Gavin replied. "Some of his patients suffer from . . ." He searched for the right word.

"Dementia?" Fox supplied.

"I was going to say from a nervous condition. Dr. Rankin has had some success in treating them."

"Really?" said Fox. "Do you know what I think, Mr. Hepburn? I think that Dr. Rankin has discovered an easy way of making money out of his patients' misery. In another twenty years, we'll look back on the medical profession and call this the age of humbug."

Gavin rarely lost his temper, but Fox's unprovoked attack on the character of a man who had given up a lucrative practice in Edinburgh to work in the slums of Aberdeen, the city of Will's birth, was more than he was willing to tolerate.

He got to his feet. "Excuse me," he said abruptly. "I believe I'm being invited to play cards."

He left Mr. Fox red-faced and sputtering. His own anger didn't show on the surface, but it seethed inside. Will Rankin was like a brother to him. They'd known each other since they were infants, when they'd caught minnows in the shallows of the river Feugh where their parents had summer homes. Over the years, catching minnows had graduated into catching salmon. To this day, fishing in the Feugh or in the Dee was a mutual pleasure that neither was willing to forgo. Even though their paths had diverged, they always managed to spend a week or two in the summer months on the banks of their favorite haunts.

A flash of memory passed through his brain: Will, seeing Maddie, his future wife, for the first time as she crossed the stepping-stones on the banks of the Feugh to get to the other side. Will had waded in to help her and had stepped right into a pothole and fallen flat on his face. Now Maddie was gone, and Will directed all his energies and his once considerable fortune to the clinics he had opened in Maddie's memory. To belittle his achievement was tantamount to declaring war as far as Gavin was concerned.

"Gavin!" a feminine voice called out.

Janet Mayberry waved him over to the card table. She'd been hounding him from the moment he'd arrived, and he'd thanked his lucky stars that he was domiciled a good half mile from the hotel. Janet was an indoors girl. She was afraid of dogs, and where he went, Macduff was sure to follow. Dogs had their uses, he thought ruefully.

"Mr. Massey has had enough of cards," Janet told him. "And we need another player."

She had bedroom eyes, a bedroom voice, and a heart that was impervious to love: just how he liked his women, but not tonight.

She pulled on his wrist and pushed him into the chair that the younger Massey had vacated. "Hearts are trumps," she said, and she dropped her lashes in a parody of modesty.

Because he wasn't a boor, he picked up his cards and pretended to study them. If he wanted to, he could win every hand, but no one liked a player who could never be trounced. Besides, it wasn't skill on his part. He barely paid attention to the cards. He was a seer of Grampian. If he won, it would be just like cheating.

He was feeling it again, a whisper-soft brush on the back of his neck. Something was wrong. Not everything was as innocent as it appeared on the surface. His eyes scanned the guests. Nothing stood out. Everything seemed normal. Will, he noted, seemed to be enjoying himself. The widow McCrae, a fresh-faced lass, would have suited Will just fine, had his heart not still belonged to his wife. But even Maddie's death had not blighted Will's spirit. It made him all the more determined to make his life count, and Maddie's as well.

He answered absently to something Miss Mayberry had said, but his thoughts had moved on to Kate Cameron. Was she a distraction, or was she the one?

"Gavin!" Miss Mayberry remonstrated.

Gavin blinked, picked up his cards, and pretended to concentrate.

Kate couldn't remember when she had enjoyed herself more. She and her old school friends had cloistered themselves in Sally Anderson's bedchamber, knocking back sherry as if it were water, as they reminisced about the scrapes they'd gotten into when they were schoolgirls. From there they'd moved on to the ups and downs of married life, and her friends had tried, without success, to bring blushes to her cheeks. They were out of luck, she told them. Her work with Dr. Rankin's patients had robbed her of her innocence. They thought she was joking, but she'd told them the truth.

They had no success with Sally, either. She was soon to announce her engagement to Cedric Hayes, Lord Aberfeldy's grandson. It was a match made in heaven, so Sally averred. On her marriage, she would come into her fortune. When his grandfather died, Cedric would come into his title. What could be more romantic than that? After the marriage, they would go their separate ways and live happily ever after.

Sally's outrageous humor had them all in stitches, but when Kate stopped laughing, her mood changed. Sally had had a brilliant future ahead of her. At school, she was the top girl. How could her brilliant prospects have come to such a dreary conclusion?

From Sally, her reflections moved to Janet Mayberry.

Janet had never been part of their group. They were schoolgirls in uniform, and Janet had been the envy of their adolescent hearts. She was the belle of Deeside whose parents had indulged her to a degree. She believed that an education was wasted on women. No one envied her now. She was an aging belle who had allowed the bonnets to pass her by while waiting for a top hat to come along. She lived in Perth, but whenever she visited her old home, she was always included in whatever was going. Mrs. Cardno saw to that.

Poor Janet. Her eyes had fairly feasted on Gavin Hepburn from the glimpse Kate had taken of them at the reception. Or perhaps her commiserations were premature? Janet had the tenacity of a predator.

The party was still going on but, because she'd begun to feel chilled, she excused herself and went to her own room for a shawl. She'd forgotten about her maid.

"Elsie, are you still up?"

The girl was only sixteen or so, and fresh off the farm. She usually worked in the kitchen, but her heart was set on becoming a lady's maid. This was her first try, and she meticulously followed every rule she'd read in *Mrs Beeton's Book of Household Management*. Mrs. Beeton's book was as revered as the Bible in Kate's house and read far more often.

"I canna go to my bed until you go to yours, Miss Kate. I have to help you undress and press your gown for the morn."

"Nonsense! I'm not the queen. I can dress and undress myself." The thought of Elsie's unskilled hand pressing her gown was alarming. The gown didn't belong to her but to her sister. "I'm only here for my shawl, then I'll be going back to party with my friends." Her eye was caught by an envelope on her bedside table. "What's this, Elsie?"

Elsie shook her head. "I must have dozed while I

waited for you. When I opened my eyes, that letter was on the carpet, just inside the door."

"Off to bed with you, then."

While Elsie slipped quietly from the room, Kate slit open the envelope with a pair of embroidery scissors she'd placed in the table drawer by the bed, then held the note close to the oil lamp to see it better. And a vise closed around her heart.

"In Scotland we burn witches," she read.

She didn't know how long she sat there in a stupor. It was a knock on the door that brought her to her senses. She gave a start and jumped to her feet.

Sally's voice. "What's keeping you, Kate?"

She wasn't going to tell anyone about the note except Dr. Rankin. He was the only one who knew her secret. Had he shared it with someone else?

The doorknob rattled. "Kate?"

Through the door, Kate said, "I think I've had too much to drink, Sally. I'm going to sleep it off."

Her mind was in too much of a whirl to make sense of what Sally said next, but she heard footsteps retreating along the corridor and heaved a sigh of relief.

She read the note again and again, and each time she read it, her nerves grew tighter and tighter. It was a lie. She wasn't a witch. She was a normal girl who had an uncanny ability to sense danger, much like a creature of the wild. Isn't that what Dr. Rankin told her?

Of one thing she was sure. This wasn't a joke. This was the threat she had sensed pervading the very air she breathed all evening. She could not, would not settle until she'd spoken to Dr. Rankin.

She put the letter back in its envelope and debated for a moment what she would do with it. She had to talk to Dr. Rankin. He would know what to do. She was sorely tempted to throw it on the fire. In the end, she thrust it in her pocket and left her chamber, carefully locking the door behind her.

Gavin sensed her presence the moment she entered the dining room. She was in the same gray gown that she'd worn at the wedding reception and earlier tonight at dinner. She wasn't the only lady who was forced to wear the same gown two nights in a row. Most guests expected to be home by now and had packed accordingly.

A smile briefly touched her lips, and he turned his head to see the lucky recipient of her favor. He might have known it. Thomas Steele, or Prince Charming, as Will called him, shook off his retinue of female admirers and quickly crossed to her. Her smile was fleeting. Thomas's smile hinted at intimacy. Gavin watched them with brows drawn as they exchanged a few words. He was on the point of getting up and joining them when she turned from Thomas and began to wend her way toward him.

So she did know he existed. A smile warmed his lips.

"Mr. Hepburn," she said, doing no more than acknowledging his presence before she moved past him to the next card table where Will Rankin was seated. There was a short conference, then Will got up and escorted Miss Cameron to the hothouse at the back of the dining room. They were in earnest conversation, and Will looked as though he'd received a blow.

"Gavin, pay attention!"

Janet Mayberry's eyes fairly bored into his. "Sorry," he said and arranged the cards he'd been dealt. He played out his hand and won the set just to please Janet. When he next looked for Kate Cameron, she was nowhere to be seen, though Will was still with the widow McCrae, looking as jovial as ever.

What in Hades's name was going on? If there was something between Will and Miss Cameron, why hadn't Will warned him off? But he had warned him off. He'd been too obtuse to see it.

He picked up his cards and glared at them.

Three

The clock on the mantel struck the hour, startling Kate from her reveries. It was time to keep her appointment with Dr. Rankin. There had been too much noise and too many interruptions earlier that evening when she'd tried to speak to him, so they had arranged to meet later, when the staff doused the lamps and guests were forced to retire for the night. All was quiet. The house seemed to have settled into its nightly mode.

He'd particularly asked her to bring the note. After folding it and thrusting it into her pocket, she scooped up a tartan shawl and slipped soundlessly from the room, then locked the door behind her. There was no need for her to carry a candle. The hotel was not in complete darkness. On every floor, a lamp was lit, but there were enough shadows to conceal her from the porters who patrolled the corridors.

Her steps slowed when she entered the dining room. There were no lamps lit here, but it hardly mattered. In the dark, she could see as well as a cat, and she moved soundlessly to the little hothouse without bumping into a single chair. "Dr. Rankin?" she whispered. There was no response, but she smelled the faint odor of tobacco smoke. Then she felt it—a draft of cold air from the French door that opened to the outside. Evidently, the doctor had gone outside to enjoy his smoke.

Her hand curled around the note in her pocket, and she slowly withdrew it. She would be glad to give it into Dr. Rankin's keeping. It made her ill to think that some warped mind could hate her so much.

She pushed through the door and hesitated. "Dr. Rankin?" she quavered. The fear she felt was natural, she told herself. It had nothing to do with her sixth sense. Then why didn't Dr. Rankin answer her? Something else filled her nostrils . . . the smell of strong spirits? Whiskey?

When the door behind her clicked shut, her whole body contracted. The door could not be opened from the outside.

Easy, she told herself. *Easy.* Maybe a servant had come out to smoke, or one of the guests. Maybe Dr. Rankin had been delayed. She heard a soft tread at her back and she whipped around with a moan bordering on pahic.

"Dr. Rankin?"

A shadow emerged from the dark.

This time, her voice quavered. "Dr. Rankin?"

Still no response.

Every cell in her body warned her of approaching doom. Her nerve broke. Picking up her skirts, she dashed through the shrubbery toward the moor.

Fear is a powerful motivator, but terror is even better.

This was the thought that passed through Kate's mind as she rushed headlong toward the dry stone dike at the edge of the moor. Beyond the dike, near the top of the incline, was the stone where the witches of Deeside were once burned at the stake. But that was three hundred years ago. No sane person believed in witches in these modern times.

That was a lie. She'd been the object of name-calling and ridicule as a child, before she'd learned to keep her mouth shut. She wasn't a witch, she reminded herself. She was a normal girl with the uncanny gift of sensing danger. As now.

It was dark on that lonely hillside, and though nothing was clear, she saw shadows within shadows and knew when to leap over an obstacle and when to go around it. Cat's eyes, Dr. Rankin told her. It was merely another indication of her God-given gifts, and everyone had gifts, so Rankin said.

Where was Dr. Rankin? Why wasn't he here to help her?

She could hear faint footfalls behind her, but sometimes the snow muffled the sound. All the same, she could sense that her pursuer was gaining on her, so she pushed herself to the limit of her endurance. Each labored step taxed her strength. Each breath she took was harder than the last. He'd planned it that way. He'd forced her to take to the higher ground, knowing that she would be exhausted when he finally caught up to her.

Then what? Was he going to kill her or maim her?

She was afraid, deathly afraid, but another emotion began to stir in her. She was a Cameron of Craigmyle. A Cameron would be ashamed to die like a wee cowering beastie. If she was going to die, she would do it with honor.

Brave words for a girl whose one aim was to find a place to hide. If only her cousins were here!

The stone dike rose from the blanket of snow like the outer wall of a Roman fort. The breath was rushing in and out of her lungs, and she bit down on her lip to smother the sound. As she climbed the dike, her hand searched frantically for a loose stone, anything that she could use as a weapon. There was nothing.

She scrambled to the top of the dike and turned to face the devil who was pursuing her. Crouched almost double, trying to make herself as small as possible, she waited. *Wait! Wait! Hold steady!*

He was closing in, making no effort at concealment. She saw a shadow emerge from the gloom. Rising to her full height, she gave a ghostly screech and launched herself at him.

She'd taken him by surprise. She heard the whoosh of air from his lungs as her body collided with his, felt the jar on her wrist as she punched him with her fist. But he had a knife. When she sensed it descend, she rolled and felt the blade glancing off her shoulder. She ignored the pain and raised her head to snap at him with her teeth. He loomed above her, with the knife raised to finish her off. Her screech of terror came out a moan. Around her, the ghosts of the auld stane began to howl their lament. Something—a man? a beast?—crouched above her, wailing like a banshee, then everything faded as she sank into a well of darkness.

Gavin tossed and turned on his lumpy bed. His recurring dream was full of images of murder and mayhem. Dark clouds scudded across the sky, obliterating the light of the moon. He could hear the wail of the North Sea as its breakers dashed against the rocky shore. He knew the time and place. His grandmother, Lady Valeria, the celebrated witch of the northeast, had summoned her three grandsons and entrusted each with a prophecy. To fail meant death, not to him, but to the one he had been sent to save.

"Look to Macbeth," his granny had whispered on a painful breath. *"That's where your fate lies. You stand on the brink, Gavin. Fail Macbeth, and you will regret it to your dying day."*

The image shifted. He was in a cemetery, standing by an open grave; his only companions were the stone angels that stood vigil and the black, prancing horses with their black plumes, the horses that conveyed the dead to their final resting place.

His heart was beating like a bird trapped inside his chest. He didn't want to be here. He wanted sunshine glinting off the distant mountains and the smell of heather in his nostrils. But he couldn't leave. He felt as though he'd taken root on that spot at the edge of the grave, waiting for his worst fears to be realized.

He saw a movement from the corner of his eye. A young woman was running for her life. He could feel the stitch in her side and the cramped muscles in her calves. The moon came out from behind a cloud, momentarily blinding him. When his vision cleared, he saw that it wasn't a cloud that had moved. It was the shadow of a man, pursuing the woman uphill toward the "auld stane," the old stone, where they once burned witches.

The scream of an animal in pain pierced his mind, and he wrenched himself from his nightmare. "Macduff!" he said aloud. The scream came again, and he shook his head to clear his mind. Where was his dog? All he remembered was that Macduff hadn't come home last night.

With the vision of his dream still fresh in his mind and the piercing howl ringing in his ears, he threw back the covers and flung himself out of bed. Panicked, he began to pull on his clothes.

He saw her in his mind's eye, lying facedown in the snow. Someone was hovering nearby. Macduff was there, keeping the scoundrel at bay. On that thought, he dragged open the door of his snug abode and plunged into a blinding snowstorm. A name drummed inside his head, but when he tried to call out to her, the wind swallowed the sound. It didn't matter. He knew where she was. The auld stane was now a favorite picnic spot overlooking the Dee valley. Few were aware of its gory history.

Macduff howled again, like a cub crying for his mother. Gavin's feet had never moved faster as he plowed through the snow to answer that call, but he was aware that time was passing. It would take him a good five minutes, maybe longer to reach the witches' stone, and in this freezing weather, she could have slipped into a coma. He'd seen it before with climbers he'd rescued from the peaks. Some recovered; others did not. How long had she been out there?

It never occurred to him that he was accepting his psychic powers as though he'd been using them all his life. He didn't debate whether or not he was hallucinating. His power had come to him full-blown. He was like one of the wizards of old—a seer of Grampian.

He found them at the bottom of the dike. Macduff was nudging her, turning her face away from the snow. It came as no surprise to Gavin to see that it was Kate Cameron whom his dog had rescued.

"Good dog," he said, sinking to his knees beside Macduff.

When he put his cold cheek to her lips, he could feel the shallow tremors of each uneven breath she exhaled. Her skin was ice-cold, and he stripped out of his coat and wrapped her in it before lifting her into his arms. All the while, however, he was straining to hear any little sound that might indicate that the villain who had done this to her was still close by.

Macduff led the way, by turns growling and whining.

"You did well," Gavin told him. His dog had stayed to watch over the girl when he might have gone chasing after the man who attacked her. "I think you may have saved her life."

Macduff licked his fingers, or he tried to, then he bounded down the slope toward their cottage.

Once there, Gavin set her down gently on the pallet bed in the kitchen. Though there was a small bedroom with a proper bed next door, it had no fireplace and was as cold as an icehouse, too cold, in Gavin's opinion, for man or beast.

The first thing he did was stir the embers of the fire and blow it to life with the bellows. As soon as a flame appeared, he added a couple of birch logs and used the poker to angle them to catch the flame. That done, he lit the ubiquitous oil lamp on the kitchen table and then turned to look at Kate. Only then did he realize how cold he was. But first things first. He had to see to the girl.

Macduff had never left her side. His stare was unwavering, as though willing her to open her eyes. When Gavin knelt beside him and began to examine the unconscious girl, Macduff retreated to the foot of the bed. It didn't take long for Gavin to assess her injuries. There was a superficial wound on one shoulder that had bled profusely but not enough to make her unconscious. His fingers found a bump on the back of her head. Was it enough to cause a concussion?

How long had she been left lying in the snow? And why was she wearing nothing warmer than the dress she'd worn tonight?

This wasn't the time to speculate. Time was of the

essence. He had to warm her and bring her out of her coma.

He began at once by removing her soaking-wet dress, uncaring of the rips he made. Not a sound came out of her as he rolled her from side to side. He was just as ruthless when he removed her underthings. Fabric ripped or fell apart in his hands. He didn't care. The one thought that possessed his mind was that he had to bring her back to consciousness before it was too late.

Inwardly, he was cursing himself. He should have taken his premonition more seriously. Because of his wavering, he'd left the girl unprotected. It wouldn't happen again.

When she was down to bare skin, he slipped one of his own shirts over her inert form, then angled it down so that he could examine her shoulder. It was just as he thought, a superficial cut that required little attention except a bandage to stem the flow of blood if she should move in her sleep. There were no bandages, so he used a clean neckcloth instead, then he wrapped her in a blanket and covered her with the bedclothes. Her hair was wet, too, so he toweled it as dry as he could make it, then fetched a dry towel and fashioned it into a turban to keep her head warm. Next to the fire, there was a kettle of water warming nicely for his morning shave. He poured the warmed water into a mug and forced it past her lips. She coughed and swallowed, but she did not waken.

He felt her skin, just a brush of his hand against her cheek, and he was shocked to see that his fingers were trembling. He'd met the woman—a girl, really—for the first time yesterday, but he knew instinctively that they were fated . . .

It took him a moment before he could complete the thought, that he'd known instinctively that their fates were intertwined. He hadn't chosen her. She'd been chosen for him.

Are you the one? There wasn't a shadow of doubt in his mind now that she was the girl in the prophecy. Her name was Cameron, but names could be changed to protect the innocent.

He turned away and began to peel out of his own wet clothes. There was a pulley in the cottage for drying laundry on rainy days. After lowering it, he gathered up both sets of garments and spread them out to dry on the slats, then raised the pulley so that their wet things fluttered just above his head.

When he next looked at the bed, Macduff was on it, nestled close to the girl. Macduff, as near as Gavin could make out, was a cross between an English sheepdog and a wooly mammoth. He made a fine blanket. Gavin didn't know his dog's pedigree, because Macduff had come to him as a stray. If any two characters were fated to meet, it was Macduff and he, but which of them was the master was difficult to tell. Macduff had a mind of his own.

"You kept her warm," Gavin said, "didn't you, boy, while you waited for me to reach her?"

No response from Macduff, not even a twitch of his tail. He was exhausted as well.

Heaving a sigh, Gavin added another two logs to the fire. This was going to be a long night. He never wore nightclothes to bed, but for the girl's sake, he slipped into a fresh shirt and drawers, then dragged on a pair of dry trousers. After fetching a spare blanket from the icehouse bedroom and wrapping himself in it, he hung the kettle on its hook over the fire to bring the water to the boil. Only then did he pour himself a generous measure of whiskey and settle himself in the chair beside the fire to watch the girl.

It would have been better for Miss Cameron if he'd taken her to the hotel, but the heavy fall of snow made that impossible. Besides, it was pitch-black out there, and even with Macduff to guide them, it would have taken a long, long time. And who knew whether the man who had attacked her was not waiting his moment to finish what he'd started?

The thought prompted him to retrieve his revolver from the dresser drawer and check that it was ready for use. Having done that, he thrust it into the waistband of his trousers and took his chair again.

Six months ago, he hadn't known much about fire-arms. All that changed when he and his brother Alex had been on the run from a mob of terrorists who had tried to kill them. Now he regarded his revolver as one of his dearest friends.

Then why hadn't he taken it with him when he'd rushed to Miss Cameron's aid? Panic, he supposed. His dream or vision was still fresh in his mind.

The first order of business, he reminded himself, was to get her warm and bring her back to consciousness. He sipped his whiskey slowly as thoughts came and went. He'd always considered himself a man of reason and intelligence. However, according to his dear departed granny, he was also a seer and possessed gifts beyond his imagining.

He drew in a long breath and let it out slowly. What did he have to lose? He closed his eyes and focused his thoughts on the woman in his bed.

The voice was calm and soothed her fears. It wanted her to emerge from the screen of darkness she was hiding behind. It wanted her to return to the land of the living.

A layer of darkness peeled away, but that was as far

as she was willing to go. For a little while longer, she wanted to hide in the cocoon she had made for herself. There was no cold here, no pain, and no shame.

Where had that last thought come from?

She gave a little shiver and turned into the woolly blanket that she was snuggled against. A warm tongue licked her face, and she smiled involuntarily. The voice spoke to her again. It was a lovely sound and brought to mind the hot chocolate she used to spoon into her mouth when she was a child. A spoon made the chocolate last longer.

"You're safe now," the voice told her. "My dog found you. He won't let anything happen to you, and neither will I. No need to be afraid of me. We met at Juliet's wedding reception. I'm Gavin Hepburn, and I have a place on Feughside, on the other side of the Dee. I want you to wake now."

She remembered Gavin Hepburn. He was a character from a gothic novel. If he went away, she would be lost. She couldn't allow that to happen.

She moved restlessly and reached for him. He didn't disappoint her. His warm hands closed around hers. The voice was speaking to her again. She didn't understand the words, but she heard the compassion behind the velvet. She did not care if she never wakened, just as long as she heard his voice.

The voice changed, became harsher, insistent, and another layer of darkness peeled away. She waited for the velvet voice to speak again, but there was no sound, only silence. On a panicked cry, she opened her eyes. Fluttering above her head were ghosts or angels. It took her a moment to realize that the ghosts were nothing more sinister than laundry hanging on a pulley to dry. She turned her head on the pillow and looked into the bluest eyes she had ever beheld, not blue like the sky, but the midnight blue of a Scottish loch, fathoms deep and impenetrable.

In a matter-of-fact voice, the man with the blue eyes said, "Drink this. It will make you feel better."

When he spread his fingers behind her neck and raised her head, she winced in pain. Her head ached, her shoulder ached, her eyes ached from too much light. But worst of all was the dryness in her throat. Her tongue seemed to be stuck to the roof of her mouth.

He put a cup to her lips, and she drank greedily. Hot sweet tea, she thought. When she drank it to the dregs, he refilled the cup and offered it to her again. All the while, her eyes were moving around the cramped interior. For a moment, she thought she might be in one of her father's estate cottages, but this one was smaller.

Dark rafters crisscrossed the ceiling. The fireplace was an immense affair with a stool at either side for, she supposed, the children to sit and warm themselves. One wall was taken up by a dresser and table. The other wall was taken up by the bed she was lying on. A long rug of indeterminate pattern covered the stone floor. She could smell the pleasant scent of peat.

As she slowly came back to herself, she recognized her dress hanging to dry on the pulley and became aware that she was in a strange bed with nothing more substantial than a flimsy piece of fine linen to cover her nakedness. Her eyes focused on the man hovering over her. Gavin Hepburn was the man whom Juliet had warned her against. She had never felt safer in her life.

When he turned away to tend to the fire, she allowed herself to drift into a blessed unknowing.

Four

The sound of his voice penetrated the haze in her mind. She wouldn't have cared if he had spoken to her in Greek, Latin, or ancient Hebrew. The words were not important. What mattered was the sense of well-being that flowed through her at the sound of his voice. He had a mesmerizing voice.

The voice changed. Or maybe it was her perception that changed. He stopped soothing her and started calling her to account.

"Oh, no," he said. "I'm not letting you slip away again, else you may never wake up. Open your mouth. Wider! Drink this!"

With those harsh words, her woolly reveries suddenly unraveled, and she opened her eyes. There was no sign now of the voice that had charmed her as she slept. This man's jaw was tight. His eyes bored into hers. Had she felt more like herself, she would have fought him, but she didn't even possess the strength to sit up.

She could have wept. As a child, she'd had an imaginary friend who was more real to her than her own sister.

He was always there to comfort her when things went wrong. *Friend*, she called him. He didn't desert her; she deserted him the day she learned that her mother was locked away for hearing voices in her head. Was she mad, too?

There was no friend. He was a figment of her imagination, a means of protecting her fragile psyche from harm.

Reality was this hard-eyed man who held the rim of a cup to her lips.

She opened her mouth and promptly choked on the tea, not because it was too hot, but because it was too sweet. How many cups of tea had she drunk, anyway? There was no relenting in him. He forced her to drink the cup to the dregs.

"Good girl," he said, as though she were his pet dog.

He helped her raise herself a little, with her head and shoulders propped against a pillow. When she was settled, he turned away and added more logs to the blaze. It looked to her as though it would be a long night.

She gave a shivery sigh. There was no escape into sleep now. Everything had come back to her. He was Gavin Hepburn, and she owed him an explanation. If it had not been for him and his dog, she would be as frozen as one of the icicles that hung from the eaves. But before she took the plunge, she wanted to make quite sure that she could trust him. After all, there was a faint possibility that he was the one who had pursued her over the moor.

To what purpose? He hadn't killed her. He had saved her. Or was there some devious point to this cat-and-mouse game?

Emptying herself of all distracting thoughts, she opened herself to what her senses were telling her, but all that she received were mixed messages. He wasn't dangerous, but he wasn't harmless, either.

What was she supposed to make of that?

He pulled a stool up to the narrow bed and sat with legs spread and his arms resting on his knees. He was getting ready to fire off his questions. It just so happened that she had a few of her own that she wanted answers to before she took him into her confidence.

"This cottage," she began and had to start over because her voice sounded as weak and wobbly as an old woman's. "Who does it belong to, and what are you doing here?"

He spread his hands. "A man with a dog is not welcome at the hotel, so Juliet offered Macduff and me this cottage. It's not far from the hotel, but in this weather, we might as well be on the moon. If it's any consolation, it has stopped snowing, so we may get out of here and back to civilization by morning."

Macduff, who was toasting himself in front of the fire, had looked up when he heard his name mentioned.

"He saved me, didn't he?" she said quietly, turning her head to look at Macduff.

"What do you remember?"

"A ferocious beast, with fangs bared, standing over me."

"That would be Macduff. He's a herder, you see, and bred to protect the flock whatever the cost to himself. Leastways, that's my opinion. He came to me as a stray, so I have no way of knowing."

"Has he done this kind of thing before?"

"Yes, but only if he takes a fancy to you."

Her smile was fleeting, but as memory returned, she shuddered. "He howled," she said. "I've never heard anything like it. It didn't sound, well, earthly. I thought, in my dazed state, that he was a banshee." She could have bitten her tongue off. Now she'd made herself sound like a hysterical, scatterbrained idiot.

He nodded. "Sometimes I wonder about that myself. I heard that howl and knew that something was far wrong. Macduff doesn't make that sound unless he is in mortal danger."

"He wakened you?"

She noted a slight hesitation before he answered. "I was sleeping fitfully." The hesitation was short-lived and he went on with relentless deliberation, "Now it's your turn. What made you leave the safety of the hotel, on such a night, without a wrap to keep you warm?"

"I had a wrap," she answered quickly. "My tartan shawl. I must have lost it in the struggle. And I had no intention of leaving the hotel."

"Was there a struggle?"

She was taken aback. "How do you think I got that cut on my shoulder? Do you think I did it to myself? And what would be the point?"

"Calm yourself," he said. "I believe you." He patted the waistband of his trousers. "See? I don't usually go to sleep with my revolver ready to hand."

He had to move his arm before she could see the butt of his revolver protruding out of his waistband. Did that mean that he suspected that the person who had attacked her was still out there, waiting for the right moment to finish her off? At least he was taking her seriously.

"No," he said, as though he could read her mind. "Whoever attacked you will be long gone, or he has turned into a block of ice. No one can survive in the open in this kind of weather."

She felt dizzy with relief.

"Now," he said, "begin at the beginning, and tell me exactly what brought you out in such a night."

She nodded, but that did not mean that he had persuaded

her to tell him the whole story. Some things, such as the contents of the note, were too personal to share. "I received a threatening note," she began, and went on to tell him how Dr. Rankin had seemed agitated when she told him about it. "He wanted to talk to me about it, so we arranged to meet in the conservatory when everyone had gone to bed."

"What did the note say?"

She shook her head. "It's not my place to say. You'll have to ask Dr. Rankin about that."

"Where is the note now?"

She couldn't hide her dismay. Until he'd mentioned the note, she'd never given it another thought. "I don't know. I think I dropped it in the chase."

He regarded her coolly.

"I had it in my hand," she protested, "but when I picked up my skirts to make a run for it, I must have dropped it."

"I see."

There was an interval of silence before he continued. "You say you agreed to meet in the conservatory? Do you mean the hothouse just off the dining room?"

"Yes."

"Why not meet in your bedchamber or his? That would have been more convenient, wouldn't it?"

"Oh, much more convenient but far more perilous. You may have noticed that at night porters patrol the corridors? The scandal of being discovered in compromising circumstances may do nothing more serious than raise an eyebrow in your circles, but in mine, the wrath of my Fraser cousins would be implacable. In short, they'd beat the man to within an inch of his life."

He arched a brow. "Then lead him to the altar? Isn't that a bit extreme?"

She gave a drowsy smile. "You don't know my family."

And she was very happy to leave it that way. A man like Gavin Hepburn would only judge them and find them wanting. They were unconventional, quarrelsome, and slightly fey, but they had the money to command the respect of their neighbors, and that made all the difference in the world.

"What about your maid? Didn't she try to stop you?"

"Elsie wasn't there. She shares a room with Sally Anderson's maid." She put her hand to her mouth to cover her yawn.

"Don't go to sleep yet. You haven't told me what happened in the hothouse."

She opened her eyes and tried to concentrate. "The French door was ajar," she said slowly. "I thought Dr. Rankin might have gone outside to smoke. So I stepped outside. I think I said his name. That's when I heard the door close. It doesn't open from the outside, so I knew that I couldn't go back in."

She paused as she brought the scene into focus. "Someone was there. I knew it wasn't Dr. Rankin. I smelled the tobacco and . . . and something else." He was silent as she took herself through the experience one step at a time. "I smelled whiskey," she said slowly. Shock rippled through her. "How could I have forgotten?"

"Why did you run? Anyone might have gone outside to smoke a cigar. And Dr. Rankin likes his whiskey."

"He . . ."

"Yes?"

"He wouldn't answer me. I've never been more afraid in my life." Her voice trailed to a halt.

"Go on. What happened next?"

She swallowed hard. "He caught up to me at the dry stone dike beside the witches' stone. Do you know it?"

"I know it."

Her voice began to tremble. "I think I must have gone

a little mad. I lay in ambush for him and leaped at him from the top of the wall."

"You fought back?" He sounded incredulous.

"I didn't know I had it in me."

There was a long silence as he considered her words. Finally, he said, "Rest up. You're safe now. Macduff and I won't let anything happen to you."

Her eyes closed. There was no dark now, no shadows behind her eyes. She felt as light as a snowflake floating on air.

Gavin adjusted the covers at her chin, then turned back to see to the fire. The stack of birch logs was low, but there was a scuttle of peat beside the grate to keep them going. He arranged the lumps, leaving enough space to allow air to ignite the peat. He wasn't used to lighting and tending fires. There were always servants in the homes he visited to take care of the menial tasks. Oddly enough, when he was out on the hills or climbing the peaks, he had to do everything for himself and never gave it another thought.

He stayed up to see to the fire. Peat was not his favorite fuel. If it wasn't placed just right, it would smother the flames, and the fire would go out. Birch logs were better, but they didn't last long. Coal would have been his first choice, but hauling coal to the Highlands was a costly business. A true Highlander would scoff at him. He was a townsman while they were a hardy lot.

When he was satisfied that the fire was not in danger of going out, he spread his blanket in front of the fire, doused the lamp, and made to lie down. Macduff got there before him. Gavin elbowed him to the side and ignored the growls and baring of teeth that met his efforts.

"Any more of that," he said, "and I'll throw you outside to fend for yourself."

The growls subsided, leaving Gavin free to contemplate what the girl had told him. She hadn't lied. He'd been with her in his dream when she'd run from the man who was pursuing her. He'd felt her pain and her shortness of breath as she tried to outrun him. He hadn't seen everything, but it was enough to convince him that she had told him the truth. But she hadn't told him everything.

Had she not been so exhausted, he would have kept on probing about the note she had received. Most people would have been suspicious when she refused to share its contents, but not he. His intuition was honed to a fine point, and he sensed an emotion behind her reluctance. What was it?

He thought about it for a minute or so, then moved on to something else that troubled him. Will had not kept his appointment with the girl. Was his friend delayed, or was there a more sinister reason for Will's absence? He remembered their conversation at the reception, and he felt deeply uneasy.

Will had wanted to confide in him, but when it came to the point, he couldn't bring himself to do it. His suspicions were too bizarre, Will said.

Murder. That was what Will was alluding to.

Gavin worried at that thought for a long, long time.

A blast of cold air had him awake on an instant, with all his faculties honed for action. The moment the intruder stepped through the door, he leaped at him, and they both tumbled to the floor. The fire had dimmed and there were no candles lit, but he knew at once that he had made a serious blunder. He lowered the fist he had raised to disable his assailant. Beneath him, covered in a blanket, a wriggling, nubile, squawking female fought to free herself of his punishing grip.

"Bloody hell!" he roared as he rolled off her. He got to his knees, then to his feet. "What game are you playing, Kate Cameron?" He turned aside to light the lamp.

She sat up, pushed out of the blanket so that she could breathe, and blew away the hair that had tumbled free of her makeshift turban to fall over her face. "Imbecile!" she hissed, as angry as he. "Do you always act first and ask questions later?" She tossed her turban on the floor and pushed the hair out of her eyes. "I went to the privy, that's all."

Her answer only added to his ire. "You went to the privy? That's why you left the cottage?"

"Don't shout! I'm not deaf!" She allowed him to help her up and guide her to the bed. When she sank into the bedclothes, she shrugged. "What else was I to do? I did not want to waken you, so I took Macduff with me instead. It's all your fault, anyway. You kept forcing me to drink cup after cup of tea till I thought I would drown in it."

Macduff chose that moment to pad behind the bed and cower in the corner with only his massive paws showing.

Gavin's temper, fueled by fear, barely softened. "There's a perfectly good chamber pot under the bed."

She squared her shoulders and answered him with all the dignity of a duchess. "As I am well aware. I, however, prefer to have some privacy. Good God, even the patients at Dr. Rankin's clinics expect privacy when they need to use the facilities, even if it's only a bedpan."

He sat on the edge of the stool and regarded her steadily. Until now, he'd never considered her one of the beauties, but with her color up and temper glinting in her eyes, he allowed that Miss Kate Cameron could hold her own. Her hair, gilded by the light from the lamp, hung heavy and straight to her shoulders. She kept flicking it back as she glowered at him from beneath her straight black brows.

"Did I say something amusing?" she asked truculently.

He shook his head.

"Then why," she demanded, "do you have that silly grin on your face?"

Because he was bemused. When he had first set eyes on her, he'd discounted her beauty and her power to make her presence stand out. It seemed that the laugh was on him.

He turned away and poked the fire to life. "Will tells me," he said, "that you're a frequent visitor to his clinic."

He sensed her wariness, and that made him more alert.

"I'm not really a visitor," she said. "Visitors come to gawk. Dr. Rankin does not encourage gawkers unless they are immensely rich and willing to endow his work."

"There are two clinics, aren't there?"

"Yes. One in Aberdeen and one in Braemar. The clinic in Aberdeen serves the poor and castoffs in our society, you know, people who can't afford to pay a doctor's bill. There's no money to be made there, but Dr. Rankin has several backers whose generosity keeps the clinic open."

Her voice had gentled considerably when she talked of Will's work, and once again Gavin wondered whether there was more to her relationship with his friend than either of them had cared to admit.

"What about the clinic in Braemar?" he asked crisply.

"There is a surgery attached to it, but it's more of a

rest home for those who have lost touch with reality or have suffered some terrible loss in their lives. I think that's where Dr. Rankin's heart lies. He says that these patients can be healed, too. We do what we can."

He thought of Fox, the retired headmaster, who sneered at Will's work. The stigma would extend to his patients. No one wanted to be known as a loony. Kate Cameron's credit rose by several degrees.

A smile lit his eyes. "You're an amateur psychiater?"

"I'm a volunteer. I do the most menial tasks." She held up her hand to stay the next question. "I don't know why you're asking me about the clinics. You're Dr. Rankin's friend. Surely he told you all this already?"

"Well, he did, but . . ."

"But what?"

He didn't want to betray a friend's confidence, but the events of that night had added a new ingredient to the mix. Will suspected someone connected to his clinics was up to no good, and that was putting it mildly. Kate Cameron was connected to the clinics, and tonight someone had tried to kill her.

He had to get to the truth.

He gave a careless shrug. "Will is worried about his clinic in Aberdeen. Do you know anything about it?"

Her eyes went very round, and she shook her head. "He said nothing to me. You should speak to him directly, Mr. Hepburn. I can't answer for him."

"Can't or won't?"

"I can't. Dr. Rankin doesn't confide in me."

She was telling the truth, or was she? He could read her, but imperfectly. This was getting him nowhere.

"We'll leave here at first light." As he spoke, he stood, reached above his head, and began to pull their garments from the pulley. "They won't start looking for you until you don't turn up for breakfast or until someone raises the alarm." A thought occurred to him. "What about your lady's maid?"

"She'll think that I have gone out for an early morning walk. What difference does it make? I don't see where this is going. Shouldn't we raise the alarm and send for the police the first chance we get?"

She was examining the gray dress he had thrown at her, poking her fingers through holes in the delicate lace bodice that was smeared with blood. He heard her sniff.

"You're not going to weep over a ruined frock, are you?" he asked incredulously.

Something flashed in her eyes, and she tipped up her chin. "This is no ordinary frock. It's a gown that was designed by a couturier from the House of Worth, and it cost a small fortune. It doesn't belong to me but to my sister. She loaned it to me for the occasion of Juliet's marriage, and I promised to return it in pristine condition."

"I'm sure she'll make allowances when she hears the circumstances.'

"You don't know my sister. There will be hell to pay."

"He's not French. He's as English as you or I."

"What?"

"Worth. He trained in France, but he is as English as you or I."

"Why would he pretend to be French?"

His look verged on the satirical. "For the cachet. Every lady wants a French dress designer, just as every bachelor wants a French chef presiding at his table. It's all for show."

She frowned down at the ruined dress. "I can't go back to the hotel wearing this. What will everyone think?"

"I'll lend you my coat. When it's buttoned up to your throat, no one will notice what you're wearing underneath. You can slip upstairs to your room and change your gown before we meet with the police."

She was shaking her head.

"What?" he asked.

"Shouldn't we go to the police at once and tell them what happened? That villain may be hanging around the hotel. He may even be one of the guests."

"You may be right, but if we want to be taken seriously, we won't broadcast the fact that we spent the night together, at least not to the rank and file. We'll do this discreetly. I'll talk to the police first. They'll want to question you, of course, but they're decent fellows. They'll keep their mouths shut and their speculations to themselves."

Her hand went to her throat, and she rubbed it distractedly. "People have such filthy minds." She spoke under her breath, then heaved a sigh. Raising her eyes to his, she went on, "Thank you for thinking of my reputation. You're more farsighted than I am."

"Oh, I don't doubt it." He touched his index finger to the dimple in his jaw in a halfhearted attempt to conceal his grin. "Your thanks are unnecessary, though. You see, Miss Cameron, I have as much to lose as you. Should it become known that we spent the night together, I might feel obliged to make an honest woman of you."

She lifted one brow. "Why should you? From what I hear, you make a practice of spending the night with women who are practically strangers to you. You haven't tried to make honest women of them."

"That's because they don't have cousins who would break my arms and legs should I be so bold as to refuse. At heart, I'm a fearful coward."

She gave an impish grin. "Don't worry, Hepburn. It will never come to that. I have enough courage for the two of us. Now, where is this coat you promised me?"

He watched her dress with a kind of grudging respect. There were more facets to this woman's character than showed on the surface. He swallowed a sigh. He might as well have been a knight in shining armor entrusted with her care. It would have helped had she been twenty years older and running to fat.

A spear of guilt twisted inside him. Why had he been sent to save this woman and not Alice? What indifferent deity had decided who should live and who should die?

"Ready?" she asked, then raised her brows when she saw his expression.

His face cleared. "You'll do," he replied.

In her tattered dress and borrowed coat, she should have looked like a scarecrow. Maybe it was her haughty smile or the way she held herself that made him feel like a supplicant in the presence of a duchess. Opening the door was easy; closing it was hard. The duchess and his dog did not spare him a glance as they sailed into that twilight just before dawn.

The sun had risen a little higher by the time they reached the hotel. It wasn't deserted as they'd hoped it would be. Several gillies in their deer hats and cradling their guns in one arm were fanning out as they made for the snow-covered moors.

"Dalziel!" Gavin called out, recognizing one of the men who wasn't dressed as a gillie. It was Will Rankin's man of business. "What's going on?"

Dalziel quickly crossed to him. He was a young man, not much older than thirty, with dark, receding hair. His usual bland expression had vanished, and worry lines puckered his brow. "It's Dr. Rankin, sir," he said. "He asked me to waken him early this morning, in case the trains were running, you know. His bed hasn't been slept in, and he is nowhere in the hotel."

Kate's hand had gone to her throat. She looked at

Gavin. All the color had drained from her face. He clasped her hand. "Don't jump to conclusions," he said softly. "Say as little as possible until we have a chance to talk things over." He motioned to Dalziel and said something she could not hear.

Dalziel nodded and offered her his arm. They entered the hotel together, leaving Gavin with the gillies.

Five

Mr. Dalziel escorted her to her room. He was discretion itself. Not one awkward question passed his lips. However, Kate was aware that he was a keen observer. "Nothing much gets past Dalziel," Dr. Rankin frequently told her. But he was referring to his business affairs, keeping track of the clinics' funds and supplies. Dalziel had no contact with the patients.

He was murmuring soothing inanities in her ear. She wasn't listening and brusquely broke into his monologue. "Tell me again, Mr. Dalziel. Dr. Rankin parted company with you last night. Then what happened?"

"He asked me to wake him early if the trains were running again. I couldn't get to the station for snowdrifts, so I turned back. I thought I'd look in on him and, if he was awake, warn him that the hotel was still cut off, but his bed had not been slept in."

She didn't tell Dalziel that Dr. Rankin had arranged to meet her after the guests had retired for the night. What had happened in the interim? Her heart beat in slow, heavy strokes.

In the same soothing tone, Dalziel went on, "I'm sure we're worrying for nothing, and everything will be fine. Perhaps he met a friend, and after a few drinks, they lost track of the time."

"You mean, they got drunk together?" If that were the case, it would ease her mind.

"It's possible, but let's not go into that right now. Stay in your room. I'll fetch your maid for you."

He reached past her and tried the door. It was unlocked. She distinctly remembered locking it when she left her room before keeping her appointment with Dr. Rankin. She supposed that she'd lost the key in the struggle. Then how had someone gotten into her room?

As soon as she stepped inside, she let out a breath. There was no mystery here. The fire in the grate had been lit and was burning brightly. There were housemaids whose first order of the day was to see that all the guests wakened to a warm room. These maids were the first to be up and doing and were on the lowest rung on the servant hierarchy.

Every morning when she wakened, there was a fire burning in the grate, but she had never given the young girl who had seen to her comfort a second thought. She made up her mind, there and then, to leave a handsome gratuity when she left for home.

Dalziel moved past her and opened the drapes. Dawn was chasing the night away. She wandered to the window and looked out. This was Deeside. How was it possible for so much beauty to conceal something dark and ugly? As she stared out of the window, a hawk suddenly dropped from the sky and snatched a pigeon from its unwary perch. Shivering, she turned away. Dalziel did not notice. He had turned aside to light the lamp.

Hugging herself, she sank onto the bed.

Dalziel came to stand over her. He spoke as though

he were speaking to a child. "Don't take on so. I blame myself for . . . well . . . getting into a panic. I'm sure everything will be fine."

She looked up at him, saw the worry lines on his face, and decided that she should be comforting him. His whole world seemed to revolve around his job. As far as she knew, he didn't have any friends.

She summoned a smile. "I'm sure you're right."

He gave her hand a quick squeeze. "Stay in your room, and I'll fetch your maid for you."

He was gone before she could thank him for his trouble. Dr. Rankin had not exaggerated. Nothing much got past Dalziel. He knew where to find Elsie.

She listened to the hotel stirring. It would be a long time before guests were up and traipsing downstairs for breakfast. These were the muted sounds of servants as they went about their business. Her mind droned on as she stared into space, cataloguing the sounds of dishes rattling, pots clattering, and laughs and giggles suddenly choked off. It didn't help. Her mind kept returning to Dr. Rankin. He was supposed to meet her in the hothouse. Had he met her assailant instead?

Elsie bustled in, blinking against the sight that met her eyes. "Miss Kate!" she gasped. "What's come over you? That nice Mr. Dalziel wouldna tell me a thing."

Kate made an effort to rouse herself. She had no desire to become an object of belowstairs gossip, though how she could avoid it, she did not know. The gillies had seen her arrive with Hepburn, wearing his coat no less, and gillies had wives who worked at the hotel. Hepburn was counting on the discretion of the policemen who would surely come and question them, but they had wives, too. It would not be long before she was regarded as a fallen woman.

She wouldn't care, if only Dr. Rankin turned up safe and sound.

"What happened," she said, "was that I went out for a breath of fresh air last night and couldn't get back into the hotel." She left it at that. The less said at this point, the better for all concerned.

Elsie clicked her tongue. "Don't you worry none, Miss Kate. Elsie is here, and I'll take care of you. Let's get these soiled things off."

Piece by piece, Elsie removed Kate's garments. Her hands fluttered when she came to Kate's borrowed gown, but she didn't shriek or moan. Magda would raise the roof with shrieks when she repossessed her gown. She never would have loaned it to Kate had their father not promised them a shopping trip to London.

It was Kate who moaned. Elsie's unsuspecting hands had gripped her shoulders, and the wound from her assailant's knife made her flinch.

"You're bleeding, miss," said her maid, all round-eyed with her bottom lip trembling. "Who did this to you?"

"It was an accident," said Kate, putting her maid off with the first thing that came into her head. Mr. Hepburn had told her to keep her mouth shut, and that was what she intended to do.

Elsie's lips thinned, but she kept her thoughts to herself, and before long Kate was down to bare skin and wrapped in a blanket.

"Don't move," Elsie told her. "I'll be back in a few minutes."

Kate nodded. An awful lethargy was stealing over her, like one of those creeping Deeside mists that blot out the sun and veil the moors and mountains in silvery lace. She couldn't see, couldn't think, couldn't get her bearings. Her eyelids felt heavy. She lay back against the pillows and closed her eyes.

The gillies huddled around Gavin as they decided where to begin their search.

"We can't make a proper search of the moors," Gavin said. "There aren't enough of us. And for all we know, Dr. Rankin may still be in the hotel."

The gillies nodded and shuffled their feet. Gavin turned up his coat collar against the biting-cold breeze that whistled down from the mountain peaks. This was the beginning of spring, and he was wishing that he was anywhere but here. The moors and mountains were too desolate, too treacherous for his peace of mind. It was light enough now to scan the horizon, but all he could see was a blanket of white snow. If Will was out there . . . He didn't want to complete the thought.

The head gillie, a quiet, thoughtful man in his late forties, broke into Gavin's thoughts. "There are no footprints to guide us. If Dr. Rankin left the building, it must have been long before the snow let up."

"And when was that?" a cultured voice asked.

Gavin turned his head and was surprised to find Gordon Massey standing at his elbow, but not the Gordon Massey he remembered from the night before. He seemed more sure of himself, more at ease. He was, Gavin calculated, a year or two older than himself and was immaculately turned out in country tweeds. It was the cultured accent that made the deepest impression on Gavin. It denoted a privileged background and the right schools, and was as different from his parents' Scottish brogue as silk from sacking. He remembered, then, that there was an uncle from whom Massey had inherited a publishing firm. He guessed that the uncle had paid for the nephew's education.

One of the gillies scratched his chin. "It must have stopped snowing two or three hours ago. Something wakened me. A dog howling, I think, and I went outside to see what was amiss. It was still dark, but it wasn't snowing then."

"Maybe it was a banshee, Jock," said another.

The gillies laughed.

Jock looked sheepish. "Aye, ye may laugh, but the good book warns us about spirits, don't it? I believe the good book afore I believe you."

No one could argue with that.

Gavin said, "All the same, we can't roust guests from their beds to search their rooms. We don't want to alarm them for no good reason."

"Then what do you suggest?" asked Massey.

"Dogs," said Gavin. "I know Henry keeps a few hounds for his own pleasure. Let's see how well they can track. Where is the kennel?"

Before he had stopped speaking, Macduff came tearing around the corner of the building, barking furiously. Gavin started forward to meet him. Having alerted his master, Macduff turned around and retraced the path he had taken. He did not go far, only to a picnic bench not twenty yards away from the hothouse. There was a drift of snow piled against one side. Here, Macduff hunkered down and began to whine. An awful feeling of doom settled in the pit of Gavin's stomach.

He went down on his knees and began to scrape the snow to the side. Massey helped him. Though the gillies were huddled around them, no one spoke, no one whispered to his neighbor. Only their breathing broke the silence.

Inch by inch, they uncovered Will Rankin's body. They uncovered something else. Close to Rankin's hand was an empty whiskey bottle.

Massey got to his feet. "It looks as though he had too much to drink, then staggered out here and went to sleep."

Gavin had other ideas that he kept to himself. Still on his knees, he was studying his friend's face. There was a scrape on Will's forehead, as though he'd fallen forward and banged his head. There was no blood on his garments. His expression was peaceful. His clothes stank of whiskey.

"Shall we dig him out, sir?" asked the head gillie.

"No." Gavin got up. "This is a matter for the police. The body can't be moved until they have seen it."

"But Ballater is cut off," Massey pointed out.

"I'll go," said the gillie named Jock. "I know my way around these hills. I'll bring the police."

Dalziel pushed out of the hothouse at that moment and joined the group around Rankin's body. When he saw what they had uncovered, he gave a choked cry and turned away.

"See to him," Gavin told Massey.

Massey nodded and went after Dalziel.

He had other instructions for the gillies—a tarpaulin to cover the body and two men on guard at all times. His words faltered and faded away as he stared at his friend's inert form. It seemed inconceivable to him that they would never fish for salmon in the Dee again or chat, man-to-man, over a glass of whiskey as the sun set. He swallowed and was reaching for the empty bottle when a hand closed around his shoulder, startling him back to the present.

"What ails you, sir?"

It took a moment for Gavin's eyes to focus. The head gillie hovered over him, his brow knit in puzzlement.

Gavin looked around him. The sun was up. There were no clouds. It looked as though it would be a fine day.

He got to his feet. "Don't let anyone touch anything," he said. "Come, Macduff. You deserve your breakfast this morning, and if anyone tries to ban you from the hotel, they'll have to deal with me."

The gillies watched him go in silence. One removed his cap and scratched his head. "He talks to his dog," he said.

"Aye," said the head gillie. "There's nothing untoward in that. Now, if his dog were to answer him, I, for one, would eat my cap."

There was a moment of silence, then all the gillies began to laugh. Suddenly remembering where they were and that a man had died tragically, they set to work.

The voice came to her like a soft breeze blowing in her ear. There were no words to begin with, only a sense of his presence.

He's dead, isn't he? Those were her words.

Shh . . . the wind said. *Trust me.*

The tension that gripped every aching muscle relaxed its hold on her one degree at a time.

The wind became a roar, and she felt herself spinning. She wasn't alarmed. She trusted the voice and knew that no harm would come to her when he was with her.

She saw a waterfall and salmon trying to leap over the rocks to the spawning grounds above. The beauty of the scene was breathtaking.

Where are we? she asked wonderingly.

Feughside.

She narrowed her eyes against the glare of the sun. Then she saw him, a much younger Dr. Rankin, waving at someone on the other side of the river, a woman.

Maddie, he called out.

The woman's face filled with joy. She held out her arms to him, and the doctor stepped lightly onto the stepping-stones that would take him to the other side.

It was only a dream.

At that one doubtful thought, the peace and harmony that wrapped around her began to disintegrate. She was doing it again, daydreaming, conjuring up her imaginary friend, as though anything he said could alter reality.

She heard something, the tread of a step, a door opening and closing. When she opened her eyes, her maid was kneeling over her.

"Oh, miss," Elsie said, blowing out a long breath, "I thought you had fainted.

Kate's eyes darted around the room. There was no one else there, no hint of another presence. "I was dreaming," she said. "Yes, that's all it was, a dream." She looked up at Elsie. "I thought that someone was here with me."

"Oh, that would be Mr. Hepburn. He left not a moment ago when he saw that you were asleep." The maid busied herself with a basin of water and odds and ends that she'd brought in on a tray. "I'm to tell him when you're up and dressed. He wants to speak to you."

Gavin Hepburn. She hoped she hadn't said anything out loud.

"Here, Miss Kate, hold this towel."

The sudden deluge of soapy water on the afflicted part of Kate's shoulder had her wheezing and gasping for air. "That hurt!" she groaned when she could find her breath.

"But it's over now, isn't it?" Elsie examined the wound and dried it off. "There, it's all cleaned up, but you're going to have a scar when it has healed."

The unfeeling wretch began to hum under her breath as she completed her ministrations, then drew the edges of the wound together with three strips of plaster and bound them neatly in place.

Kate ran her fingers over the dressing. "How did you learn to do that? What a stupid question! You've been reading Mrs. Beeton's book again."

Elsie nodded. "There's not much that lady doesn't know about doctoring."

The maid was still humming when she went to the clothes press and shook out a set of clothes for her mistress to wear. "He's a real gentleman, isn't he, miss? Lovely manners and a sweet smile."

Kate was silent. She was watching her maid hold up the traveling ensemble she'd worn for the journey. It was a brown challis with a cinched waist and a jacket to match with a rabbit's fur collar. It looked better against Elsie than it did on her. Magda always said that brown was not her color.

"What else did Mr. Hepburn say to you?"

Elsie sighed and laid the traveling gown over the back of a chair. "That I was to stay with you until he came to relieve me. Look, I've brought you a nice cup of tea and toast to go with it. Drink your tea, then I'll help you get dressed."

Kate sipped her tea and nibbled on toast while she watched her maid. Her blood seemed to slow and her heart clenched.

Will Rankin was dead. She refused to believe it until Hepburn himself told her.

She pushed out of the blanket and told Elsie to help her get dressed.

Six

Kate had just finished dressing when there was a knock at her door. When Elsie answered it, Gavin stepped into the room. He crossed to Kate at once and took her hands in his.

Before he could say a word, she shook her head. Her lips formed a denial, but all that came out of her mouth was a hoarse whisper.

Elsie cried out, "Miss, what is it?"

Gavin said at once, "We found Dr. Rankin not far from the hothouse. It looks as though he had been drinking heavily and knocked himself out on a picnic bench. The cold did the rest. I'm sorry, so sorry. I've sent for the police, but it may take some time for them to get here."

Elsie burst into tears, which she scrubbed away with the hem of her frock.

Turning to her, Gavin said, "Your mistress is in shock. Find a footman and have him bring a glass of whiskey here. Oh, and have one yourself. Tell one of the kitchen maids to make a fresh pot of tea for Miss

Cameron. Tell them nothing about Dr. Rankin. Do you understand?"

Elsie's tears dried, and she hastened to do his bidding.

Kate searched Gavin's face. She could tell by his pallor and the way he clenched his jaw that he was just as shaken as she, if not more so. He and Dr. Rankin had been friends since they were infants. He'd known Mrs. Rankin before her death, though Kate, herself, had never met the lady. His grief far outstripped hers. She felt so inadequate and frightened.

She reached out and pulled him into the chair beside hers. "You look bone-tired," she said, "and more in need of a restorative than I. You must be hungry. Shall I ask Elsie to bring a tray for you?"

He shook his head. "We don't have much time, Kate, so listen carefully to what I tell you. I know how the police work. Until they are sure that Will's death is an accident, they will treat it as"—he hesitated over his words—"as a suspicious death, and they'll look around for someone to blame."

"The man who pursued me and tried to kill me—won't they look for him?"

His answer was immediate. "Can you prove that someone tried to kill you?"

She swallowed hard and shook her head.

He let out a short breath. "Do you have the note, Kate?"

"No. I told you. I must have lost it when I ran."

He sat forward, arms braced against his knees, and stared at his loosely clasped hands. In a voice that was just above a whisper, he said, "You have to tell me what the note said. Will's death changes everything. You do see that, don't you?"

It was the voice of her dreams, the same voice that

she'd heard when she was in the cottage, only half aware of where she was and what had happened to her, the velvet voice that soothed all her fears and slipped by all her defenses.

There must be something about this man's voice that appealed to her if she'd taken it as the model for her long-lost friend.

When he lifted his head and looked into her eyes, she was struck again by the intensity of his stare. There was no sign of the easygoing, charming rogue whom Juliet had warned her against. His gaze, now, was so probing, so intense, that she felt as though he was trying to mesmerize her.

"Kate," he said, reaching for her.

She jerked back and stared at him warily. "What does it matter what it said? I felt threatened. That's why I wanted to talk to Dr. Rankin."

He looked down at his hands again. One corner of his mouth lifted. "Don't you trust me, Kate?"

"With my life. I think that's obvious." And before he could completely demolish her defenses, she said quickly, "What about the cut on my shoulder? Won't that prove that I've been attacked?"

He let out a breath. "They'll only put it down to a lovers' quarrel. You and Will . . . well . . . you seemed very close."

"I had a professional relationship with Dr. Rankin," she protested.

Once again her unwary gaze was caught in his stare. She couldn't look away, couldn't breathe, could only wait for him to release her.

His eyes crinkled at the corners, and he gave her his crooked grin. "I believe you," he said, "but it's the police we have to convince. You spent the night with me. What do you think they will make of that? They'll think Will was jealous—"

"It was entirely innocent!"

"Was it, Kate? Who undressed you? Who put you to bed? Do you remember? Or were you"—his grin lifted both corners of his mouth—"completely insensate?"

Her jaw dropped. What he hinted at wasn't impossible. She remembered the velvet voice of her dreams and how she would have done anything to keep that voice with her.

The sound he made was close to a growl. When her eyes flew to his face, she saw that he was scowling.

Through his teeth, he said, "I am not in the habit of seducing innocent young women. You have nothing to fear from me."

She shot him a nasty look. "I was never afraid of you, Hepburn." It was the truth. She was more afraid of what he would find out about her.

He smoothed his frown with the tips of his fingers. "We don't have much time to discuss this," he said. "The footman will be here in a moment or two. Here's how I think we should play this out. We'll stick to the truth as far as possible. You were in your room when you heard a dog howling. You went downstairs to investigate and left the hotel by the hothouse door. You followed the sound of the dog but became disoriented. It was snowing heavily by then. Let's say you tripped and something sharp pierced your shoulder. You have to say something about that wound if you're asked. If your maid mentions it to the police, they'll want to know how you came by it." He stopped, then said gently, "Are you with me so far?"

"I'm ahead of you," she replied. "Your dog found me and led me straight to your door."

"And as soon as it was light enough, we set out for the hotel."

"What?" he asked when she was silent.

She heaved a sigh. "What an accomplished pair of liars we are!"

He got up. "We're not liars. We're simply not telling the whole truth, not at this point. However, I will defer to your conscience. By all means, tell the police everything, but be prepared for the consequences. Oh, one other thing. Say nothing to anyone until we've spoken to the police."

His face was set and forbidding when he walked to the door. She would have said something conciliatory to prevent him from leaving, but a footman arrived with the whiskey, and the moment was lost.

He tried to put his conversation with Kate out of his mind and spent the next little while looking for the note she said that she had dropped in her mad dash for freedom. Without betraying his purpose, he wandered through the hothouse before idling his way outside. It was hopeless. The snow blanketed everything as far as the eye could see. He'd hoped that he would detect anything out of place with his psychic power, but it was not to be. When it came to detecting, he was no better than the next man.

He could have told Kate a lot more—and when had he started to think of her as Kate? She always referred to him as Hepburn, and sometimes as Mr. Hepburn. As though her formality could keep him at arm's length! He'd been chosen to protect her, and whether Miss Kate Cameron liked it or not, they were fated to see a lot more of each other.

What in blazes was in that note that she didn't want

anyone to know about? He corrected himself. She had told Will, and they had agreed to meet late at night in the hothouse. This is where things got tricky. How did the villain know that Kate and Will had agreed to meet? Was the attack random? Was there a deranged patient of Will's waiting in the wings to kill her, too?

Will had suspected something was amiss in his clinic in Aberdeen. He'd mentioned the word "murder" and then retracted it. Kate had received a note.

No, this was no random attack.

She was grieving for Will, but it was grief for a friend not a lover. He had deduced that much when he had come to her door earlier and found her asleep, moving restlessly and mumbling to herself. He had tried to slip into her mind, but it wasn't his gift. All he'd gotten was a multitude of unconnected impressions and a brick wall at the periphery to keep thieves out.

What was she hiding from him?

She'd called him "friend," but she wasn't thinking of him. Then who? He had to know, not from any base motive, not because he was jealous, but because the more he knew about her, the easier it would be to keep her safe.

They were connected, and one way or another, he was going to smash the wall she had built to protect her secrets. They were connected. How could he make her accept it?

The police had yet to arrive, and guests were beginning to come downstairs, so he found the hotel manager and gave him an edited account of what had taken place.

"You should assemble the guests," he said, "and tell them that there has been a dreadful accident that the police will want to investigate. No one is to leave the premises until they get here. Oh, and post a footman at every door to prevent anyone leaving."

The poor manager stuttered and stared until Gavin barked out, "See to it, man. At once, do you hear?"

The dining room staff had already begun to set out chafing dishes for the influx of guests for breakfast, so Gavin took the opportunity of helping himself to beefsteak and scrambled eggs. When he sat down to eat, however, he discovered that he didn't have the stomach for it. He still couldn't take it in. At any moment, he expected to hear Will's belly laugh. He'd look up, and Will would be grinning down at him.

He did look up, visualizing Will's red hair and freckles, but the face he stared into was evenly tanned and framed by dark, windblown locks.

"May I join you?" asked the younger Massey.

"By all means." Gavin pulled out a chair.

Massey sat down, cradling a cup of coffee in his hands. He looked at Gavin's untouched plate of food and smiled faintly. "Yes," he said, "appetite is the first thing to go when one loses someone close." He looked over his shoulder. "Do you think anyone would mind if my parents were to go on to Braemar as planned? This is all very upsetting for older people."

Gavin followed the direction of Massey's gaze. Mrs. Massey was weeping into a voluminous handkerchief, and her husband had his arm around her, his hand patting her in a consoling gesture.

"They would never get through," Gavin said, "even if they could find a conveyance to take them. I'm afraid we're all marooned here until the roads are open."

Massey nodded. "That's what I told them, but your opinion will carry more weight. You live in the area, don't you?"

"Across the river." He swallowed a mouthful of coffee. "Even so, I wouldn't tempt the elements unless I had a good reason to try for home."

"That's what I thought." A moment of silence went by. Finally, Massey said, "Have you spoken to Dalziel?"

"Dalziel?" That got Gavin's attention. "Is he ill?"

"No, not exactly, but he's taking it very hard. He shouldn't be alone, but he refuses to leave his room." He swallowed another mouthful of coffee. "He has this odd idea," he went on, "that because he is an employee, it's not his place to fraternize with his betters. That's the likes of us, by the way. I can't talk him out of it, but I think you may succeed where I failed."

Massey drained his cup and got up. "I need more coffee," he said, and he moved away, leaving Gavin feeling rather abashed.

He had known that Will held Dalziel in high esteem. Will was hopeless at keeping records and writing letters, while Dalziel excelled at it. It was more than that. He took a pride in it. "My factotum," Will said when referring to his assistant, but Gavin had always thought of Dalziel as an employee. He knew little of the man's origins. His position was awkward and not unlike that of a governess. Most governesses were invisible.

He drummed his fingers on the white tablecloth. Rising abruptly, he left the dining room and went in search of Dalziel.

It wasn't Dalziel he found, however, but Janet Mayberry, on the point of leaving her room to go in search of sustenance.

"Gavin," she exclaimed, "just the man I want to see." She grabbed his arm, yanked him into her room, and shut the door. "What is this my maid tells me? Is it true? Did Dr. Rankin meet with a terrible accident?"

In as few words as possible, he gave her an account of how things stood. He was reaching for the doorknob when she collapsed against him.

"I feel faint," she mewed softly. "Please, help me to the bed."

At any other time, he would have been hard-pressed to keep a straight face. Janet didn't know how to be subtle. She was already unbuttoning her jacket.

"I can't breathe," she fluttered. "It's all been such a shock. Gavin, help me, please?"

He wasn't given time to answer. Her arm looped around his neck, and she dragged him down for an openmouthed kiss.

"Hurry," she moaned. "My maid will be back in another minute. Don't worry, I locked the door."

For one insane moment, he was tempted, but his thoughts strayed to Kate, and with a furious curse, he fought off Janet's stranglehold and lurched to his feet.

"Gavin, what is it?" she cried out.

"She knows," he said with a violence that made Miss Mayberry cower away.

"You're not making sense," she cried out.

He was in no mood to explain. Torn between outrage and embarrassment, he went in search of Kate, but Kate did not wish to be disturbed, her maid told him, and nothing he said could persuade Elsie to unlock the door to him.

Seven

The police arrived on foot late that afternoon. Constable Hamilton, the officer in charge, explained to the assembled guests that there were no detectives with them because the gillie had already told them at the station that Dr. Rankin had accidentally locked himself out of the hotel when he'd had one too many and had subsequently died of exposure. So the body was put on a stretcher without ceremony, and two gillies were commandeered to convey it to the village.

A babble of voices broke out at this point, with many of the guests asking questions and shouting across each other. Hamilton silenced them by holding up his hand. He looked as though he'd been dragged out of retirement and knew how to handle a rowdy crowd.

"You'll be free to go," he said, pinning malefactors with a steely eye, "after I've taken your statements."

"Statements?" queried his fellow officer, a new recruit, Kate surmised, who didn't look as though he knew how to tie the laces on his boots.

"Statements," Hamilton repeated. "We take statements

from everyone before we let them go. Make sure they sign them. Have you got that, Officer Binnie?"

Binnie looked askance at the sea of faces in the crowded dining room and gave a little nod.

"You take the hotel staff, then," Hamilton said, "and I'll begin here with the guests."

Binnie gave another nod and beat a hasty retreat to the door that gave onto the kitchens.

Kate felt queasy, and it wasn't only because of the statement she would have to make to the police. Without warning, a door that she'd hoped she had closed for all time had opened, and she was seeing visions again. It was because of these visions that she'd been labeled a freak as a child. That's what had brought her to Dr. Rankin's attention all those years ago. He'd taught her how to keep the visions at bay, and when that was impossible, to keep her mouth shut.

Gavin Hepburn and the Mayberry woman? Her vision might not be true, but even if it were, she had to shut her mind to it. It was the only way to stay sane.

With a will of their own, her eyes strayed to the table where Hepburn and Dalziel were seated. The Mayberry arrived at that moment, fluttering like a brilliant butterfly, and made straight for Hepburn's table. After some rearranging, she managed to squeeze in between Hepburn and Dalziel. It was all very amusing, Kate thought, frowning. Macduff was right beside his master but staring at her with mournful eyes. Evidently the rules had been relaxed about allowing dogs inside the hotel. Or perhaps Hepburn was breaking the rules, and no one was brave enough to point it out to him.

His face was turned away, and she could see the line of his jaw. It was granite hard, just like the rest of him. His attention seemed intent on whatever Dalziel was saying. Without warning, he turned his head, and their eyes met. She felt the power of that stare all the way to her toes. It felt as though he knew about her vision and had smacked her hand for her vulgar curiosity.

Assuming her most innocent expression, she pretended an interest in what Constable Hamilton had to say.

She'd anticipated that the guests would be interviewed one by one, but it was far more informal than that. Paper and pencils were distributed, and guests were asked to give an account of their movements from dinner the night before until they came downstairs for breakfast that morning. Obviously, it was nothing but routine. Officer Hamilton wasn't expecting anything shocking to come to light. She chewed on the end of her pencil, wondering what to put down and what to leave out.

She couldn't help chancing another quick look at her nemesis. He was looking at her, too, his eyes narrowed and dark with menace. He couldn't know that she had trespassed in his mind. Then what had put that look on his face? Was it because she wouldn't let her maid open the door to him? She couldn't have faced him then. Now that she had herself well in hand, she gave him a cool smile, then bent her head and wrote exactly what they'd agreed on earlier that morning.

Her eyes had begun to tear by the time she'd finished. She'd forgotten Hepburn and Janet Mayberry by then, and her thoughts had turned to Will Rankin and how unjust it was that such a good man had been struck down in his prime. She owed him so much, and she hadn't told him how grateful she was for all he had done for her. She'd tried, but every time she'd begun to stammer out her thanks, he'd cut her off with a smile. He was only doing his job, he'd said. So she had repaid him by helping out at his clinic in Aberdeen and had been well and truly caught. She'd found something bigger than herself to give her time and energies to.

Murder. It didn't seem possible. But neither did what had happened to her when she'd been locked out of the hotel last night. Then there was the voice and her vision. No wonder she was confused.

Sally Anderson, who was sitting on her left, broke into her thoughts. "I think," said Sally, "that your admirer has just put Janet Mayberry in her place, and about time, too, if you ask me."

Kate looked up just in time to see a red-faced Janet rushing out of the room.

"What admirer?"

"Why Mr. Hepburn, of course. Have you two had a falling-out?"

"Why should we? I hardly know him." Kate folded her sheet of paper and held it loosely in one hand. Hepburn had told her to say nothing of the night they'd spent together until he'd had a chance to explain things to the police. It would get out soon enough, if she knew anything about belowstairs gossip, but by then she and Hepburn would have gone their separate ways.

Sally laughed. "Strange," she said, "he has been looking daggers at you since he walked in here."

Kate looked up with a start. He *had* been looking daggers at her since he walked into the dining room. What was the matter with the man? He couldn't possibly know that, in all innocence, she'd wandered into his assignation with the ever-so-ripe Mayberry—could he?

Officer Hamilton made another announcement. They were to leave their statements with him, signed, of course, then they were free to go. That didn't mean much. There were no trains running yet, and the roads were still impassable, except for the old drovers' road that came out at Braemar.

With her eyes carefully averted, Kate got up, crossed to the table where Hamilton sat, and added her statement to the stacks of others that were lying there. That done, she attached herself to her friends and exited the dining room with her head bent and eyes on the floor.

It didn't do her a bit of good. He was waiting for her in the corridor, and before she could take evasive action, he had cut her out of the herd.

"This will only take a moment, ladies," he said. His eyes crinkled at the corners. "I have a favor to ask Miss Cameron."

A few brows went up. Others tittered, but her friends backed away, saying that they would see her later.

As soon as they were out of earshot, she lifted her chin and shot him a scorching look. "I did what you asked me to do," she said. "I wrote what we agreed upon in my statement to the police."

"Oh, I'm sure you did."

"Then why all the ferocious glares?"

"You're mistaken. I was lost in thought, that's all." He paused, then went on, "Look, about this afternoon . . ."

He was searching for words, and that amazed her. He always seemed so sure of himself.

He shook his head. "When I came to your room, your maid wouldn't allow me to see you. I just wanted to make sure that you were all right."

She answered him with all the composure she could muster. "I had a headache, a severe one. I wasn't fit to see anyone. I'm sorry if that inconvenienced you, but we've said all that needs to be said, haven't we?"

"No," he replied. "I wanted to tell you that I'll be away for most of the day. Dalziel and I intend to visit the police station to have a word with the medical examiner.

He's an old friend of the family, so I know that he'll share his findings with me. I've asked Mrs. Cardno to look after you in my absence."

She was startled into a laugh. "Mrs. Cardno? She's an old lady. What can she do?"

He framed his answer as though she were a slow-witted child. "I've known Juliet's mother since I was an infant. She knows what to do in an emergency. There's no need to worry. I'm leaving Macduff with you as well. Don't let him out of your sight. Remember what happened to Will. Remember what almost happened to you. Never forget it for one moment."

"Now you're frightening me."

"Good! Just remember to keep Macduff with you at all times."

"And what's the favor you wanted to ask?"

"Don't frown so much. It makes you look angry."

It looked as though he might say more, but he shook his head again, then strode along the corridor to the exit, where Dalziel was waiting for him.

Mrs. Cardno passed around the plate of sponge cakes and regarded her companions with a satisfied smile. "It's such a pleasure for an old woman to have young people about her," she crooned. Her gaze touched briefly on each one. "You were just young girls in pinafores and pigtails when I first met you. And now look at you! All married or soon to be married. Where did the time go?"

The "girls" she referred to were Juliet's school friends, Kate among them, who had good-naturedly accepted her invitation to an after-dinner hen party to cheer an old lady who was beginning to pine for the company of her only child. Kate was wondering if the hen party was Hepburn's idea, something to take her mind off her troubles. It worked, up to a point; then her mind would stray to Dr. Rankin, and she would blink away the sting of tears.

They were in Mrs. Cardno's private parlor, a commodious room that was usually reserved for paying guests. As the mother of the bride, Mrs. Cardno evidently took precedence. It was on her say-so that the rule about dogs in the hotel had been relaxed.

As she sipped her glass of sherry and nibbled on the delicacies laid out for them, Kate's thoughts turned to her school days, when she and her friends were senior girls. They'd felt so grown-up then, at the end-of-term parties, when they were allowed to stay up late, sipping sherry and making small talk under the watchful eyes of their teachers and parents. Not that she'd had much to say. Even then, she'd known that she was different.

Macduff nudged her knee, and she surreptitiously passed him the remains of her minuscule sponge cake, which he swallowed without even biting into it. When he nudged her again, she scowled down at him, and he slunk behind a chair.

"Kate isn't soon to be married," said Lorna Dare. She popped a tiny custard tart into her mouth and swallowed it—just like Macduff, Kate thought. "You're becoming a confirmed spinster, Kate, an old maid before your time."

Kate had never taken to Lorna, maybe because she did everything well. No, that wasn't it. Sally did everything well, and she liked Sally. The difference was that Lorna wanted everyone to envy her.

She was going to make light of the jibe, but Sally got there before her. "Lorna, do you have eyes in your head? Gavin Hepburn took one look at our little mouse, and he was smitten. Who is looking after his dog? Our Kate, of course, and you know how Hepburn feels about his dog."

Sally's green eyes, blond hair, and alabaster skin were, she liked to boast, Viking in origin. When her temper was up, as now, no one doubted her claim, and a wise person kept out of her way.

But Lorna's last name wasn't Dare for nothing. She tossed her head. "Hepburn," she said, "is a rake. He takes advantage of women. Watch your step, Kate, or you may find yourself no more than another notch on his bedpost."

"Now that," said Sally with a laugh, "sounds like the voice of experience. What happened, Lorna? Did he resist your charms?"

Kate had expected a ribbing after Hepburn had singled her out, but she took instant umbrage to Lorna's remarks. She wasn't the least bit interested in Hepburn.

"Mr. Hepburn," she said, "was Dr. Rankin's friend. He has been very kind to me. That doesn't mean that I am smitten with him or he with me. Isn't it possible for a man and woman to be friends?"

"No," came a resounding chorus of female voices followed by giggles.

"It's just as well," Lorna replied. "I have it from my maid, who had it from Miss Mayberry's maid, that your Mr. Hepburn whiled away the afternoon in her mistress's boudoir."

Into the awful silence that followed, Mrs. Cardno said, "May I pass the decanter around?"

The glasses were replenished. Kate was just beginning to relax when Lorna spoke again. "There's a rumor going around that Hepburn is one of those Grampian wizards, you know, an heir of Lady Valeria, the celebrated Witch of Drumore. Not that I believe in such things myself."

"What?" Kate's head jerked up.

"His grandmother, the late Lady Valeria McEcheran," Lorna amplified.

"Don't believe everything you hear," responded Meg Brown. She was the oldest in the group and the shyest. "Lady Valeria's gifts died with her. They pass through the female line, you see, and there were no females to inherit."

"How do you know so much?" asked Sally.

"My grandparents live in Drumore. The village, I mean, not the castle. They told me."

Sally said, "I think our little Meg has been making too free with the sherry decanter."

Meg shook her head. "I've hardly taken a sip. Strong spirits don't agree with me. Don't look so worried, Kate. Lady Valeria was a good witch. But you know the family best, Mrs. Cardno. Is it true? Is Mr. Hepburn one of the heirs to Lady Valeria?"

Mrs. Cardno treated them all to a benign smile. "It's true that Lady Valeria was his grandmother, but as for the rest, well, if you accept legends and the old knowledge, I suppose it's possible. But as you said, Meg, Lady Valeria's gifts were supposed to pass to the females in her family, not to the males."

"But there were no females. Only Mr. Hepburn and his brother and a cousin."

"True," replied Mrs. Cardno, and she popped a small macaroon into her mouth.

"What kind of gifts would a good witch pass on?" asked Sally, sounding truly interested now.

"Clairvoyance," replied Mrs. Cardno, "visions and dreams, and the ability to read minds. That sort of thing. Some of them are healers. But the gifts are selective. Not every seer has the same gifts. But I'm only speculating. The old knowledge died away, and we're all more skeptical now."

Kate wanted to hear more, but Mrs. Cardno veered off in another direction. "Sally," she said, "have you set the date for your wedding yet? And when are we going to meet your betrothed?"

There was a twinkle in Sally's eyes, as though she, too, was aware that the old lady had deliberately turned the conversation. "Didn't Juliet tell you?" she said. "The wedding is in June, and that's when you will meet Cedric—if he remembers to turn up. I don't mean to shock you, Mrs. Cardno, but this will be a marriage of convenience. Cedric in not the least bit romantic, and neither am I."

Mrs. Cardno nodded sagely. "Such marriages were common in my day, and very happily they turned out, too. I think young people expect too much from their partners these days. Love can grow from friendship, you know."

From there, the conversation moved on to children, and how impatient Meg and Lorna were to get home to theirs. Everyone complained about the inconvenience of being marooned in the Highlands, especially as they had packed only enough garments for a three-day jaunt.

Macduff began to scratch the door. It was the perfect moment for Kate to excuse herself. She had nothing to contribute to the rearing of children. "I should take Macduff for a walk," she told Mrs. Cardno. "Then I think I'll toddle off to bed."

Once in the corridor, she inhaled a long breath and let it out slowly. All this talk of wizards and witches was making her light-headed. Gavin Hepburn a wizard? She didn't believe it! That was the thing about the Highlands. It was so isolated that the old superstitions continued to flourish.

Whoever had sent her that note believed in the old superstitions. He thought she was a witch. That was why he wanted to kill her.

Gavin Hepburn had saved her. She really was the most ungrateful wretch. She should be kissing the ground he walked on, not finding fault because he indulged in a little dalliance with Janet. She couldn't be jealous. She hardly knew the man.

She let out a sigh. "Come along, Macduff—" She stopped. There was no sign of the dog. He must have trotted downstairs while she was woolgathering. Damn and blast that dog! What was she supposed to do now?

"Macduff," she whispered fiercely. "Where are you, you bad dog? Get back here at once!"

Macduff either did not hear her or he had found an interesting scent to chase down. She could well imagine where that scent would lead him. The kitchen staff had taken to feeding him tidbits. They weren't the only ones. When he cocked his head and looked up at her with those huge, mournful eyes, she couldn't resist him, either.

There was such a thing as loyalty! Macduff was supposed to protect her! She was sorely tempted to leave him to his doggie vices. What stopped her was Gavin's instructions. She could well imagine how he would react if she told him that she had mislaid his precious dog.

She took a moment to absorb her surroundings. No sense of danger came to her. All was quiet in the hotel. Normal. It was dark outside, but the corridors were well lit. The odd footman passed her and murmured a civil greeting. Emboldened, she walked to the end of the corridor and pushed through the door to the servants' staircase. At the bottom of those stairs, two flights below, were the kitchens, and that was where she was sure she would find Macduff.

It took a moment for her eyes to adjust to the gloom. There were fewer lamps here than in the hotel's corridors, but that came as no surprise. The hotel staff were early to bed and early to rise. All the same, she expected some of them to be up and about. Someone had to answer the bells that summoned servants to the guests' bedrooms. And, obviously, someone had to be up to tempt Macduff with morsels of food. Step by slow step, she began to descend the stairs.

She was halfway down when the staircase door below her opened, letting in a shaft of light. With one hand on the rail, she froze, ears straining. Then it came to her, danger, not the kind of danger that made her skin crawl, but that odd apprehension that turned her bones to slush.

"Gavin Hepburn!" she said under her breath. It had to be him.

"What in hell's name do you think you're doing?" he demanded angrily.

When he drew level with her, he came into the light, and she had a clear view of that frozen jaw and lips pulled back in a snarl.

With some idea of delaying the evil moment when she had to confess that she'd lost his dog, she blurted out, "So what happened in Ballater?"

He did not unlock his jaw. "We'll get to that later. What I want to know is what you are doing hiding out in the staircase? Didn't I tell you not to let Macduff out of your sight?"

Because he had frightened her, her temper flared. "Your dog," she said, "got away from me. What was I supposed to do? I was sure I would find him in the kitchen."

Her answer seemed to inflame him more. "When you entered the servants' staircase, you shut him out. He can't open doors."

"He deserted me! I didn't desert him! And where is the traitor, anyway?"

"I sent him to bed."

"Where did you find him?" Her voice was rising to match her frustration. Another thought occurred to her. "And how did you know I was in the servants' staircase?"

"I didn't know. I met you by chance. That isn't the point. You were supposed to keep Macduff with you at all times. Have you forgotten what happened to Will?"

She was totally unprepared for the rush of emotion that swept through her. Her petty grievance with the man who was glowering at her seemed insignificant when she remembered what had befallen Will Rankin. How could she have forgotten even for a minute?

"Kate," he said and reached for her. "I'm sorry."

She took a quick step back.

He paid no attention to her involuntary movement, but reaching for her shoulders, he pulled her into his arms. "It's all right to grieve," he said, "but you can't grieve every moment you're awake. Will wouldn't expect it of you. And this isn't over yet. You are a target, too. Never forget it. All I want is to protect you. Will you remember that?"

She needed to be comforted, but not by him. She wanted her mother. Even her sister would do. She wanted petting and a shoulder to cry on. She wanted to unburden herself and share the horrible events of the worst night of her life.

She pushed out of his arms. "I was in the wrong," she said. "I'm sorry. My mind wasn't on Macduff, and I let him wander away. I didn't think I was putting myself in danger. I was more worried about what you would say if I couldn't find him."

"You were more worried about a dog than you were about yourself?"

"No. Yes." She lifted her shoulders in a tiny shrug. "Macduff saved my life. That makes him special."

"What about me? Am I special, too?"

She tilted her head to get a better look at him. "Every woman thinks you're special, Hepburn. Why should I be different?" She managed a convincing chuckle. "My friends were right about you," she said. "You can make a female forget her own name. Now tell me what happened at the police station."

He said something harsh under his breath and then indicated with a gesture that she should precede him up the stairs. When they pushed out of the staircase, Macduff came loping along the corridor to meet them. Not far behind him was Mrs. Cardno, leaning on a cane.

"I take it," said Mrs. Cardno, "that all has ended well?"

Kate was staring at the cane. She couldn't remember seeing it before. Who did Mrs. Cardno think she was—her bodyguard? The thought made her want to laugh.

"Yes," said Gavin. "No thanks to one reckless young woman."

"Then I'll leave you to it," replied Mrs. Cardno, and turning smartly, she hobbled toward her own door.

Kate was beginning to feel like a precocious schoolgirl who had to be kept on a tight rein. As they walked in the opposite direction from Mrs. Cardno's, she said, "I thought you sent Macduff to bed?"

"I did, but of course, the door to my room is locked. As I told you, Macduff can't open doors."

"Your room?"

He had her by the elbow and was propelling her along the corridor. "I thought it best to be close at hand. I did mention, did I not, that you are probably still a target of some deranged killer? We have a lot to talk about, and we'll be private in my room."

He released her and unlocked the door to his room. It seemed ridiculous to protest. Shrugging negligently, she brushed by him and crossed the threshold. Macduff followed and made straight for the tall dresser and squeezed himself underneath it as though he wanted to hide.

Preoccupied with the dog's strange behavior, she barely registered the key turning in the lock, and she gave a startled cry when she found herself grabbed by strong hands. Her eyes flew up to meet Gavin's furious expression. She was so shocked, she could only stutter.

Eight

"What?" Her hands balled into fists. "What do you think you're doing, Hepburn?"

Between his teeth, he replied, "I'm thinking how satisfying it would be to give you a good shaking. You did not obey my instructions, Kate."

She dragged herself free and retreated, rubbing her arms where his fingers had dug in. She wasn't afraid. Her temper was the equal of his, but her breathing was far more audible.

"You arrogant ass! I am not your dog to run and fetch on your command. I am my own mistress. I come and go as I please!" She continued to give ground as he pursued her. "I'm warning you, Hepburn. My Fraser cousins will break you into little pieces if you harm a hair on my head."

She had retreated to the bed. It was too undignified to crawl over it, so she stood her ground and tried to stare him down.

"Your Fraser cousins," he said pleasantly, "are not here. In their absence, I have appointed myself as your guardian until someone more suitable turns up to fill the slot."

"Guardian!" she flung at him. "I came of age a long time ago!" Inch by slow inch, she edged away from the bed. If only she could reach the door, she would be home and free. "Unlock the door," she commanded stridently, "or I shall scream the house down."

Her threat made no impression on him. With the same pitiless stride, he closed the distance between them. Her hand lashed out, but he easily deflected the movement. Clamping his arms around her, he used his weight to flatten her against the wall. Despite her prodigious experience in ministering to the sick and drunks at the clinic, she realized that she was abysmally ignorant of male anatomy, at least when the male was aroused. His body ground into hers. His lips moved on hers in a sensual caress that betrayed a wealth of experience that she did not possess. His hands circled her throat, holding her head up to prolong the kiss. Against her lips, he whispered, "I've been dreaming of this from the moment I first saw you." He increased the pressure of his lips, and the sudden surge of emotion staggered her. Nothing in her life had prepared her for the leap of awareness of everything that was feminine in her nature. She felt like the bewitched beauty in the children's fable, the girl who had been awakened by a kiss.

He pulled back slightly, his brow puckered in a frown. He was staring at her as though he had fallen off a horse and landed on his head. She knew the feeling. He was stupefied. And she was stupid.

She wrenched herself free and swung away from him, then swung back again. The angry words bubbled up and spilled over. "If you're looking for a night of debauchery, go find Janet Mayberry. Or is one woman a day not enough for a man of your prodigious appetites?"

His mouth tightened. "How do you know about Janet?"

Her mind froze, then thawed when a way out of her dilemma opened before her. She felt quite smug. How did she know about Janet?

"Ladies have maids, and maids gossip. Ask Mrs. Cardno. Ask my friends. They were highly diverted."

"Bloody hell! Can't a man have a private life? Look, nothing happened. I kissed her. So why are you so put out? What does it matter to you?"

Good question. To give herself time to think, she fussed with the trim on her gown.

"You haven't answered my question," he said gently.

"It matters," she said, "because our names are being linked as well. How do you think that makes me feel? You, me, and Janet Mayberry, a ménage à trois."

He grinned devilishly. "A ménage à trois? Where did you learn about that? A gothic novel?"

"I may be innocent, Mr. Hepburn, but I'm not ignorant. I read the newspapers." She would never admit to this man that she read gothic novels.

"Innocent?"

She let out a long breath. "Innocent, inexperienced, call it what you will. Now that I've gained a little experience, I promise not to attack you again."

Without a trace of mockery, he said, "I'm afraid I can't make the same promise. You have been forewarned, Miss Cameron. Now, take a chair. We have a lot to talk about."

It wasn't a request. His eyes glittered with a warning. She thought it prudent to accept the chair he indicated by the fire, but she was sore pressed not to pick up the poker.

"I came into your room," she said, "because I thought you would tell me what happened at the police station."

He took the chair opposite hers, and after giving her one of his enigmatic stares, he slouched down and inclined his head. "The police were satisfied with the obvious explanation, that Will's death was an accident. I spoke to the medical examiner, and he was of the same opinion. Of course, they didn't know about the attack on you."

"What about our statements?"

"I was getting to that. I told them exactly what we'd agreed on, that you heard a dog howling, went to investigate, and became disoriented. They know we spent the night together."

When she bit down on her lip, he quickly interjected, "Kate, we can't pretend that it didn't happen. The gillies saw us. And it's in our signed statements. You knew that."

"It's not that."

"What then?"

"Isn't it possible that Dr. Rankin's death *was* an accident?"

"No. Hear me out. I overlooked something I should have noticed before. There was an empty whiskey bottle beside Will's body. You remember that you smelled whiskey in the hothouse?"

"I remember."

"The bottle was at the police station. I had a chance to look at it more closely. It was the wrong whiskey. Will only drinks . . . drank single malt. This was an inferior whiskey, possibly from some local still. I pointed this out to Officer Hamilton. His response was to look at me as though I'd imbibed one too many myself." He gave a deprecating smile.

When she tried to interrupt, he went on in a level voice, "I'm not finished yet. Dalziel told me that Will had received a note, too, but being Will, he didn't take it seriously. In fact, he laughed it off. He said that it was the ravings of someone who detested psychiaters." His eyes narrowed on her face. "What?"

"That must be why he seemed agitated when I told him about the note I'd received. That's why he wanted to meet with me when everyone had gone to bed." She looked up at him, her eyes tight with horror. "Someone must have overheard us arrange to meet. Whoever murdered Dr. Rankin must have heard every word of our conversation." She gave a ragged breath. "If only I hadn't involved him, he might still be alive."

"No! Will took the threat seriously, whatever he may have told Dalziel. I know, because he tried to confide in me but couldn't quite bring himself to tell me anything, except that murder was involved. It was Dalziel who told me that three people connected to the clinic in Aberdeen had died accidentally: Dr. Rosner was the first."

"Dr. Rosner?" She nodded. "I'd heard that, but he retired a long time ago. Who would even remember that he was once connected to the clinic?"

"The other victim was someone Dalziel knew only as Daft Daffy. He fell into the harbor and drowned."

Again, she nodded. "He was a vagrant. His only connection to the clinic was that he'd come in for a hot meal or a place to sleep when the weather drove him in." She looked up at him. "Who was the third victim?"

"A prostitute who plied her trade down on Regent Quay. She went by the name of Annie Laurie. She was beaten to death."

She shook her head. "Poor girl. There are so many of them. No one mentioned it to me."

"It's not the kind of thing Dalziel would mention to a lady."

"No, I suppose not."

He leaned forward in his chair. "Will said that he

would tell me more when he talked to someone in Aberdeen. That was where he was going if the trains were running. Have you any idea who Will might have been thinking of? Who would he talk to in Aberdeen?"

She shook her head. "I don't know. But you should talk to Dr. Taggart. He has been at the clinic long before my time."

"I know I've asked you this before, but is there anyone who might wish you ill?"

"No."

Her mind was still dwelling on the people who had met with suspicious accidents. Her voice was whisper soft. "That would mean," she said, "that the vile creature who attacked me has already murdered four people, five if we count Annie Laurie."

"Yes," he replied tonelessly.

"Maybe more."

"It's possible."

She jumped to her feet, paced to the window, then returned just as abruptly to the chair she had vacated. "We have to tell the police everything," she said. "They *must* listen to us now. If we can't convince them, other people may die."

"It won't work."

The conviction in his voice infuriated her. "How can you say that? The police aren't stupid. They know what they're doing."

He shook his head. "It's too late now. As I said before, anything we would say would be highly suspect. Let's not complicate things. We can't prove that someone attacked you. As it is, they think that we invented the story about the howling dog to make it appear that our night together was innocent. I'm sure in my own mind, however, that the police believe we are lovers and that you slipped away to be with me."

"What? That's nonsense! No one in his right mind would think that you'd be interested in someone like me or vice versa. We're too different. Opposites, in fact."

"Opposites attract, or so I've heard." One side of his lip curved.

She scowled. "Don't start that again."

He laughed. "Oh, we'll get to that later, but right now I want you to pay attention to what I say. Here's the conundrum. Assuming that all the victims received notes like yours, what was the murderer's purpose in advertising the fact that his victims were all connected to the clinic?"

She thought for a moment and shook her head. "I don't know. What do you think?"

His eyes were no longer blue but as black as coal. "I think that there was only one target. I think that the others were camouflage, you know, misdirection to confuse the authorities."

She wasn't following his logic. "But the police don't have the notes, so how can they be misdirected?"

"Oh, I'm sure that this villain will think of a way to correct his error."

Now her mind was going in circles. "Who was the real target?"

He gazed at her through the thick veil of his lashes.

Her voice came out a squeak. "Not me!"

"We'll have to wait and see."

"What does that mean?"

"We'll put my theory to the test."

She stopped breathing as she scanned his words. "How do we do that?" she asked slowly. A horrible suspicion was beginning to take root in her mind.

Hands clasped, he leaned forward and pinned her with his stare. "You'll never feel safe till we catch this monster. We have to lure him into the open. Don't worry. I won't let anything happen to you."

"You mean . . ." She could hardly believe what he was suggesting. "I'm to be the bait?" In her mind's eye, she saw a little goat tied to a stake, bleating for his mother, while a big black panther edged closer and closer.

"No!" The violence in his voice made her start. "You're a target, not bait. I let that monster get to Will. I'm not going to let him get to you, too. I'll do everything in my power to keep you safe."

She realized that this wasn't about her. It was about his friend Will Rankin. This was about revenge, and she would be the pawn to entice Dr. Rankin's murderer to overreach himself. She wasn't unwilling. She owed Gavin Hepburn her life. Dr. Rankin had not been as lucky as she. Her only defense was that she wasn't that brave.

When he closed the distance between them and grasped her hands, she flinched from the contact. He sank down on his heels till they were eye to eye. "I'm not letting you out of my sight until that murdering devil is behind bars or hanging from a gibbet."

"And how will you mange that?"

The tense lines in his face relaxed, and he managed a faint smile. "You, my dear Kate, are about to acquire a bodyguard, two, if you count Macduff. Where you go, we go. We'll become inseparable. I've also arranged for a chaperone to keep tongues from wagging."

She thought that a chaperone just to convey her to her home was a bit excessive, and she wondered whose good name he hoped to protect—his or hers.

She said dryly, "A chaperone won't help. Tongues are already wagging about you and Miss Mayberry."

When he scowled at Kate, Macduff pushed between

them and started to whine. "That's right, boy," said Kate. "You look after me, and I'll look after you."

Gavin ignored his dog. His voice was tight. "It was a lapse in judgment, nothing more. Let me repeat myself. Nothing of any significance happened."

She raised her brows. "Oh? Why not?"

"Because, my dear Kate, I felt as though you were looking over my shoulder."

The oddly speculative look in his eyes made her skin heat. He couldn't possibly know how close he was to the truth, could he? She answered him lightly. "A ménage à trois? You must be dreaming." To distract him, she said quickly, "So, who is this respectable chaperone you mentioned? Oh, no, don't tell me it's Mrs. Cardno."

"How did you know?" He sounded surprised.

"She said that she was ready for an adventure. Is that why she carries a cane? To protect me?"

"It wasn't my idea, but it's a good idea."

She thought for a moment. "What if you're wrong? What if someone else is the target, someone who has no idea that a murderer may be stalking him or her?"

He shrugged. "I can't protect everyone."

His indifference shocked her. "That sounds heartless!"

His lips flattened, and he rose to his feet, forcing her to look up at him. "Contrary to what you may think of me, I haven't washed my hands of them."

She watched as he walked to the table by the bed and turned up the lamp. "That's better," he said. "Now I can see your face."

He took his chair again. "When I was in Ballater, I took the opportunity of telegraphing my brother. He and his family are in London right now. I know I can count on him to be on the first train to Aberdeen and start making inquiries at the clinic. Does that satisfy you?"

His face was carved in stone. Obviously, she had offended him. She modified her voice. "Your brother? That would be Alex Hepburn, wouldn't it? He's some kind of policeman?"

"He's attached to the Home Office as a special agent."

She had no idea what that meant, and the coldness of his response did not encourage her to press for answers. She did, however, remember something Juliet had told her about the Hepburn brothers, that they had foiled a plot to assassinate the queen. Official channels had suppressed the story so that only a few insiders knew the details.

"Any other objections?" he asked in the same cold tone.

His hauteur was beginning to grate on her. She lifted her chin. "We're going to become inseparable?"

"I won't let you out of my sight. And if I have to leave you for any reason, I'll make sure you are well protected."

"How am I going to explain your presence to my family?"

He gave a negligent shrug. "Let's sleep on it. I'm sure something will occur to us."

There were a million questions buzzing inside her head, but they stilled when he thrust something into her hand. "What's this?"

"The note that Will received. Dalziel found it inside the book Will was reading."

Her heart picked up speed as she smoothed out the note and silently read the message: "Psychiaters are the spawn of the devil."

"Does it look familiar?" he asked.

She nodded. "The script is the same."

He took the note back. "My brother will want to see this," he said. "Was the note you received in a similar vein? I ask because Alex will want to know what it said, to compare it to any others he may find."

It seemed pointless to conceal what she was beginning to see might be a crucial clue. "It said, 'In Scotland, we burn witches.'"

He didn't look shocked or puzzled or curious.

"Alex will know what to look for when he arrives at the clinic," was his only comment.

She didn't know whether she was drooping with relief or fatigue. All she knew was that she wanted her bed.

He got up. "Through there," he said, pointing to a door, "is the bathroom and water closet." His eyes filled with laughter. "We don't want a repeat of what happened at the cottage when you crept off to the privy without telling me. Your clothes are in the wardrobe."

She was mulling over his words, trying to make sense of them, but she couldn't seem to think straight. "I don't have any clothes except what I'm standing up in."

"Oh, I took the liberty of asking Mrs. Cardno if you could borrow some of Juliet's things. She was happy to oblige."

She took exception to the way he had taken charge. It would have been nice to be consulted. She set her jaw. "Has it occurred to you that Juliet might not feel the same way?"

"Juliet would not be so small-minded. The bed is yours. Macduff and I will make do with the floor."

Finally, his words made sense. Appalled, she burst out, "I can't stay here! This is your room. What will the maid say when she arrives to light the fire?"

"This room is supposed to be unoccupied. No one will come to light the fire. Kate, I'm not letting you go back to your own room. It's not safe. Can't you see that?"

He had a point. "What about my maid? Elsie will have a fit if she can't find me."

"Dalziel will tell her about the switch. When you wake up in the morning, she'll be here."

Arguing with this man was useless. She really, really hated take-charge men, even when they were in the right.

She was hardly aware that he'd lit a candle for her to take to the bathroom. Fatigue was beginning to dull her mind. She'd been tossed around by so many emotions, she hardly knew whether she was coming or going.

When she studied her reflection in the mirror above the sink, she shook her head. No one would notice her in a crowd. But Gavin Hepburn had noticed her. Truth to tell, she had noticed him, too. Was it chance that had thrown them together, or was it something else?

According to gossip, his grandmother had been a celebrated witch. In her own time, she'd been called a witch, too, but that was before Dr. Rankin had taught her how to protect herself. It was all humbug anyway, wasn't it?

She spent the next little while washing the day's dirt from her skin. When she cleaned her teeth, she grimaced at her reflection. Magda said that her teeth were her best feature. But who noticed teeth? She let down her hair and fluffed it out. In another minute, her hair would hang straight and heavy as it always did. And why was she bothering?

When she crawled into bed, she had to admit that she felt safer knowing that Gavin and his dog were right there with her. She listened to their breathing, then she listened to the soft hiss of the rain as it painted patterns on the small windowpanes. Rain. The temperature was warming, melting the snow. Tomorrow, the trains would be running again.

Her eyes closed; her thoughts began to drift. *Bait.* Her head moved restlessly. Her muscles tensed. But something soft and silky slipped into her mind, soothing, beguiling, drawing her away from all her fears. She breathed out a sigh when she recognized the voice.

Pictures formed behind her eyes, and by degrees her muscles relaxed. She wasn't alone, the voice told her. An army of powerful protectors ringed her in. She listened to the voice whisper their names, and when the voice hesitated, she said the names for him. Her family was there, even Magda, and her Fraser cousins. But out in front were her two stalwart defenders, Gavin and his dog. And right at her back was Mrs. Cardno, wielding her cane as though it were a spear.

Mrs. Cardno? What was she doing there?

She grew restless again. This wasn't right. She wasn't helpless. She wasn't a coward. She wanted to do her part. But the voice wouldn't hear of it. The more she struggled, the tighter his hold became.

Suddenly, the picture changed. She saw herself sleeping in her secret hiding place in the priest's hole high above the cellar stairs. It was so secret that not even her father knew about it. It was the one place she felt really safe. Gradually, her breathing slowed. She drifted.

When Gavin felt her slip into a dreamless sleep, he gently released his hold on her mind. The pictures and images that he'd put there had obviously worked. She was sleeping soundly.

He wished that he could read her thoughts, but that wasn't how his gift worked. He could, however, read her emotions, sense when she was frightened or angry or upset. That was how he had known that she was on the servants' staircase, and that was how he had known she was running for her life on the moor. Her panic had transferred itself to him and, naturally, he had rushed to her defense.

She thought he was heartless. Her jibe had stung, but he made allowances for her, because she didn't know as much as he. Sighing, he linked his fingers behind his head and stared up at the ceiling. His convoluted theories to persuade her that she was the target of a deranged killer were unconvincing at best. A horse and carriage could have driven through the holes in his logic. How much easier it would have been if he could have said simply and truthfully, *I know that you're the target because I'm a seer, and I've been sent to save you.* As though she would believe him!

But it was the truth. That was why he'd felt a jolt of recognition when he'd first set eyes on her. That was what his dreams and visions were *trying* to tell him. The cemetery, the stone angels, the black horses with their funeral plumes, that was what the future held for her, but the future could be changed and, by everything he held holy, he would change it.

"In Scotland, we burn witches."

He let out a breath. He'd only known one witch, his granny, Lady Valeria, and Kate wasn't in the same class. She was intuitive, but so were many people. What had she done to incite someone to murder? He had to probe into her past, her mind, her secret thoughts to find the thread that would lead him to a killer.

He thought of Janet Mayberry and cursed under his breath. Janet was a mistake that he was sure Kate would make him pay dearly for. The thought turned in his mind, and he began to smile. She must care for him a little, or she wouldn't have been so scathing when she confronted him with what she knew. The question he was asking himself was, how did she know? Was it maids' gossip, or was it something else?

He didn't regret kissing Kate. It was either kiss her or shake her. His anger had changed to something quite different the moment he'd felt her yield to him. It had been a long, long time since he'd wanted to know a woman so intimately. He wasn't thinking only of sex; he was thinking of everything that made Kate who and what she was.

He wondered how soon it would be before she heard about Alice.

He'd drunk himself insensate for weeks after Alice drowned. It was his granny who had been the saving of him. Her psychic power had sent her from the Highlands to London like a homing pigeon. She'd known that he'd sunk into a melancholy. And it was in the Highlands that he'd finally managed to crawl out of the pit.

He'd tramped over miles of drovers' roads, climbed the peaks, and fished for salmon with his friend Will. They hadn't talked much at first, but he'd learned that there was healing in silence. And when he finally shared his guilt, Will had been a good listener.

Now Will was gone, and Kate Cameron's fate hung in the balance. The words sounded melodramatic, but they were the right words. He had to find a way to change her future.

He thought about the way she had responded to his kiss for a long, long time. He could still taste the sherry on her tongue. He swallowed, filling himself with her taste and flavor. He wanted more. After tomorrow, however, he would be lucky if she would give him the time of day.

On that sobering thought, he turned on his side and willed himself to sleep.

Nine

"No. There must be some mistake, Elsie. I'm not going to Aberdeen. I'm going home."

Even as she said the words, Kate knew that she'd been tricked. Perhaps *tricked* was the wrong word. It had never occurred to her that Gavin would take her to Aberdeen. And when had she started to think of him as Gavin?

Elsie didn't stop packing all the lovely garments she'd found in the wardrobe, Juliet's garments. That was what was beginning to convince Kate that the misunderstanding was all on her part. When he'd mentioned that Mrs. Cardno had picked out a few of Juliet's things for her to wear, she'd assumed that he meant a change of clothes to tide her over until she got home.

Elsie was no happier with this turn of events than Kate. "There's no mistake," she said, tight-lipped. "I'm to take a letter to your father explaining your absence, while you take the train to Aberdeen. I'm your lady's maid. I should go with you."

Mistress and maid were both banging around the

room, opening cabinets and slamming doors. There wasn't a scrap of clothing in that room that belonged to Kate. According to Elsie, Mr. Hepburn had packed all her bits and pieces in a small valise and taken them downstairs when she was asleep.

She ground her teeth. She had no choice; she had to don the outfit Elsie had laid out for her, a cherry colored wool with a fitted red and black plaid jacket.

And where was the knave who had promised never to let her out of his sight? Elsie didn't know. She didn't know, nor could she go and look for him. Macduff had planted himself squarely in front of the door and bared his fangs whenever she got too close.

She didn't feel let down; she felt betrayed.

"Oh, miss, you do look nice." Elsie was looking at her as though she were a mouthwatering dessert. "No wonder Mr. Hepburn fell head over heels in love with you at first sight."

"What?" Kate spun to take in her reflection in the mirror. The woman who stared back at her seemed like a stranger. She wasn't sure that she liked what she saw. The outfit was too showy, too flamboyant for her quiet personality. She couldn't live up to it, nor did she want to. Besides, whenever she borrowed someone else's finery, disaster zoomed in like a shark drawn by the scent of blood. Magda's beautiful gray silk gown was a case in point. Juliet didn't have Magda's temper, but Kate knew that she, herself, would feel horribly, horribly guilty if anything happened to Juliet's immaculate outfit.

She turned back with a scowl. "Don't believe everything Mrs. Cardno tells you." She could see from the maid's expression that she'd hit the mark. "She has a romantic turn of mind. And I'm not going to Aberdeen. I'm going home. There has been a colossal misunderstanding, that's all."

There was a discreet knock on the door, and Gavin entered. Kate folded her arms across her breasts. Macduff wagged his tail, and Elsie muttered something incomprehensible before making a quick exit.

"What's the matter with your maid?" Gavin asked, staring at the closed door.

"I think she wants to be out of the battle zone," Kate replied coolly.

"Ah." He smiled as he perched on the arm of a chair. "What is it this time? Was the bed lumpy? Did I snore? Don't you like the garments Mrs. Cardno chose for you?"

She came straight to the point. "I'm not going to Aberdeen with you. I thought I made it clear that I was going home to my family."

He frowned. "It was all settled last night. What made you change your mind?"

She sat on the edge of the bed. "I think," she said, "we must have been talking at cross purposes. My family will be worried about me and . . . What?" she demanded when he shook his head.

"I'll wager that our villain has set himself up nicely in Braemar. That's the nearest village to your father's house, isn't it?" When she nodded, he went on, "Don't you see, Kate? He's probably somewhere close by, waiting to make his move. Of course, he'll know where you live. Can't you see the danger you'd be in?"

"I have cousins who will protect me if it becomes necessary."

He was on his feet. "If it becomes necessary?" he roared, making her cower. "You are the target of someone with a deranged mind or an ax to grind. I'm going to keep you safe. That means I'm going to be as close to you as your own shadow until I find out who he is, and since I'm going to Aberdeen to make inquiries, you will have to come with me. Do you understand?"

"What inquiries?" she asked.

His lips flattened fractionally, then relaxed. "Dalziel tells me that all Will's records of patients past and present are in the Aberdeen clinic. I'd like to examine them. I'd also like to find out who it was that Will wanted to talk to. Apart from that, I have to see Will's solicitor, make arrangements for the funeral, that sort of thing."

She wasn't worried about the records. She'd taken care of that problem a long time ago.

"I thought your brother was going to make inquiries for you?"

"Alex will help, but he may not know what to look for."

"What about my family?" she asked. "I realize that you and your brother are close, but you have to understand that I'm close to my family, too. I was supposed to be gone for three days, but it's closer to a week. I have to tell them what happened here. I can't let them hear it from strangers."

They stared at one another for a long moment. His eyes were dark and intense, so she tried to copy his look of sheer determination.

"Your family means a lot to you," he said gratuitously.

"Obviously."

"What are they like?"

She shrugged. "Like most families, I suppose. We don't do things together because we're so different. My father's best friends are books; my mother is the custodian of the family, you might say, and by that I mean the family far and near. She is forever arranging get-togethers so that we'll remember that we were once part of a clan. My sister Magda is the beauty. She has broken more hearts than is good for her. Oh yes, and we quarrel a lot. The Camerons and the Frasers have short tempers, and when they are angry, they breathe out fire."

He laughed at this. "And where do you fit in?"

She said simply, "They're larger-than-life characters. I live in their shadow."

He cocked his head to the side. "I find that hard to believe."

"Trust me. Everything is turned into a drama in my family. If you're not part of the drama, then you're part of the audience."

He smiled at this. "I can't make you change your mind?"

"No!" she said emphatically.

"You're as stubborn as a mule."

Since he seemed resigned, she allowed the jibe to pass.

"Be discreet. Don't tell anyone what your plans are. If you are asked a direct question, answer it vaguely. Don't try to leave the room. I'll be back in a few minutes to take you down for breakfast."

She was still digesting his words when he walked to the door.

"Wait!" She was too late. He'd already left, and once again Macduff had planted himself in front of the door.

"You wouldn't bite me, would you, Macduff?" she asked coaxingly.

When she stretched out her hand, Macduff pulled back his lips and showed her his fangs.

She gasped and took a quick step back. "How can you treat me like this?" she said. "I thought we were friends."

She stopped. She must be out of her mind, trying to reason with a dog.

"May I join you?"

Kate looked up with a start. Gordon Massey was

hovering at her elbow with a plate of food in his hand. "Please do," she said automatically.

He set down his plate and pulled up a chair, squeezing in between her and Mrs. Cardno. Kate's eyes flicked to Gavin. He was selecting various items from chafing dishes that were set out on a long table. He had yet to notice that Mr. Massey had joined their little group. But Dalziel, who was sitting opposite Kate, noticed, and his expression was sour.

This, she thought, was excessive. What did Dalziel imagine Mr. Massey would do? The dining room was full of people who would be leaving soon to complete their journeys to Aberdeen or Braemar. No one in his right mind would attack her here. Besides, she had a sixth sense about danger, and her heart hadn't lost a beat yet with one exception—when she looked at Gavin Hepburn.

Massey gave her a smile that dazzled her eyes. "So," he said, "where are you off to this morning?"

She took a quick bite of toast and chewed on it to give herself time to think of a vague answer. Mrs. Cardno filled the void. "First, we're going to Ballater to do a little shopping," she said. "What about you, Mr. Massey?" She waved to his parents, who were sitting at another table. "Are you bound for Braemar?"

"Only long enough to see my parents settled, then I'm off to Aberdeen to keep an appointment I made long before . . . well, before we were cut off by the storm."

Kate was sure he had been on the point of mentioning Dr. Rankin's death and respected his tact in avoiding the subject. She could not think of it without breaking out in shivers.

Mrs. Cardno had no such qualms. "We shall all be in Aberdeen for Dr. Rankin's funeral," she said. "No doubt we will see you there, Mr. Massey."

"Naturally, I'll be there. Has the time and date been arranged?"

"No!" said Dalziel, angry color running under his skin. "The notice will be in all the local papers. I suggest you watch for it."

"Oh, I shall, I shall."

Massey bit into a piece of toast, but nothing could hide his smile, and he winked at Kate. She was mystified by Dalziel's conduct and dipped her head to hide her embarrassment.

A shadow fell across the table, and she looked up to find Gavin staring at her with knotted brows. What, oh what had she done now?

The moment passed when Dalziel got to his feet. "I shall pack and get my boxes downstairs," he said.

There were handshakes all round, then Dalziel left them to finish their breakfast. Kate couldn't concentrate on the chatter that went on around her. The antagonism issuing from Gavin was almost palpable. She was confused. Mrs. Cardno, on the other hand, seemed to be highly entertained.

Finally, it was time to go. They were all milling about in the hall, saying their good-byes. Sally Anderson gave her a hug and made Kate promise to be her bridesmaid at her wedding. Kate readily agreed, knowing that if she ruined her bridesmaid's gown, at least it would be her own loss.

After securing Kate's promise, Sally turned a speculative gaze on Gordon Massey. Her look was returned. Kate was taken aback. Sally was engaged to Cedric Hayes.

"Don't gawk, Kate," Mrs. Cardno said in a stage whisper. "You're already taken. What's the poor man to do?"

Kate gritted her teeth and feigned to be as amused as everyone else who had overheard Mrs. Cardno's comments. At Kate's side, Gavin chuckled and linked his fingers through hers in a proprietary gesture, as though, thought Kate, he was proclaiming to the company that she belonged to him. She wasn't flattered. She wanted to hit him. He was only doing it to annoy her.

"Smile," he whispered in her ear, a whisper that no one else could hear.

She smiled dutifully, but her thoughts were chaotic. Once again, she felt that she was participating in a drama, only this time, she was one of the lead actors.

The trouble was, she didn't know her lines.

It seemed that everyone wanted to leave the hotel at the same time. The result was that there was a run on the carriages the hotel kept to convey its guests to and from the station. All that was available were a pair of two-seater vehicles that looked as though they'd been rescued from a graveyard.

Gavin helped Kate into the cab and climbed in beside her. The hood was up to protect them from the light drizzle that had begun to fall. Kate could see that the journey to Braemar would be miserable beyond bearing. They'd be lucky if they did not come down with pneumonia by the time they reached their destination.

She was on her best behavior since she felt that she had won the point. Gavin would escort her home and, she assumed, catch a later train to Aberdeen. Though he seemed rather stern—a poor loser, she supposed—she made up for his sobriety by adopting her most charming manner. She was, however, not nearly as bright-eyed as she appeared. Only to herself would she admit that she was becoming a tad too fond of this irresistible rake. The sooner they went their separate ways, the better for all concerned.

When they came to the crossroads and the carriage turned left, Kate stirred herself. "We're going the wrong way," she said. "We should have turned right."

"No," responded Gavin. "We're going to the station. If I miss this train, I won't be able to leave until tomorrow. There's only one train running, you see."

She was taken aback. She'd assumed that he would escort her home. Surely he would not let her go alone?

"Who is going to escort me home? Dalziel?"

Her eyes were on Macduff. He was trotting beside their buggy. Was he going to trot the eighteen miles to Braemar? She did not think so. So he was going to Aberdeen, too?

"No," he said, "I'll take you home after our business in Aberdeen is completed."

It took a moment for his words to register, and when they did, she tried to jump to her feet. There wasn't room, of course, so she hit her head on one of the hood's slats, and before she knew it, he had a hand clamped around her wrist. She tried to drag her arm away, but it was held fast in fingers of steel.

"You're hurting me," she hissed and tried to wrench her arm out of his grip.

"You can make a scene," he said, "but it won't do you a bit of good. I told you, where you go, I go, and vice versa. You've got to take our killer more seriously, Kate."

She was breathing through her teeth. "You won't get away with this. I'll scream 'abduction' to the first policeman I see."

"And I shall be forced to kiss you into silence." The shadow of a smile touched his lips. "Grin and bear it, Kate, else people will think you're touched in the brain."

The color washed out of her cheeks, and something inside her seemed to flare to life. She struggled for air as the familiar litany of taunts beat inside her head: *freak, lunatic, bedlamite.* They were only words, Dr. Rankin had told her. Only words. She could lock them out and control her visions with mind games. *Lock them out, Kate.*

She retreated to her safe haven and locked the doors.

There were plenty of people milling about in the station, and not all of them were guests from the hotel. Gavin released the pressure on her wrist, but she sensed his fingers were like the claws of a trap, ready to clamp on her arm if she tried to bolt. She'd become strangely passive, and that troubled him, because it was so unlike her. He slid his hand up to her elbow as he guided her to one of the first-class carriages. Mrs. Cardno was waiting inside with a big smile on her face.

Kate stopped, undecided, but the fingers on her elbow tightened their grasp and propelled her into the window seat. Mrs. Cardno chattered about nothing in particular, then withdrew to the other compartment of their private coach, leaving Gavin and Kate to face each other in silence. His eyes were grave but not unkind. Hers were unseeing, as though she were sleepwalking. He tried to engage her in a rational conversation, but every overture he made was met by silence. He tried to apologize for the steps he felt he'd had to take to keep her safe, but that, too, was met by silence. As a last resort, he closed his eyes and focused on entering her mind with some idea of soothing her fears. What he met was a medieval castle ringed around by a moat. The bridge over the moat was up, and the portcullis was down. There was no way in. What was he supposed to make of that?

His eyes jerked up to her face. Her eyes were closed, and she was breathing softly.

"My time will come," he whispered in her ear, and

he smiled when a little frown flashed across her brow before tranquillity settled on her again.

She wakened on the last leg of their journey feeling refreshed and ready for anything, even for her obnoxious captor, who was watching her with wary eyes.

"It's been almost two hours since you fell asleep," he said. "We'll be arriving in Aberdeen soon. There's a great deal still to be settled between us."

"Why don't you tell me what you've decided? I know my opinions count for nothing."

He was silent a moment. Heaving a sigh, he said, "We shall need a convincing story to explain why we are always in each other's company."

"And?"

He shrugged. "We're eloping because your family doesn't approve of me."

She laughed. "That's not very convincing." Her family would move heaven and earth to see her married, and Gavin Hepburn was definitely a catch.

"It's the best I can come up with, unless you have something to offer."

She shook her head. It hardly mattered what story he invented, because the first chance she got, she would be on her way home.

"One thing I'd like to mention," he said. "No flirting with other men. You may get more than you've bargained for with Massey, but I don't want Dalziel's heart to be broken, and I have no wish to fight a duel over your honor."

Sometimes, like the present moment, it was hard to remember that this man had saved her life, and she should feel grateful. "I don't flirt," she said with as much restraint as she could manage. "I wouldn't know how."

He laughed. "Kate, you flirt with Macduff. You can't help yourself."

It was on the tip of her tongue to mention Janet Mayberry, but that would only invite a war of words, and she wasn't as clever with words as he. All the same, it rankled. First Janet Mayberry, then her. Some stalwart defender he was turning out to be.

"What did I say, Kate?"

"The same as you always say." Her voice was laced with sarcasm. "Nothing of any significance. Where is Dalziel, by the way?"

"I sent him with your maid to answer any questions that your family might raise about our trip to Aberdeen. He'll be on the next train."

She shouldn't have been surprised. Gavin Hepburn seemed to relish disposing of everyone's life. She'd wager that he was a master at chess. They were all pawns in his capable hands, or so he liked to think. He'd learn his mistake soon enough.

"You trust Dalziel implicitly, don't you?" she asked, still thinking of pawns and chess.

He nodded. "I believe I do, firstly because he has been with Will for a number of years, long before our villain came on the scene, and secondly, because no one could manufacture the grief he feels for Will. It's real."

Macduff chose that moment to creep from the corridor and settle at her feet. She didn't want to pet him. In fact, she was sorely tempted to kick him, she, Kate Cameron, who had never met a dog or cat she did not like.

She wanted badly to kick something, but she also wanted to maintain her dignity, so she made do by staring out the window in frigid silence.

Ten

Flanked by Gavin and Mrs. Cardno, Kate stood on the front steps and gazed at the granite mansion where they were to stay for the duration of their visit to Aberdeen.

"It doesn't look like a hotel," she said. "Where are the carriages? Where are the people coming and going?"

"It's a private hotel," Mrs. Cardno replied, "and my good friend Miss Hunter owns the place. It has been in the family for years and years. Too big for one person, so she had the idea of making it over into a sort of guest-house. It's *very* comfortable. I know you will love it."

"And," Gavin interjected, "it's for ladies only. For propriety's sake, Dalziel and I have been domiciled in the gatehouse, but one or both of us will always be close by. Macduff and Mrs. Cardno will be at the house, keeping an eye on you."

Kate ignored the warning behind his teasing grin. Though her temper had cooled considerably since she'd realized that he was abducting her, she was still a long way from being won over by his cozening smiles and asides. As much as possible, she addressed all her remarks to Mrs. Cardno.

"It's a lovely house," she said.

Inwardly, she was sizing up its proximity to other buildings in the area in this cul-de-sac off King Street. The house was in its own grounds but not far from the new Town House on the corner of Union Street, and within easy walking distance of the docks where the clinic was situated. Another point in its favor was that Sally Anderson's house was only a five-minute walk away.

The thought of making a run for it was only a passing fancy, something the heroine in a gothic novel might attempt. She didn't know how long Gavin intended to stay in Aberdeen, but she was sure that her parents would want to attend Dr. Rankin's funeral. So in three or four days, she would see them again, and they could all return to Braemar together.

Heaving a sigh, she climbed the granite stairs and entered the hall. There were, she noticed, no stags' heads or paintings of hunting scenes on these walls, but portraits of men in uniform that obviously catalogued the long line of Hunters who had served in the military. The silver-haired lady who came forward to greet them looked as though she had stepped out of a page of Jane Austen's *Pride and Prejudice*. She wore a high-waisted gown of diaphanous muslin and had a paisley shawl draped artfully around her arms.

"Jessica," Mrs. Cardno trilled, propelling Kate forward. "How lovely to see you again. Allow me to present Miss Kate Cameron, my nephew's fiancée."

Kate threw a scorching look at Gavin, who lifted his shoulders in a negligent shrug. Miss Hunter did not stand on ceremony but put her hands on Kate's shoulders and kissed her on both cheeks.

"It's about time," she said, "that this wandering gypsy settled down. I couldn't be happier, my dear." She linked her arm through Kate's. "Come along, Kate, and I'll show you to your room. You must wonder at my Regency getup, but after dinner, the Jane Austen Club meets, and I'm to read from *Emma*. Now, we have a few rules you should know about . . ."

As she was swept up the stairs, Kate threw Gavin a beseeching look. His response was to wiggle his fingers in a gesture of farewell.

Thirty minutes later, Kate was pacing in her room as Gavin looked on with a bemused smile. He was lounging in a chair, watching her from below his dark lashes.

"What I don't understand," she said, "is how Miss Hunter knew that I would be arriving at her door. She was expecting us. When was this arranged?"

"When we arrived at the station," he replied easily. "Mrs. Cardno telephoned Miss Hunter, and it was all settled."

She stopped pacing. "Miss Hunter has a telephone?" she asked, diverted.

He was watching her intently, but there was a trace of humor in his eyes, too. "Telephones are becoming all the rage in Aberdeen. I wouldn't be surprised if we'll have them all through the Highlands in another year or so."

She sank down on the bed. "Why didn't you tell me on the train about Miss Hunter and her boardinghouse? Why have I been kept in the dark?"

"Don't let Miss Hunter hear you call this house a boardinghouse. She prefers the term *guesthouse*. And the reason I didn't mention it was that you were giving me the cold shoulder. You wouldn't even look at me."

Something else occurred to her, another grievance to lay at his door. "Do you know how many rules the inmates here have to obey?" She ticked them off on her fingers. "No gentlemen callers unless a chaperone is present. No late-night parties; no wine or strong spirits. The doors are locked at nine o'clock. I could go on and on. This isn't a guesthouse. It's a prison." She clenched her hands into fists. "What I'd like to know is why Miss Hunter has made an exception in your case. Why aren't we chaperoned?"

He scratched the bridge of his nose. "She's very romantic," he said and paused.

"And?"

He shrugged. "I had to tell her the sad story of our elopement, you know, that your family does not approve of me. So she knows that you are in hiding."

Her brow creased. "I wouldn't have thought that she would have approved of an elopement. She's a stickler for rules."

"Oh, she has been known to make exceptions. You see, she trusts me. I've known Miss Hunter since I was a babe. She and my mother were close friends. That allows me a certain latitude. All the same, we've only been granted five minutes alone in your room; then I have to go."

She was aghast. "You're not going to leave me here to fend for myself?"

"Certainly not. If you look out the window, you'll see the gatehouse. That's where I'll be staying, and when I'm not here, Mrs. Cardno will be your constant companion. Then there's Dalziel. There's a telephone at the gatehouse, so if you need him for anything, anything at all, give him a call. And, of course, there's Macduff."

"And where will you be when you're not here?"

"I'll see Will's solicitor first, to make arrangements

for the funeral. Then, if I have time, I'll go to the clinic and have a word with Dr. Taggart. I'm hoping he can tell me about those accidents that worried Will." He cocked his head to the side, studying her. "Stay close to the house, Kate. If you want to walk in the grounds, make sure someone is with you."

So much vigilance to keep her, and only her, safe made her wonder. She stared at him in silence, then slowly shook her head. "You know something I don't know. That's it, isn't it?"

His eyes went suspiciously flat. "Why do you say that?"

"Because you're acting as if you know . . . as if you're *certain* that I'm to be the next victim."

The velvet in his voice turned to steel. "What else should I think? Will was murdered, and then his killer came after you. I know that Will would want me to do everything in my power to protect you."

His words brought to mind the mad chase across the moor, and she shivered. Gavin was beginning to make sense. The killer hadn't given up easily. He'd taken a big chance following her into the snowstorm. Why had he bothered? That was the question that gripped her mind. She didn't know anything that could provoke someone to go to such lengths. She was nobody.

He left his chair and sat beside her on the bed. She didn't resist when he took her hands in his. "Trust me, Kate. I won't let anything happen to you."

She lifted her head to look at him, but she didn't say anything.

"I promise you," he went on formally, "as long as I'm alive, you'll be safe, and I intend to live for a very long time." He got up. "I'll look in on you later. Remember what I said about Macduff and Mrs. Cardno."

After he left, she got up and went to look out the

window. The gatehouse was beyond the lawns but half-hidden behind a clump of rhododendrons and other shrubbery. Gavin appeared and strode purposefully across the lawn.

Her intuition had absorbed more than his words told her. His determination to protect her wasn't about Will Rankin as she'd thought. There was more to it than that.

Or was she just havering?

Macduff nosed her hand. "Let's see," she said, "my intuition is telling me that you want to go for a walk or eat your dinner. Well, dinner is out. You already . . ." She stopped. Why was she speaking to a dog? She must be more lonely than she realized.

"Let's see if Mrs. Cardno is free," she said, "and we'll go for a little walk."

Dinner was a nerve-racking affair. There were a dozen elderly ladies, much like Miss Hunter and Mrs. Cardno, whose names Kate forgot almost as soon as she heard them, ladies who were avidly curious about the fledgling who had flown into their coop. She left Mrs. Cardno to field their questions, since she had only a vague idea of what story Gavin had concocted to explain their situation.

At first, she was amused by Mrs. Cardno's embellishments, but her amusement soon turned to horror. Her family wasn't as bad as all that! In an effort to change the subject, she complimented her hostess on the succulent steamed sole that Cook had prepared for their enjoyment. She wasn't exaggerating. It made a pleasant change from the salmon that was so plentiful on Deeside.

After that, her mind wandered, and she came to

herself with a start when she realized that the table had gone quiet and all eyes were on her.

Miss Hunter answered the question in Kate's eyes. "Alice's death was tragic, of course, but it's more than time for Gavin to put the past behind him. We are so happy for both of you, my dear."

Kate looked at the faces staring at her. Mrs. Cardno, she noted, was tying knots in her handkerchief. She'd get no help there. What had she missed when she was woolgathering?

Who was Alice? Why had everyone's expression turned somber? Apart from Mrs. Cardno, they seemed to think that she would know.

Sighing softly, she murmured, "Yes, poor Alice." She chanced a quick peek through her lashes, wondering if she was overdoing it. It wasn't fair to Gavin, it wasn't right, but her curiosity was at boiling point. "I never really did understand what happened there."

"No one does," said one of the ladies. "All anyone knows is that Alice and Gavin went out on a boat. Alice jumped into the water as a lark and drowned. They weren't engaged or anything like that. He didn't go into a decline or drink himself to death, as far as I know."

Another voice added, "He was the one to find her. No one in the crew knew how to swim. Men who don't know how to swim shouldn't be sailors, in my opinion."

In an aside to Kate, Mrs. Cardno said, "I've known the family for years, and they have never hinted that Alice and Gavin were more than friends. You have nothing to fear there, m'dear."

Another lady—Mrs. Black?—joined the conversation. "I knew Alice slightly when I lived in London, before my husband died. Everyone said that she would come to grief sooner or later. She was a law unto herself and took the most appalling risks."

Someone else added with a chuckle, "I think we're exaggerating Alice's hold on him. He hasn't exactly avoided feminine company these last few years."

Miss Hunter said coyly, "Oh, the stories I could tell you—"

At this point, Mrs. Cardno clutched her throat and said hoarsely, "I think I've swallowed a fish bone."

By the time she had chewed on a piece of bread to dislodge the bone, Gavin was forgotten, and all the ladies were relating incidents where they, too, had choked on a morsel of food or knew someone who had. Miss Hunter brought an end to the chatter when she got up and indicated that it was time to withdraw to the parlor for the next installment of *Emma*.

Kate sat through the reading without hearing a word of it. Gavin's high-handed methods to keep her safe were becoming much more comprehensible now that she knew about Alice. The image of him pulling the body of the girl he loved from her watery grave made her wince. No one should have to endure that. First Alice, then Will. She sympathized, truly sympathized, but he had to accept that people should be free to make their own choices, and choices often had unforeseen consequences.

A round of applause dragged her from her reveries. The reading was over.

"Tea and cake, then off to bed," Miss Hunter announced in a ringing voice.

Kate looked at the clock. She couldn't believe it. It was only nine o'clock. She wouldn't sleep a wink for hours and hours. This was purgatory.

No, this was Gavin Hepburn's doing. The more she thought about it, the more her resentment simmered. By the sound of it, Alice wouldn't have accepted his strictures. She was a law unto herself. Then what was she? A mouse?

She sat there simmering, choking on the minuscule bites of cake she was chewing, dreaming of ways of getting out from under his thumb.

By the time bedtime rolled around the following day, Kate would gladly have strangled Gavin Hepburn. She was used to walking for miles, tramping the moors with the sun in her face. The scent of Deeside heather would perfume the air. The air in Aberdeen was, literally, fishy because of the fish market nearby. Not that the residents noticed it. Familiarity had obviously blunted their sense of smell. And all she could see when she looked out her window beyond the grounds was row upon row of depressing gray granite. So what if the houses were practically indestructible and lit by gas? She'd rather be at home in the ramshackle labyrinth of a house her great-grandfather had built, with its oil lamps and candles.

This was Saturday. She should have been out shopping in the fashionable shops of Union Street, but because she was supposed to be hiding from her parents, the most she was allowed was to walk in the small park by the house. And where she went, Mrs. Cardno was sure to follow.

Twenty-four hours had passed since she had last seen Gavin, and though he'd telephoned the house, he hadn't spoken to her directly but had left a message with Miss Hunter to tell her that he had seen the solicitor and would drop by the clinic before coming on to see her. Kate didn't know what annoyed her more—the brevity of his message or the fact that he hadn't asked to speak to her. She had a million questions she wanted to ask him. Had his brother arrived from London? Had he found anything out of place or suspicious in the accidents that Dr. Rankin had mentioned? Who was in charge of the clinic now? Was it still Dr. Taggart? How had her parents reacted when Dalziel told them she wasn't coming home? And where was Dalziel, anyway? He was supposed to be at the gatehouse, but she hadn't seen him.

She hadn't undressed for bed and sat on top of the covers thinking, thinking, thinking. She could not turn around but Mrs. Cardno was right by her side. And when she got too close to the great iron gates, Macduff herded her back to the house as though she were a stupid sheep. But that wasn't the worst of it. She was supposed to go to bed when things at the clinic were just about to get hectic? That was where she should be, helping at the clinic, not sitting here feeling sorry for herself.

He had telephoned her. The thought revolved in her mind. Not too many people had telephones in their homes. She supposed that some of the big hotels would have installed them. Where would he be where a telephone was available?

It was possible that he was at the gatehouse. She didn't want to speak to him; she just wanted to know where he was so that she could make her own plans.

There was also a telephone at the clinic. Perhaps Dr. Taggart or his substitute could tell her where Gavin was. Failing that, she would call the gatehouse and ask to speak to Dalziel.

On that thought, she opened the door and poked her head out. Nothing was stirring. All she could hear were a few muffled snores from behind closed doors. The telephone, for some odd reason, was on the dining room wall. She kept her voice low as she gave the number she wanted. She did not have long to wait.

"Madeline's Hospice," the voice said. *His* voice. She hung up at once. Her temper flared. He was at *her* clinic while she was incarcerated here? Intolerable!

It was only nine o'clock and although the sun had recently set, it still was not dark outside. She didn't minimize the danger, but she didn't exaggerate it, either. There were only two obstacles to overcome: Macduff and Dalziel.

She knew how to get around them.

Eleven

Madeline's Hospice, or the clinic, as it was commonly known, was on two floors. The ground floor had two wards, one for men, the other for women, a surgery, and an office. Upstairs were Dr. Rankin's private apartments and plenty of storage space. It was ten o'clock on a Saturday night, and Dr. Taggart and his nurse were run off their feet attending to knife wounds, broken bones, and a plethora of cuts and bruises. Dockworkers, sailors, and fishermen, Gavin had discovered, were a rough lot. Hard drinkers and hard fighters, every last one of them, and the women were no better.

He had hoped to put a few questions to Dr. Taggart before going on to see Kate but had found himself indispensable the moment he set foot inside the door. There weren't enough hands to go around. So he'd taken off his coat, rolled up his sleeves and donned a voluminous bib apron of a sickly green color, and meekly obeyed whatever orders came his way. He'd been here for hours, and there was no shortage of patients.

"It's not so bad during the week," Dr. Taggart told

him. He was as bald as a coot and, in spite of his advanced years, looked as though he could flatten an obstreperous patient with one punch from his massive fist. "They get paid on Saturday," he amplified, "recover on Sunday, and Monday they go back to work. It's not much of a life."

Gavin nodded and clenched his teeth. Someone behind him was vomiting into a basin, and his own stomach was beginning to heave. Sweat beaded his brow as he tried to ignore the patient who was vomiting and concentrated on the man on the surgery table. It was his job to hold him down while Taggart stitched up his face.

Dr. Taggart didn't notice Gavin's distress. "You've never been here on a Saturday night, though, have you?"

Gavin did not dare unclench his teeth. The stench of urine, whiskey, and unwashed bodies was working on him, too. He swallowed hard and shook his head. His visits to the clinic had taken place during the day. The only smell he had associated with the clinic was the pungent odor of antiseptic. The clinic at Braemar was as different from this madhouse as heaven from hell. It was quiet and orderly, as were the patients who entered its doors. It was in Braemar that Will had done most of his research on the human mind and how it worked.

He swallowed again. *Mind over matter,* he told himself. He had the happy knack—one of the gifts he had inherited from his granny—of calming his mind and diminishing his discomfort by thinking positive thoughts. It was a technique he'd used on Kate when he'd found her on the moor. It seemed to work, and that had surprised him. Not only was he out of practice, but he was also a tad skeptical. It would have helped if he had managed to get through to his brother, but Alex was on assignment and, so his aide said, would get back to him as soon as possible.

He was dragged from his thoughts when the nurse, who was holding the basin for the vomiting patient, let out a shriek, dumped the basin on the floor, and went tearing to the door.

"Miss Kate," she cried. "You're a sight for sore eyes. Have you come to help?"

"What else?" Kate smiled at the nurse and gave Gavin a spare nod.

Nurse Proctor blinked, and big fat tears rolled down her plump cheeks. "Dr. Rankin," she began, and shook her head. "I canna believe he has gone." She sniffed back more tears.

"I know, I know," Kate crooned. Tears were beginning to pool in her eyes, too.

"Nurse Proctor!" Dr. Taggart barked out. "Miss Cameron! The best testament you can offer to Dr. Rankin is to see to the patients. We're swamped here."

"This is no place for Miss Cameron," Gavin interjected. "I'll take her home."

"You'll do no such thing," Dr. Taggart snapped. "She's needed here." He snipped the catgut from the stitches he'd made, then examined his embroidery. "You almost lost an eye that time, Mac," he said. "When will you learn?"

Mac was too much under the influence of raw whiskey to do more than mumble something incomprehensible.

To Gavin, the doctor said, "You think this is bad? In another hour it will be like Bedlam in here. Nurse Proctor and I need all the help we can get."

Gavin's spine was poker stiff. "I'll stay," he said, "but first, I'd like to have a word with Miss Cameron."

Kate ignored him, turned on her heel, and crossed to a large closet in the entrance hall. Gavin followed her.

"What do you think you are doing?" he demanded in an angry undertone.

He could see what she was doing. She removed her jacket and donned a bib apron that was the exact match to his. "You heard Dr. Taggart," she said. "Oh, don't look so . . . so shocked. I help out here whenever I come up to town."

She pushed past him and walked into the surgery.

"If you can tidy up, Kate," Taggart said, "it would free Nurse Proctor to help me set bones."

She nodded and picked up the basin of vomit from the floor, then walked out the door. Once again, Gavin followed her. This did not sit right with him. Even without the stench, this was no place for an innocent like Kate. Naked bodies, putrid flesh, excrement, and the dregs of humanity making lewd suggestions—those of them who were still conscious—that made him want to tear their heads off. Most of all, though, he was stewing because she had obviously circumvented all his stratagems to keep her safe.

His fury seemed to register with Kate. She spoke to him quietly but forcibly. "Will you get a hold of yourself? I know what I'm doing. As I said, whenever I'm in Aberdeen, I come here to help out, and I'm not the only one. The doctors and medical students at Woolmanhill take turns to relieve Dr. Taggart and Dr. Rankin." Her voice faded and she breathed deeply. "I'm needed here. I don't want to spend hours shut in my room, wide-awake, with nothing to do."

His temper was still simmering. "Where is my dog?" he abruptly demanded.

She'd filled a basin with warm water and was pulling up a stool beside the patient who had vomited so violently. A smile edged onto her lips. "Macduff is quite safe. I left him eating a pork pie in the kitchen. The doors are closed and, as you once pointed out, he can't open and shut doors. Now, if you don't mind, I have to clean up my patient."

His jaw flexed. "And Dalziel? Did you shut him up, too?"

"No. I telephoned him and told him that your dog had run off. He was combing the grounds looking for Macduff when I slipped away."

She appeared to be quite proud of herself, and that incensed him. The sharp words that gathered on his tongue died, however, when Taggart bellowed his name. "Hepburn, over here!"

Nurse Proctor gave up her place to him and moved to the other side of the surgery table where a young man was flapping like a fish out of water, fighting off the doctor who was trying to administer chloroform. There were jagged pieces of glass embedded in his torso. Blood was everywhere. It looked as though his leg was broken.

"He was knocked through a window," Taggart explained cheerfully. "No more brawls, Billy," he shouted into the patient's ear, "or next time we report you to the police."

This threat produced a spate of curse words from Billy.

"Hold him!" roared Taggart.

Gavin and the nurse tightened their hold, and the mask with chloroform finally did its work.

The next hour passed in much the same way. For the most part, Gavin was kept so busy that he couldn't keep a watchful eye on Kate. Nevertheless, he was aware of her quiet presence as she moved from one ward to the next, emptying bedpans, administering bed baths, and he didn't know what all.

Relief came when a couple of medical students from Woolmanhill arrived. Dr. Proctor soon put them to work. "Take her home," he told Gavin, nodding in Kate's direction. "And thank you for helping out."

Gavin didn't waste time. "Get your jacket, Kate. I'm taking you home."

She took one look at the determined set of his features, nodded, then went to the closet where she'd hung her jacket. She had just slipped into it when a woman screaming in terror burst through the front doors. A heartbeat behind her, a man built like Goliath pushed his way in.

Everyone froze.

In a soft undertone, Taggart spoke to one of the medical students. "The telephone is in the front office. Phone for the police and tell them that Giant is here and looking for trouble."

The command came too late. The big man blocked the exit. The woman backed away and suddenly grabbed a pair of scissors from a set of surgical instruments and raised them threateningly. "Animal!" she screamed. "I'll kill ye before I'll let ye beat me."

The man called Giant advanced with his fist raised to strike. "Ye stole my money, ye thieving bitch," he hissed.

"To feed your children," she shouted. "Ye promised ye wouldna spend your wages on drink, but ye lied."

"It's my money," he roared. "I earned it. I can do as I like with it."

Kate stepped between Giant and his wife and put her hands up in a placating gesture. "Giant," she said soothingly. "You don't want to do this. Remember what happened the last time?"

Far from soothing the big man, her words seemed to enrage him. From out of nowhere, he produced a knife and raised it threateningly. Gavin felt the ground shift beneath his feet. Time slowed, and he had a vision of Alice before she had jumped from the rail of the yacht into the waters that were to become her grave. Kate was just as reckless.

All this passed through his mind with lightning speed, so when Giant took a step toward the diminutive figure who held him off with nothing but her own puny strength, his pent-up fury boiled over. Snarling like a wounded beast of prey, in one flying leap, he knocked Kate out of the way. Giant was startled, but he soon recovered. With a furious roar, he lunged at Gavin. Kate let out a cry, but Gavin was ready. He twisted the big man's arm, snapping it, and sent him toppling to the floor with a well-aimed knee to his stomach. Giant moaned and groaned, but he did not get up.

Dr. Taggart clicked his tongue. "Another patient to see to," was his only comment.

Gavin crouched down and took hold of the big man's collar. "Who sent you?" he demanded angrily. He gave him a shake. "Who sent you?"

Giant moaned.

"Gavin!" Kate kneeled down beside him. "Leave him be! We know him!"

"He's a regular," Taggart amplified. "Who did you think he was?"

Gavin got up. He was breathing hard. "Obviously I made a mistake," he said.

He walked to the closet, stripped out of his apron, and donned his coat. "Let's go," he said. His eyes were still leaping with fury as he looked at Kate.

"Wait!" she cried. She crouched over the big man, felt in his pockets, and produced a handful of coins. "Here, Bella," she said. "Take this. Feed your children with it."

Bella snatched the money from Kate's hand, hesitated, nodded, and hurried out.

Gavin snared Kate's wrist. "Don't argue," he said. "Not one word."

He gave a satisfied grunt when he saw her meek demeanor. Only then did he stride for the door, dragging her behind him.

She could hardly keep up with him as he dragged her up the steep hill of Marischal Street toward the market cross in Castlegate. There were no drunks or prostitutes here, largely because police headquarters were strategically located across the road. There were, however, more lights and cabs with drivers waiting for fares.

"He could have killed you!" He sounded more composed.

"Giant? No. He's a bully but not stupid. I could have talked him into giving me the knife." It looked as though he was losing his composure again, so she said quickly, "Did your brother arrive? Have you talked to him?"

"No. Alex is on assignment. He'll get back to me as soon as he can."

"What about Dr. Taggart?"

"I didn't have a chance to ask him anything. He put me to work as soon as I arrived. I did, however, see Will's solicitor. I'll tell you about it once we are clear of this sewer!"

He halted a cab and bundled her into it, then, after giving the driver directions, jumped lightly in beside her.

"We're not going back to Miss Hunter's?" she asked. The directions he had given were for a hotel on Union Street.

He had positioned himself to look back the way they

had come. A sound resembling a hiss slid from between his clenched teeth.

"What is it?"

"We're being followed. I was afraid of this." He turned to face her. In the same hard voice, he went on, "Can't you do anything right? I told you not to leave Miss Hunter's house. You were safe only as long as you stayed hidden."

She shook her head. "No one followed me." She was sure of that, or she would have sensed danger. "I was very careful."

"I'm the one our villain is watching. I should have expected something like this. I *did* expect it. I should have taken better care of you."

Exasperated, she said, "Stop blaming yourself for circumstances beyond your control. *I* decided to come to the clinic, *me*, Hepburn, not you. Stop trying to play God."

He wasn't listening. His attention was still on the cab that was following them. "He's still with us," he said.

She looked out the window. There were cabs coming and going, but nothing to rouse her suspicions.

She tried to close her mind, to use her gift to determine whether they were in danger, but, as ever, when she was with Gavin, her gift gave her mixed messages.

"So what do we do now?" she asked glumly.

Even in that dim interior, she could feel his eyes boring into hers. "What we do," he said, "is give him the slip and get you back to the house, only this time, I won't let you out of my sight."

She shivered and hugged herself with her arms.

"Afraid?"

"No. Just tired." Before he could berate her, she went on quickly, "I can't stay at Miss Hunter's forever. You can't protect me forever. You have your own life to live, and so do I."

"That's not how it works."

His words puzzled her. "That's not how *what* works?"

He shrugged, and it seemed that he wasn't going to answer. Finally, he said, "I promised myself that I would hunt down Will's murderer and see him brought to justice. Can you imagine how I would feel if he got through my defenses to you? You and Will. I can't separate you in my mind. Ah, here we are. Stay close. And do as you're told."

The cab slowed. The hotel was close to the Music Hall, and people were exiting from the theater and spilling onto the pavements. When the cab stopped, Gavin tossed a coin to the driver and propelled her not into the hotel lobby but into the Music Hall. The hand cupping her elbow urged her to move faster, and she was sure that in the morning she would have bruises where his fingers gripped her. He didn't look to the right or left. He didn't stop until they came out of the building by the back door. She sucked in a breath when she saw the gun in his hand.

"What—" she began.

"Hush!" He gave a shrill whistle, and a passing cab drew to a stop.

"Where to, guv?"

"King Street," Gavin replied tersely.

Within minutes, they were making a detour along Union Terrace and going back the way they had come.

Twelve

The voice was changing, fading, and she didn't want to let it go. It kept the shadows at bay, and the visions of a beast of prey stalking her, gaining on her. The sun, so brilliant only a few moments ago, was obscured by a bank of thick clouds. She heard the tread of footfalls behind her and the sound of branches snapping as the beast moved in for the kill. Her own feet felt like iron and moved in inches. Just as the beast leaped for her, she sucked in a breath to scream and opened her eyes.

It wasn't a beast. It was Macduff, and he was licking her hand. Her pulse gradually slowed. It took a moment for her to get her bearings. Gavin hadn't taken her back to the house but to the gatehouse. It was small and sparsely furnished, and she was resting on the only bed, or the only bed she knew of in that small building.

Dalziel was talking in whispers, but she could just make out what he was saying. Poor Dalziel. He couldn't stop apologizing for not making sure that she was tucked up for the night in the main building. He'd rescued Macduff but had never imagined that she had slipped away.

She turned her head on the pillow and gazed through the open door into the adjoining room. They'd moved the table so that she was in view even while she slept. She wondered how Gavin would make good on his promise to keep her in sight at all times. Miss Hunter might have something to say about that. They couldn't stay here. Then where would they go?

She couldn't summon a sliver of ire. For one thing, she was too comfortable and far too drowsy. It was well past midnight, and she could scarcely keep her eyes open. But there was more to her compliance than mere fatigue. He had helped out at the clinic as though he were the lowest lackey, he, a man of the world and a self-confessed pleasure seeker. He wasn't all bad.

Dalziel was still apologizing for not taking better care of her. She'd have to make it up to him for causing him so much trouble.

"You're not to blame," said Gavin. "She's as obstinate as a mule when she makes up her mind to do something. She wanted to go to the clinic, and nothing anyone could say or do would have stopped her."

She'd heard words like these from her father, too, but her father's words didn't have the power to sting her. He always said them with a smile in his voice. Gavin Hepburn's voice was threaded with impatience. It was pathetic that she should care for his good opinion.

"When is the funeral to take place?" Dalziel's voice.

"I haven't had time to see the minister yet, but the service will be held in St. Nicholas Kirk. Perhaps you would take care of that?"

Dalziel nodded. "I'd be happy to. I have many happy memories of St. Nicholas. My father was an assistant there when I was a boy."

"Your father was a minister?" Gavin sounded surprised.

"He still is, though he has retired to a smaller parish in Kintore."

"What about you? Did you ever consider taking the cloth?"

Kate felt her eyelids drooping. She knew Dalziel's background. He was the eldest in his family and had gone into commerce to support his younger brothers. He was doing quite well for himself, too, when he was set upon and robbed by thugs on one of the docks. Passersby carried him to the clinic, and that was where he had met Dr. Rankin. According to the doctor, Dalziel was never quite the same after the beating, but he'd found a position at the clinic that suited him. He was shy, rather sweet, and very good-looking, or he would have been if he didn't frown so much.

A bell went off, and she opened her eyes. Gavin had moved out of her line of vision, but she could see Dalziel. He snapped his fingers, and Macduff trotted after him, evidently going out for the dog's nightly constitutional.

"Hello?" Gavin's voice. She hadn't been dreaming. The bell came from the telephone. "Alex? Where are you?"

Alex Hepburn, she thought drowsily, the secret service agent.

"London? Yes, I know you're on assignment. I understand. Can I at least tell you what's going on here? I could do with a second opinion."

She listened as he began with finding her on the moor and ended with their present situation, where they were pretending to be an engaged couple so that he could keep her out of harm's way.

"Absolutely not!" She jumped at the vehemence in

Gavin's voice. "I refuse to use her as bait to catch Will's murderer, and that's final."

She would hope not! Alex Hepburn wasn't the nice man Gavin had described to her. In fact, she didn't like him at all.

"What?" Gavin laughed, but it sounded forced to her ears. "You need your head examined, Alex. This escapade is not going to end as yours and Mahri's did."

His voice became more testy. "Yes, yes, Cousin James and his Faith. I know what you're saying, but you're reducing our granny to little more than a matchmaker."

She was sure that she could hear the laughter traveling all the way along the lines from London to Aberdeen. Gavin was obviously not amused. "Of course I remember the prophecy," he said. "It doesn't work in this case."

What prophecy? It was so frustrating to hear only one-half of a conversation.

Gavin again. "The name Macbeth has never come up." A long pause. "Alex, are you there?"

At that dread name, Macbeth, Kate's heart didn't race, it began to sprint. How could he know about Macbeth?

Gavin's whisper was unequivocal. "She's the one, I tell you." Another pause. "I just know it."

He was silent for a long time, obviously listening intently to what his brother was telling him. Her eyes began to droop. The room was too hot, though the fire had burned itself out. It was raining fiercely, and the wind from the North Sea rattled the windowpanes in violent gusts.

"You're awake," he said.

He had startled her, and her eyes flew to his. He was

propped against the doorjamb, glass in hand, watching her warily. She couldn't tear her eyes away. He'd removed his jacket and neckcloth, and at his throat a pulse beat slow and strong.

She felt as though she'd been caught red-handed, like a dog drooling over a stolen bone, and she gestured weakly to the other room in an effort to distract him. "Who was that on the telephone?"

"My brother," he said and took a sip from his glass. "He won't be joining us after all."

Her relief was overwhelming. Anyone who thought of her as bait was no friend to her. "I never understood," she said, "what you hoped he could do for us."

He strolled into the room and sat at the end of the bed. She was still fully dressed apart from her jacket, and she resisted the urge to check the buttons on her bodice to make sure they were all done up. She kept her eyes on his, but that was no help. He had beautiful, long-lashed blue eyes that had the power to make any woman's heart beat just a little faster. She'd seen him work his charm with the old biddies up at the house, but it was all done artlessly, without conscious thought. What woman could resist that?

"Alex has connections," Gavin said. "He can go into any police station in the country and get access to information that only the police know. Besides that, he is very . . . gifted. We work well together."

"Gifted?" She said the word carefully. It was how Will Rankin had described her.

"Alex," Gavin said, "has a lot of experience in his field. He sees things that most of us would overlook." His lips curled in a private smile.

When he paused to take another sip from his glass, she said, "Your voice changes when you speak about your brother."

"How does it change?"

"It gets warmer." She shrugged. "Are you a close-knit family?"

He thought about it for a moment. "Our parents died when we were young," he finally said. "I suppose you could say that Alex took their place for me. And, of course, my grandmother McEcheran was always there. If we are a close-knit family, then my grandmother can take the credit for it. She had three grandsons. Besides my brother and me, there's Cousin James. He is a railway magnate and part financier. He manages the family fortunes, thank God, or Alex and I would be as poor as church mice."

"Interesting," she said in an undertone.

"What is?"

She shook her head. "Just a stray thought."

"Tell me!"

She sighed, then went on reluctantly. "Your brother is a secret service agent, your cousin is a financier. They sound . . . industrious . . . purposeful men of the world."

"Meaning that I'm an indolent pleasure seeker?"

"I didn't say that!"

His eyes filled with laughter. "You didn't have to. Your expression said it for you. But you're wrong. My life *is* purposeful." He leaned toward her and pinned her with his wickedly amused eyes. "I'm a connoisseur of fine whiskey, fine horseflesh, and fine women."

"As I am well aware," she said coolly, thinking of Janet Mayberry. She was tempted to ask him about Alice but was afraid that her curiosity might be misconstrued, so she turned the conversation back to a safer topic.

"Do you see much of your brother and cousin?"

"A fair amount. Family gatherings. That sort of thing. There will be more of those in the coming months. I'm to be an uncle twice over. Faith and James's child is due in July—and Alex and Mahri's sometime after that. Why the smile?"

"Your voice got warmer again. I take that to mean that you like Mahri and Faith?"

"You're very perceptive. Yes, I like them immensely, but . . ."

"But?" she prompted when he stared into space.

He shrugged. "I'm glad I'm not married to them. You wouldn't want to meet Mahri in a dark lane if you were looking for trouble. She can handle herself like a . . . well . . . like a secret service agent." He grinned.

"I see," she said, not seeing anything at all. "And Faith?"

"She's an antiquarian and a classics scholar. You'd better know your facts before voicing an opinion on the ancient Greeks when you're with Faith. She doesn't say much, but she can make you feel like a dunderhead."

She could hear it again, the warmth in his voice. "She sounds like my father. If he's not debating points of law, he's whipping up interest for the Knights Templar. Yes, I know, they were discredited centuries ago and had to surrender their wealth and monasteries, but their name and relics still live on in Deeside."

"Then I shall be careful not to provoke my future father-in-law."

He was joking, of course. "You should be married," she said, voicing the thought that occurred to her. She was thinking of his lost love, Alice.

Amusement glinted in his eyes. "Are you offering, Kate?"

"I meant . . . oh, forget what I said. It's none of my business anyway."

"No, seriously. I could say the same to you. You should be married. Why aren't you?"

"I haven't married," she said, "because I'm fussy." She was quoting what she'd heard Magda say many times. "Besides," she went on flippantly, "no one has asked me."

She chewed her bottom lip, wishing she could take the words back. The truth was, she didn't want to marry anyone, couldn't take the chance of exposing herself.

"I find that hard to believe."

She tried to make a joke of it. "You wouldn't say that if you knew my sister. Men take one look at Magda, and they can't remember their own names, much less that I was the one who brought them to the party."

His eyes were grave, as was his voice. "Not every man is seduced by a pretty face."

"Thank you," she said. "I take that to mean that there's hope for me yet."

Her tart response made his lips quiver. "I wonder what Magda will say when she hears that we're engaged?"

Her lips quivered, too. "She won't believe it."

"Oh? Why not?"

She gave him a look that was meant to tell him that the answer to his question was obvious.

"Well?" he goaded.

She sighed. "Because you're a catch, and I don't know how to go about catching someone like you." She gave a tiny shrug. "I'm awkward around men."

"Yes," he said seriously, "I've noticed, but not all men, only me."

The corners of her lips turned down. "What does that mean?"

He drained his glass and got up to put it on the table. When he came back to the bed, he sat down so close to her that she inched away.

"That's what I mean," he said. "You're always putting

distance between us." He put his hand on her shoulder, and she jumped, dislodging his hand.

He smiled. "If we're going to convince the world that this engagement is real, you'll have to do better than that."

Pride kept her immobile when he captured her wrist and put her hand on his shoulder. His voice was velvet soft. "Lovers like to touch each other. Touch me, Kate. I won't bite you."

When she remained frozen, he said softly, "Let me show you."

He held her fingers and stroked them down the length of his arm, from shoulder to wrist. When her brows rose, he said, "What is it?"

"I had no idea," she said, trying to sound bored, "that there were muscles concealed beneath your fine clothes."

He chuckled. "Kate, I climb mountains. I rescue damsels in distress. I slay Giants."

She smiled at this, but he wasn't finished yet. This time, he pressed her fingers to his throat. The beat of his pulse had her own pulse racing in counterpoint. When she looked up at him, his eyes were closed. He stroked her fingers up the strong column of his throat and then brushed them over his mouth.

"Very good," he said. He opened his eyes. "No, don't tense your muscles. Remember, we're engaged. We should look comfortable together, as though we're in love." His fingers traced her jawline. "This is a love match, isn't it?"

She gave a refined snort.

He laughed softly under his breath. "No. It must be a love match." His lips were only a hairsbreadth from hers. "We have eloped," he murmured, "and we wouldn't do that unless . . ." His words slowed and faded away. "Ah,

Kate," he finally said. Against her mouth, he murmured something unintelligible, then he framed her face with his hands and kissed her.

She had some idea of showing him that she was immune to his practiced lovemaking, but when his lips moved on hers, it was just like the first time. Everything inside her melted and, just like the first time, she twined her arms around his neck and strained against him, so that not even a shadow could slip between them.

"Bloody hell!" His hands clamped around her wrists and dragged her hands from his neck. In a low, angry voice, he said, "Don't you know how to say no, woman?"

Fatigue and the emotions that were churning inside her were taking their toll, and she hardly knew what she was saying. "No," she said. The awful thought that emerged from the chaos in her mind was that she might be falling in love with this impossible, dazzling man. "No," she repeated, meaning that it was the last thing she wanted.

He was on his feet, pacing, dragging his hand through his hair. He suddenly stopped and glared at her. "No?" he roared. "It's bad enough that I have to protect you from a vicious killer. Must I also protect you from myself?"

As sensible thought returned, she began to discount what she was feeling. It was this awful situation that had blunted her natural caution. He was her savior, her protector. It was bound to have made an impression on her. He couldn't help being what he was any more than she could help what she was. When the danger was over, when he had unmasked the killer, as she was sure he would, she'd find her balance again.

Through gritted teeth, he said, "I don't believe you've heard a word I've said."

She clasped her hands and stared down at them. "I

heard you, and the answer is yes. You have to protect me from yourself. You see—" She looked up at him and looked away quickly when she saw that he was still glowering at her. "I haven't had your experience with the opposite sex. I didn't know that kissing could be so . . . well, I didn't know."

"And now I suppose you'll want to repeat the experience?"

His irate tone made her lift her chin. She said the first thing that came into her head. "Not with you. What I had in mind was a variety of men, you know, to compare notes, and yes, to put your kisses in proper perspective."

She almost smiled when she saw that her little barb had found its mark. His face looked like thunder.

"One of us is insane," he muttered, "and I know it's not me." His voice rose alarmingly. "If you start kissing other men, no one will believe we are engaged to be married."

"When this is over, is what I meant."

A knock at the door made them both jump. Dalziel stood on the threshold drawing great gasps of air into his lungs. "There has been a break-in up at the house. The odd thing is, nothing was taken. Mrs. Cardno thought she heard glass breaking. When she went downstairs, one of the windows was broken. She heard footsteps running away. She called the police. They should be here soon."

"Bloody hell!" Gavin combed his fingers through his hair. He looked at Kate. "Our villain has found us."

"The man who followed us?"

"I think so."

"What do we do now?"

"We go back to the clinic and hide out in Will's

rooms." To Dalziel, he said, "It's best if we don't have Macduff with us. He may not be welcome at the clinic."

"I'll take care of him," Dalziel promised.

"Thank you," Gavin replied. "Anyone seeing him will know that I can't be far away. Do you think you could find someone you trust to get him back to Feughside?"

"Consider it done," said Dalziel. "Come on, boy. Let's go for a walk in the grounds."

Macduff gazed at his master with mournful eyes. "Go!" Gavin commanded, and Macduff obediently followed Dalziel from the room.

Kate's head was spinning. She was comfortable where she was and didn't want to move. "Isn't this a bit excessive?" she demanded.

"Please yourself," he replied indifferently. "You can answer any questions the police may want to ask."

The thought was daunting. "Wait for me," she cried. She was fully dressed and had only to pull on her shoes and throw a scarlet wrap over her shoulders, and she was ready to go wherever he commanded.

"Good girl!" he exclaimed as he ushered her through the door.

The door to Will's rooms was at the side of the building, and Gavin used the key that the solicitor had given him to unlock it. He left Kate sitting on the bottom step while he went upstairs to light the lamps. That done, he got their small traveling bags and led the way to Will's bedroom and ushered her inside.

"Get changed. Go to bed. And don't try to leave."

Satisfied that she was too exhausted to cause him trouble, he made his way to Will's office. His friend had been sometimes careless about his appearance, but where his clinic was concerned, whether in the care of his patients or their records, he was meticulous. Gavin wasn't sure what he hoped to find. A former patient who held a grudge? It soon became clear, however, that it would take him hours if not days to read through all the files. The telephone call with Alex had keyed him for action. Now he felt deflated. It was only Alex's reminder of his granny's prophecy that made him persevere. He tried another tack and flipped through the folders, looking for anything that struck him as odd or familiar. His fingers froze when he came to a file with the name Macbeth scrawled across the top. He didn't recognize the script, but he knew it wasn't Will's.

He knew before he opened the file that it would be empty, just as in a card game, he knew who held which cards.

He gazed into space as he tried to recall the moment his granny had given him the prophecy that would bring Kate Cameron into his life. His brother and cousin were there, too, at Granny's deathbed, skeptics all three of them, and wanting only to please their granny before she drew her last breath.

The frail rasp of her voice echoed inside his head. *"Look to Macbeth. That's where your fate lies. You stand on the brink, Gavin. Fail Macbeth, and you will regret it to your dying day."*

Fail Macbeth? Fail Kate? Kate and Macbeth. What was the connection there, apart from the obvious one of the clinic?

Alex had told him that the more he used his gifts, the more powerful his gifts would become. He had already experienced the truth of that. He'd had a vision of Kate running from her would-be killer. But that was a response to moments of extreme danger. He didn't know if he could call on his gift at will.

"Nothing ventured, nothing gained," he said under his breath. He placed the empty folder on the flat of the desk and spread his fingers over its surface.

"Focus," Alex had told him. *"Don't think. Don't talk. Let your senses be your guide."* He closed his eyes.

It came to him faintly at first, then more strongly as he inhaled the sweet scent of heather and lavender: Kate's scent.

Heaving a sigh, he opened his eyes. So Kate had been here before him. There had been something in that file that she didn't want anyone to know about. It was possible that she had found the file empty, too, but if that were the case, he would have sensed another presence. There was only Kate's.

He went through the same process of focusing and opening his senses, and he noted something else. As Kate's scent faded, the folder gave off a musty smell. It was an old folder. So when had Kate purloined its contents? And what, he wondered, was so revealing that she would go to such lengths? He considered asking her point-blank but decided against it. It might put her on her guard. There were other ways of discovering what he wanted to know.

He put the file back where he had found it and returned to Will's bedroom. No one answered when he knocked on the door, so he pushed it open gently. The outfit she'd worn that day was carefully draped over the back of a chair. One corner of his mouth turned up. He was thinking that he'd never met a woman who was so particular about her clothes. He'd seen more emotion from her over her sister's ruined frock than he'd seen over her close escape from the hands of a murderer.

There was another chair in the room. He pulled it close to the bed and folded himself into it. His gaze fixed on Kate's face. She was resourceful, obviously.

She'd managed, somehow, to get into Will's office and steal the file, no mean feat when the door from Will's rooms to the clinic was always locked from the inside. The trouble was, he had difficulty catching her likeness, as though she had moved when he was taking her photograph. Everything with Kate was blurred at the edges.

He searched his brain, trying to remember what he had heard of her before they had met. Juliet had never mentioned her friend in his hearing. What did she think he would do, pounce on Kate and carry her off? Mrs. Cardno had been more forthcoming, but he hadn't really been listening. He certainly hadn't expected lightning to strike him when Kate's eyes met his. And what had he done? He'd pounced on her and carried her off against her will. The corners of his lips twitched.

It was her eyes that fascinated him, her eyes that told him far more than her words. When they weren't shooting sparks at him, they were . . . fragile, sad, soft eyes that made him wonder who or what had put that look in them.

There was another side to her, one that irked him excessively. She took the most appalling risks. He frowned when he recalled her account of her race across the moor. She shouldn't have left the hotel at all. His frown intensified when he remembered his shock when she'd turned up at the clinic and set about performing the most menial tasks—washing vomit from drunken dockworkers, emptying bedpans, and God only knew what all. He pressed his hand to his eyes, recalling those few moments of panic when she had thrown herself between the giant and his wife.

She wasn't fascinating; she was frightening. In some ways, she was not unlike Alice. How was he supposed to keep her safe when she defied him at every turn?

He shook his head, remembering Alex's laughter at

his expense. If he ran true to form, Alex said, his mission to keep the girl safe would turn into a lifelong commitment. "Look what happened to James and me," Alex said. "Ha-ha!"

He let out a sigh. Who was he trying to fool? She did fascinate him. And though she frightened the hell out of him, he couldn't deny that he admired her, too. If it were only that, but she appealed to him on another level. He remembered the delicate brush of her hands on his neck and shoulders and how her brown eyes had darkened with desire. Where he had found the will to resist what his body clamored for was a mystery to him.

Focus. He would never do anything to harm her, just the opposite. Her welfare had become the most important thing in his life.

He brooded on that thought for a long time.

Thirteen

The stealthy creak of a stair on the landing brought Gavin out of a restless sleep. He was fully dressed on top of the bed, and Kate was curled against his back like a trusting child. During the night, his cramped muscles had made him seek something softer than the confines of the chair. He reached for his revolver on the floor by the bed. His hand had just grasped his gun when the door burst back on its hinges.

The gas lamp on the wall was turned to low, but with the stirring of dawn filtering a soft glow through the window, he counted two assailants. He held himself immobile, then suddenly launched himself at the man in front. The man howled and kicked out, the second man spewed out a string of oaths, then he lurched forward, and Kate shot out of bed.

"Stop!" she shouted.

No one listened. Gavin crouched in attack position. They were too close to chance a shot, so he put down his revolver on the bed and kicked out, his foot catching the man advancing on him in the groin. The stranger gasped and keeled over, moaning in pain.

"Get my gun, Kate," Gavin yelled. "Guard him!"

He could hear Kate babbling, but his mind was so focused on taking down anyone who threatened her that he couldn't hear her words. A murderous rage possessed him. All he wanted in that moment was to tear her assailants to shreds so that they would never threaten her again.

A low growl erupted through his clenched teeth as he closed with the man who was still standing. He was built like an oak, solid and unyielding. Strength would not work here, only guile. As the man charged, Gavin twisted away and chopped him with a blow to the back of his neck. Then he fell on him, and they both sprawled on the floor. A split second later, Gavin was on top with a knee pressed against the man's chest. He raised his fist to punch him in the throat when a howling virago launched herself at him and dragged his arm back.

"Are you deaf?" Kate yelled. "I know these men. They are my cousins. They won't harm us."

It took a moment for the murderous rage to ease its grip on Gavin, and another moment for him to take stock of the situation. One man was groaning. The man beneath him wasn't moving, and Kate was mewling apologies as she helped the groaner to his feet.

"Your cousins?" Gavin said woodenly.

"My Fraser cousins, Hamish and Rory."

He rolled off the man he'd been willing to disable permanently a moment before and turned up the gas lamp to get a better look at these Fraser cousins. The one who was built like an oak had risen to his feet; the other was slighter, but both were little more than boys, nineteen, twenty, or so. They looked like any well-turned-out bucks one might meet in the streets of London and bore no resemblance to his preconceived notions—no tartan, no kilts, no tweed, and no red hair or freckles. They were dark-haired, blue-eyed Celts like himself.

He was considerably relaxed and willing to shake hands and make up when Kate suddenly darted in front of him, arms stretched out in a protective gesture, facing the two young men.

"Now you listen to me, you . . . you heathens." Her voice was low and fierce. "This is the man I'm going to marry. Touch one hair of his head, and I'll blow your heads off. Gavin, get the gun."

Gavin was amused, then he was touched, but his softer feelings evaporated when he remembered how she'd tried to face down Giant. Reckless was too tepid a word to describe this woman. Reckless, but quick-thinking. At least she had remembered to stick to their story.

"He has offered to marry you," said the oak tree, beaming. "D'you hear that, Rory? Katie is getting married." Looking at Gavin over Kate's shoulder, he went on, "I'm Hamish Fraser, by the way, and this is my brother Rory."

He held out his hand.

Kate had not budged, so Gavin put his hands on her waist and, over her protests, lifted her to the side. He turned with a smile on his face. "I'm Gavin Hepburn," he began, then doubled over in agony when the oak tree's fist connected with the softest part of his gut in an almighty wallop.

Kate had the gun. "Touch him again, and I'll pull the trigger," she screamed.

The brothers paid no attention to her threat but hauled Gavin to his feet and, linking their arms through his, tightened their grip.

Hamish said, "Now, Katie, you know he deserves a worse beating than that. You should thank us. We'll make damn sure he marries you. Now get your things."

Gavin was getting his wind back. "How did you find us?"

Rory answered the question this time. "We visited all her friends first, but Kate's mother was sure that she'd turn up at the clinic eventually. So here we are."

"But—"

He stopped when a disembodied voice reached them from the staircase. "Hallo? I know you're up there, and you should know that I've sent for the police."

"Alistair," Kate said. "He's one of the medical students. He must have heard the racket you made."

Hamish chuckled. In an ear-splitting roar, he yelled back, "We *are* the police, so mind you keep out of our way." Then to the others, "Let's go."

"Where are you taking us?" Kate demanded.

"To your parents. They're here in Aberdeen. Oh, Katie, you have no idea of the trouble you're in."

That silenced her. In an undertone to Gavin, she said, "Don't worry, Gavin. My parents are reasonable people. They're not like these hotheaded imbeciles." Her voice rose on the last word, then she went on softly, "I'll see that no harm comes to you."

The cousins laughed. Gavin chuckled. He was sorely tempted to show the buffoons who were hustling him down the stairs that it was unwise to tangle with an opponent whose wrestling partner was a hardened secret service agent. He could have disabled them very easily. What stopped him was Kate's obvious affection for her cousins in spite of her violent words. And the same could be said of Hamish and Rory. They had Kate's best interests at heart. He couldn't fault them there.

Besides, he was basking in a novel experience.

Granny and his mother excepted, he had never known a woman who had his best interests at heart. He was their quarry, either as a husband or a conquest.

There was no sign of Alistair or the police when they exited the building, only a horse and buggy tied to a hitching ring.

"Well, what did you expect?" Hamish was grinning. "This is Sunday. No God-fearing person would dream of going anywhere but church. No customers, no cabs."

There was a short conference between the brothers, then they all squeezed into the buggy.

As the buggy moved off, Gavin scanned the streets and lanes they passed, but there was no sign of anything untoward, no one watching their movements. The streets were practically deserted, so he would have noticed if someone was following them. All the same, he kept up his vigilance until they reached their destination, the Regent Hotel on Constitution Street.

"This is the man I'm going to marry," said Kate.

They were in a small private parlor with Kate's family on one side of the room and Gavin on the other. Kate's eyes were on Gavin, but his gaze was riveted on Magda. Kate had seen that look on men's faces before, but she'd never felt this hollow feeling in the pit of her stomach. He was bowled over by Magda's beauty. Wasn't everyone?

Magda took after their father and the rest of their Cameron kin. She was tall and willowy with an abundance of delicate blond hair and cat's eyes the color of emeralds. Not one freckle marred her perfect skin. Her generous mouth was turned up in a smile, assessing, inviting, and reveling in the admiration she no doubt saw reflected in Gavin's eyes.

"Well, sit down, sit down!" said Kate's father, and everyone found a chair. "Have you had breakfast, Mr. Hepburn?"

"Ah, no sir."

Kate's mother interjected, "Iain, that can wait until Kate gives us an explanation of her bizarre behavior."

Gavin crossed one ankle over the other and relaxed against the back of the chair. He wanted to see how this family worked. Kate had piqued his interest. She'd called them larger-than-life characters who enjoyed drama. She'd said that she was an audience of one. Well, she was center stage now. He wondered how she would handle it.

"Well," said Kate carefully, "it was like this—"

Magda cut her off. "Why do we have to listen to this? We know what happened. She slipped away from her maid and spent the night with Mr. Hepburn in his cottage. They were caught in flagrante delicto."

"Flagrante what?" asked Hamish.

Magda threw him a quelling glare. "They were caught in the act." Her cat's eyes flashed to Kate. "Don't try to deny it. It's common knowledge all over Deeside. You're a scarlet woman, Kate."

Gavin was sorely tempted to intervene, but he crushed the impulse. He wanted to hear what Kate had to say. Magda, he reflected, was a sad disappointment. At first sight, her beauty was staggering, but he saw it now as a cultivated gloss that concealed a mean-spirited mind. What puzzled him was Magda's spleen. He smelled jealousy. Magda jealous of Kate?

His gaze shifted to Kate, and everything inside him softened. Her borrowed brown dress was crumpled and mired along the hem. The jacket had lost a button. Her hair was a mass of tangles.

"Katie," said Mrs. Cameron gently, "no one who knows your character would dream of calling you a scarlet woman. Now tell us what happened."

Kate's chin lifted in a gesture that Gavin knew only too well. He uncrossed his ankles.

"It's just as Magda said. I spent the night in Gavin's cottage. Make what you will of it."

Gavin silenced her with a scorching look. "It was all very innocent," he interjected, cutting across the cousins' hoots of derision and Magda's gasp, and he went on to give them the story they had concocted for the police.

"A likely story," was Hamish's provoking comment. "We found them in bed together in Rankin's clinic!"

"Hush, Hamish!" commanded Mr. Cameron. "This bickering is useless. I want to hear what my daughter has to say."

Mrs. Cameron gave a sad, gentle smile. "Kate, you must see that you owe us an explanation. Mr. Dalziel told us only that Mr. Hepburn needed your assistance at the clinic but that you would be returning home almost directly. We thought nothing of it when we heard that Juliet's mother would be chaperoning you at all times. So where is she? And why did you stay away so long?"

Rory snorted. "There was no chaperone in that bedroom, only Kate and her lover."

Gavin spoke through his teeth. "Both of us fully dressed. And we are not lovers."

Mr. Cameron stood up, and everyone fell silent. "None of this is to the point," he said. "Kate, no one is going to force you into a marriage you do not want. Tell me one thing. Do you love this man?"

Gavin's spine straightened. Kate turned her head to

look at him. "It was love at first sight," she said. "Wasn't it, Gavin?"

"That it was, Kate," he replied quietly.

Mr. Cameron said, "Then the sooner this wedding takes place, the better."

"A wedding," said Mrs. Cameron, her eyes gazing at some distant vision. "We'll have the ceremony in the church in Braemar. The hotel there is large enough to accommodate all our guests. All the Frasers and Camerons will be invited, of course, and no doubt Mr. Hepburn—"

Magda's grating voice cut across her mother's words. "It's always the same with 'our Katie.' She can do no wrong." She jumped to her feet and crossed to her father. "Father, is she to be forgiven so easily? Have you any idea how her folly will affect me? My reputation will be tarnished just by association. People will laugh at me behind my back."

"Magda," her mother reproved gently.

Magda turned to meet her mother's gaze. "She has always been your favorite, and I have never understood why. She's . . . odd, peculiar, you know she is. She has the strangest ideas." She turned her flashing eyes on Kate. "You steal my beaux, you borrow my clothes, you—" She broke off. "What?" she demanded.

Kate was chewing on her bottom lip, another habit that Gavin recognized. She cleared her throat. "The frock you loaned me for Juliet's wedding?"

"What about it?"

"My fault entirely," Gavin quickly interrupted. He gave a sardonic shrug. "I lost it in transit. I'm sure it will turn up sooner or later, but you must allow me to replace it. House of Worth, was it not?"

Magda's jaw literally dropped. Coming to herself, she gave a choked laugh. "I should have known how it would be. I can never win, can I?" No one answered. No one was expected to. She dismissed them with a flick of her lashes and made a regal exit.

"I should go to her," said Kate.

She made to get up but sank back again when her father spoke to her forcefully. "You'll do no such thing. The world does not revolve around Magda. The sooner she comes to realize it, the more comfortable it will be for us all. What we are going to do is go down to the dining room for breakfast, and when we have eaten, Mr. Hepburn and I will have a few quiet words in private."

Gavin stood by the window in his bedchamber looking out at nothing in particular. He was wondering what was keeping Kate. He'd been sure that she would want to discuss how they could forestall this trumped-up marriage before he talked to her father. He knew that she was with her cousins, because he'd told them that she was distraught, and they should keep an eye on her. As watchdogs, they were almost as good as Macduff. Even so, he'd expected Kate to come to him before the interview with her father.

He shook his head, wondering why he had allowed himself to become engaged to a slip of a girl he'd only known for a short time. Oddly enough, it didn't feel like playacting.

"It was love at first sight. Wasn't it, Gavin?"

He smiled at the memory of their first encounter. No words were spoken. Their eyes had met, and from that moment on, he'd become her shield. His smile faded as his thoughts shifted to her family. He understood now what she meant by dramas and larger-than-life characters, but there wouldn't be a drama if it were not for Magda. It was hard to believe that Magda and Kate were sisters. They'd been raised by the same parents. How had one girl, the elder, turned out to be such a sour plum, while the younger was . . .

He had to think about that. Kate was too complex a character to be summed up in a word. Magda said that Kate was odd and that she had the strangest ideas. Is that why someone wanted to kill her?

"In Scotland, we burn witches." He knew that she was intuitive, but a witch?

There was something he was missing. What was it?

His thoughts moved on to her parents. They were not exactly larger-than-life, but they were a tad eccentric. Kate's father had read a book all through breakfast without a word to anyone, and her mother had refused the tea and imbibed her customary morning diet, a generous tot of whiskey to, as she said, clear her mind and set her up for the day ahead. Nothing, it seemed, could shake her equilibrium, not even the prospect of her younger daughter's hastily contrived marriage.

As for Kate, she was a peacemaker. She had wanted to go to her sister. She wouldn't let him hurt her cousins, and she wouldn't let her cousins hurt him. No wonder Macduff was smitten with her. They were kindred spirits. Macduff did not like hurting people, either.

He turned from the window when he heard the door open. "Kate," he said.

It wasn't Kate who entered, however, but Magda, her beautiful eyes moist with tears. Her voice was husky. "Kate and Hamish are playing chess in the lounge, so I thought this would be an ideal moment to offer an apology for my behavior earlier. Do say you forgive me."

"It's not to me you should make your apology, but to Kate."

She angled him a teary smile. "I've done that already. Kate has a very forgiving nature, I'm glad to say."

She approached him slowly. "I should never have loaned her my gown. That was what set me off. You were right. It bears Worth's label. Not that that would matter to Kate." She gave an elegant shrug. "Even as a child she was clumsy."

Gavin was more curious than angry. This beautiful woman had deliberately sought him out. Not for one moment did he believe that it was merely to offer him an apology. Then what was she up to?

He managed a half smile. "Siblings never do get along, do they, not when they're children. My brother and I came to like each other as we got older, and now we're the best of friends."

She gave a brittle laugh. "Kate and I are not children. We are not going to grow to like each other. It's too late for that." She gave a little sigh. "It's not her fault. From the day my mother brought her into the house, she has been feted and fussed over like a little princess. Of course, I was jealous." Her shoulders lifted in a helpless shrug. "I was afraid of her then, and I'm still afraid of her."

Now, thought Gavin, they were getting to the crux of the matter. "Afraid of Kate? I think you've got that backwards. There is no spite in Kate."

There was a moment of silence, then Magda's eyes flared. "Are you saying that I'm spiteful?"

"Aren't you?"

A moment passed, and she gave a creditable laugh. "Oh dear, Mr. Hepburn, you have a lot to learn about our little Katie." The laughter went out of her voice. "Why *are* you marrying her? You must know that she is not an heiress. She isn't a beauty. She has no style, no accomplishments."

He put his hands in his pockets as a precautionary measure, and gave a suggestive smile. "Kate's appeal lies in the kind of person she is. She is warm. That's what a man wants in his woman. She appeals to his . . . shall we say . . . softer, better nature? Haven't you noticed that plain women marry handsome men and that the reverse is true? You'd be a much happier person if you had a heart."

When she raised her hand to strike him, his fingers manacled her wrist.

Panting, furious, she spat the words at him. "You don't know my sister at all. Ask her about the clinic. Ask her about Dr. Rankin and how she met him. Ask her where she spent her summers when she was a child." And, turning on her heel, she stalked from the room.

Thoughtful now, Gavin stared absently at the door. Magda's words revolved in his mind. The clinic. Dr. Rankin. Kate's summers. Other things occurred to him. *"From the day my mother brought her into the house."* What did Magda mean by that?

Kate was keeping secrets from him, and it was the worst thing she could do. Hadn't he tried to impress on her that a killer was after her? He'd be damned if he'd allow her to fob him off now with evasions and half-truths. There had to be a reason for someone to want her dead. Every little piece of information mattered. Without her cooperation, they were merely playing a game of blindman's buff.

Slow down, he told himself. There was a right way to go about this. One Magda in Kate's life was enough. All the same, time was of the essence. He couldn't keep her in protective custody forever. Could he?

On that thought, he left the parlor and went downstairs to keep his appointment with Kate's father.

Fourteen

To say that Kate's father was a take-charge kind of person didn't do the man justice, in Gavin's opinion. Only six hours had passed since that fateful interview in the private parlor, and they were there again, a small gathering of family and friends, to witness his marriage to Kate Cameron.

He wasn't sure that the thing was legal.

Mr. Cameron, who ought to know, since he had practiced law in both England and Scotland in his time, affirmed that it was, as long as the couple lived together as man and wife. Since this was a civil marriage, there would be no church setting and no minister officiating. The couple could choose anyone they wanted to perform the ceremony, or they could say the words themselves.

"As is the old custom in Scottish marriages," Mr. Cameron elaborated, as though that validated what was about to take place.

Everybody seemed satisfied by Mr. Cameron's explanation except, perhaps, the bride and groom. The tears swimming in Kate's eyes, as Gavin was well aware, were not tears of joy as the assembled guests seemed to think. They were tears of frustration. Having convinced her parents that this was a love match, she couldn't come up with a credible excuse to put the wedding off.

He sympathized with her parents. Everybody knew that he and Kate had spent the night at his cottage on the moors, so it was imperative that they appear in public as a married couple. And their first public appearance would be at Will's funeral on Friday.

"Smile, Kate," he said.

"I feel like such a cheat," she hissed under her breath.

"Well, just look at them. They're all silly with happiness."

She was right about her mother. Not that Mrs. Cameron was enthused about this civil ceremony, but her husband had promised that there would be another ceremony in Braemar, a church ceremony with a lavish reception to follow in the local hotel.

"Magda doesn't look silly with happiness," he commented.

"Is she glaring at me?"

"No. She looks bored."

"Then she's as happy as Magda ever gets."

When he stifled a laugh, she smiled.

"Your father doesn't look happy, either," he said in an undertone. "I don't think he trusts me."

"Of course he doesn't trust you. He knows that this is a trumped-up affair, that, in fact, it's not precisely legal, and he's wondering if you know it, too." Her brows drew together. "How did you know that the bride or groom had to be domiciled in the parish for three weeks before their marriage could go forward?"

"Will told me. This is how he married Maddie. They thought it would be more romantic than to have a priest or minister say the words over them, not that they could find a priest or minister to marry them. She was Catholic, and Will wasn't."

"I see," she said and sighed.

"Yes," said Gavin. "The old enmity between Catholics and Protestants is as fierce as ever in the Highlands."

He'd promised that before that proper wedding service in Braemar could take place, whether they had caught Will's murderer or not, he would break the news to her family that they had inadvertently broken the law, and their marriage was null and void.

Had she even considered the uproar that would ensue? The disgrace? Her father might call him out. Did she care?

His thoughts were diverted when the door opened to admit Mrs. Cardno and Dalziel. The former was all smiles; the latter looked deeply disgruntled. It was then that Gavin remembered that Dalziel had a sweet spot for Kate. To ask him to officiate at the service was adding insult to injury. But who else could lead them through the labyrinth of promises and vows? Kate didn't know what to say, and neither did he.

"What is Mrs. Cardno doing here?" Kate asked, barely mouthing the words. "She's a dreadful gossip. By this time tomorrow, half the townspeople will know about our wedding."

"That's the point. Besides that, Juliet's mother will lend credibility to the proceedings."

He went to greet Dalziel and in short order had introduced him to the others. In an aside, Gavin said, "Thank you for agreeing to help us out. I thought of you at once, of course, because you were raised in the manse."

Dalziel did not waste time on pleasantries. "You do realize that neither you nor Miss Cameron meet the residency requirements?"

"That won't matter," Gavin replied, trying to sound

confident. "The church wedding will take place in Braemar. Kate's father decided to move things up a little to save her embarrassment, you know, at Will's funeral."

A moment went by, then Dalziel sighed. "I hope you know what you're doing. My father would never sanction this. Nor would the Church."

Gavin's response was cut off by Mr. Cameron's impatient interjection that it was time to get the thing done now that everyone was present.

When he and Kate joined hands and took their places in front of Dalziel, Gavin took a moment to study his bride. Her simple gown of cream-colored taffeta added a luminous glow to her skin. Her dark hair was pinned up and showed to perfection her delicate earlobes with diamond pendant earrings and the slope of her throat. Her eyes . . . he could never do justice to how they affected him. He'd seen them flash with temper; he'd seen them shimmer with a private sorrow she could not bring herself to share. But the look that could make him forget to breathe was the look of appeal she sometimes directed at him, a look that said, he was sure, far more than she wanted him to hear.

He bent his head to hers. "What's borrowed?" he whispered.

"What?"

"The bride is supposed to wear something borrowed on her wedding day."

"Everything," she said smartly. "Everything is borrowed, including my wedding ring."

Dalziel was still leafing through what appeared to be a book of Church discipline and order, so Gavin went on softly, "When we're married, I'll see to it that your wardrobe is stocked with garments. You'll never have to borrow anything again."

Her eyes jerked up to meet his. "Don't get carried

away, Hepburn. I warned you about drama, didn't I? It's infectious."

"Can we get on with it?" Mr. Cameron's steely voice commanded.

Dalziel found his place in the book. "Dearly beloved," he began, and the room fell silent.

Gavin glanced at Kate's small hand that rested on his own. Her fingers were trembling, and he wondered what she was thinking.

Kate's mind was too numb to think much of anything except that she wondered what defect in her brain or character had brought her to this pass. As the evening progressed, however, and the sherry (for the ladies) and the whiskey (for the gentlemen) flowed freely, she began to mellow.

She listened to the ebb and flow of conversation around her, watched the smiles and nods of well-wishers, and thought that something was missing.

"Penny for your thoughts," said her father. He brushed back his coattails and sat down beside her.

She blinked up at him. Everyone should have a father like hers, she thought. He had never been particularly demonstrative, not even when she and Magda were children. If her mother was the eternal optimist, her father was the eternal realist. There was no trouble he could not fix. When she was little, she'd thought that he *was* the Bank of England. Everyone knew that that was one bank that would never fail.

Things were different now. She was a big girl, and no one could solve her problems except herself.

"I repeat," he said, his gray eyes disturbingly assessing, "a penny for your thoughts."

She forced a smile. "I never thought I would hear myself say this, but I miss the brawl that usually concludes any celebration where Camerons and Frasers get together. This seems so . . . tame."

Her father laughed. "Brawls," he said, "are for young men. You wouldn't want to see Hamish and Rory pick a fight with your new husband, would you?"

Her eyes wandered over the guests and came to rest on Gavin. As usual, he looked as though he'd just stepped out of the pages of the *Gentleman's Companion*. "It might do him a bit of good," she said darkly.

Her father's hands closed around hers. "Listen to me, Kate," he said. "Mr. Hepburn and I had a long talk in private before you joined us this afternoon." He waited until he had her full attention. "I want to know only one thing—is my daughter happy with her choice?"

She gazed into her father's shrewd eyes and gave an involuntary nod. She must have let her smile slip before he'd come to quiz her on the state of her soul.

"He's everything I could hope for in a husband," she said.

Her father smiled. "That's all I wanted to hear."

"Father?" she said when he made to rise.

"What is it?"

She rushed on before she could change her mind. "Was Mama the first woman you ever loved?"

His eyes crinkled at the corners. "It would be more accurate to say that your mother was the only woman who ever loved *me*. What she saw in me, I have no idea. I was a crusty old bachelor immersed in my law practice. I was bewitched. Three months after I met her, we were married. People said it wouldn't last, because we were so different." He chuckled.

Kate had heard this story before, but the warm glow

she usually experienced on hearing it was absent this time. Her pseudo-marriage seemed a travesty of her parents' marriage.

When Dr. Rankin's killer was caught and all came to light, her parents would understand, she promised herself.

Her father's shrewd eyes missed nothing. "What is behind your question, Kate?"

"Nothing, nothing at all."

"Hmm!" His eyes searched her expression, which she tried to keep unrevealing. "When I met your mother," he said, "all other women ceased to exist for me." He lowered his voice. "It will be the same for you. I see how he watches you, you see."

How she could keep her tongue still was a mystery. It wasn't the same for her. In the first place, this was not real. It was playacting, though there was a serious purpose behind it. In the second place, Gavin could never claim that all women had ceased to exist for him after he met her. Janet Mayberry was proof of that. Then there was Alice. She lived on in his heart, if rumor was to be believed.

It was obviously a tradition for parents of the bride to impart a few morsels of wisdom to prepare their daughters for married life, because when Kate was getting ready for bed, her mother bustled in and dismissed the maid so that she could have a "wee" word with her daughter.

She waited until Kate was in bed with her knees drawn up to her chin before she began. Stumbling over her words a little, she said, "Events moved so quickly that we did not have that heart-to-heart talk a mother and daughter usually have before the wedding. Every mother wants to prepare her daughter for marriage. It's a duty that must not be neglected—"

"Mama," said Kate, cutting off her mother's spate of words, "I'm not an ingenue. I've worked at the clinic. I've seen and heard things I could never mention to my sister, let alone in polite society. I'm not unfamiliar with masculine anatomy. Without boasting, I can say that I know more about the birds and bees than I want to know." She squeezed her mother's hand. "You don't have to put yourself through this, Mama. I'm not nervous or afraid. I know what to expect."

"You're not nervous?"

"No," Kate answered truthfully. Nothing was going to happen, because this wasn't real. She couldn't tell her mother that, so she added, "As I said, I learned all I need to know at the clinic."

Her mother laughed. "If you know so much, perhaps we should change places. Maybe you could tell me a thing or two about the birds and the bees." She shook her head. "There's more to marriage, though, than what a couple do in bed. Of course, I know that your work with Dr. Rankin gave you an education that few young women receive. Your father and I are very proud of you, oh, not only for your work, but because you care about people. We've raised a fine daughter."

Kate felt horribly, horribly guilty. If she cared about people, she wouldn't have embarked on this harebrained marriage. If she were a fine daughter, she wouldn't be planning to bring disgrace on her family.

All would be forgiven, she reminded herself, when the truth came out.

Her mother took a breath as she searched for the right words. "My only misgiving—no, no, that is too strong a word—but it troubles me sometimes that you keep everything locked tightly inside you. Your sister, of course"—she let out a resigned sigh—"is the opposite. What I'm trying to say, Kate, is . . ." She got off the bed and looked at Kate with a smile in her eyes. "I want you to be happy, dear, that's all."

Kate felt as though all her past sins had come home to roost and were draped around her shoulders. She did keep things tightly locked inside her. The only person she'd ever allowed into her secret world was Dr. Rankin. She was what she was and couldn't change now.

She had to say something. Her mother was waiting with an expectant look about her eyes.

"I am happy," she said so softly it was almost a whisper.

"Then tell him about the past."

"I will. I intend to."

"You won't regret it. Husbands and wives should share each other's burdens. That's my philosophy, for what it's worth."

Kate waited until she heard the door click before she got up and went to lock it, as instructed by Gavin. Not that he was expecting trouble. The hotel was small, with only a sprinkling of guests. But Gavin was careful. He knew where everyone was domiciled and had arranged with the manager that if any traveler came seeking a bed for the night, he would be the first to know it.

A fine bridal night this was turning out to be. She didn't even have Macduff for company. She and Gavin were expected to spend the night together. But what about the next night and the night after that?

"Tell him," her mother advised. She stretched out in bed with a horrible sinking feeling in the pit of her stomach. *Tell him.* She was under no obligation to tell him anything. It happened so long ago. It could have nothing to do with Will Rankin's murder.

There was more to her reluctance than that. She didn't know what she knew. All she had to go on were her dreams and the notes she had taken from the file in

Dr. Rankin's office, the file with the name of the woman who had given her birth, Mary Macbeth.

She was five years old when the Camerons adopted her. Her memory did not go back that far. She had dreams, but whether she could trust them or not was debatable. Everyone had bad dreams . . . everyone had dreams.

When Gavin entered their bedchamber, it was to find his bride asleep. A fine state of affairs for an eager bridegroom! Not that he'd had any hopes in that quarter. He might as well make love to a marble statue.

No. That wasn't precisely true. He wasn't a seer for nothing. From the beginning, he'd recognized Kate's latent sensuality. Hell, a man didn't have to be a seer or a wizard to recognize it. Any red-blooded male could sense it. But Miss Cameron was unattainable. No wonder Magda had lost all her beaux to her sister. There was nothing men loved more than a challenge.

One corner of his mouth curled up. He was remembering Kate's words, that she had lost all her beaux to her beautiful sister. It wasn't true. He didn't believe for one moment that Kate had suitors. The only men she wanted in her life, that she allowed, were safe men like her father and cousins. He wasn't safe, because he persisted in treating her as a desirable woman.

He wondered about her relationship with his friend Will.

Brooding now, he removed his jacket and draped it over a chair. Next came his shoes and socks. He knew what he was supposed to do. They had arranged it beforehand. He was to take the quilt and one of the pillows from the bed and make his own bed in front of the fire.

He did none of these things. He turned the gas lamp down to a peep, settled himself in the comfortable armchair, and studied the girl in the bed. She moved slightly and let out a low moan. He half rose from the chair with the intention of going to comfort her. When she moaned again, he sank down and clasped his hands.

Alex's voice, as he'd heard it on the telephone, came back to him. *"The more you practice, the stronger you'll become. If you don't use the gift Granny gave you, you will lose it altogether. Concentrate, focus, and you'll be surprised at the results."*

And when he'd protested that his gift was erratic, Alex had scoffed at him. *"You're lazy, Gavin, that's your trouble."*

Concentrate. Focus. Gavin closed his eyes and opened his mind to Kate.

Nothing happened. He tried again with the same result. His trouble was that he was bone tired. He'd spent half the night making sure that the hotel was shut up tight and laying a false trail, just in case. All he wanted now was a nice soft bed and a good night's sleep. A quilt in front of the fireplace was not what he had in mind.

Kate was sleeping soundly. What was to stop him stretching out beside her? She need never know. And what if she did? He wasn't going to lay a finger on her.

On that virtuous thought, he crossed to the bed and gingerly eased himself down beside Kate.

Fifteen

She knew where her dream was taking her, and she tried to resist, but the dream was stronger, more persuasive than her hold on reality. Reality, now, was her mother's hand: thin fingers, dry skin, nails bitten down to the quick. She didn't care. It was her mother's hand, and she clutched it to her breast as if it were a holy talisman.

They crept soundlessly from the children's dormitory into the long, dark corridor. There was a door there, Mama said, that led outside. There was a friend waiting for them. Soon they would be free and live together in a lovely cottage in the Highlands. Nothing and no one would ever separate them again.

In spite of her mother's words, her child's mind was numb with dread. The door to the outside was always locked. What if Matron discovered them? Matron never went to sleep. She had eyes in the back of her head. She would make them sorry they had broken the rules. Mama would be dragged back to the hospital wing, and she would be locked in a cupboard.

Mama was whispering to her, but her whispers were

drowned out by a fit of coughing. When the coughing stopped, she tried again. They were giving her something, Mama said, to make her sleep. Whatever happened, Kate mustn't look back. She was to go through that door where Mama's friend was waiting for them. If Mama couldn't come now, she would come later.

A light behind them. Someone shouting. Footsteps. Matron raising the alarm.

"Go, Catherine, and don't look back!"

The urgency in her mother's voice gave wings to her feet. She had never run faster than she did during the next few moments. Tears streamed down her cheeks as she turned the doorknob and pulled the door open. Cold air streamed in. Her mother's screams had her head whipping round. She had to go back. Mama was in trouble. Matron was shaking her. Before she could retrace a single step, someone flung a blanket over her head, and she was lifted off her feet. Kicking, screaming, she tried to fight free of the arms that restrained her.

Someone cursed. A man's voice. Her struggles only made him tighten his hold. She began to panic. She couldn't breathe. Darkness swam at the edges of her mind.

"Wake up, Kate. It was only a dream! It's me, Gavin. You're perfectly safe. Wake up!"

She stopped struggling and sucked great draughts of air into her lungs. "Gavin?"

He was on the bed, half sprawled over her, and she found his weight more comforting than his soothing words. Her arms wrapped around him, and she held on tight. He kissed her tears away, then he brushed her lips with his. The dream had seemed so real, more like a memory, and she burrowed closer to his warmth to stave off the shivers that racked her whole body.

"Kate," he said, and his kisses changed. They were no longer comforting but darker, sensual, passionate.

It never occurred to her to stop him. She was ready to break. She wasn't thinking about consequences. If only for a few minutes, she wanted to blot out the paralyzing despair that still held her in its grip. All that had ever come to her in her dreams were fleeting impressions. Tonight, her dream was sharply etched and had seared her mind. But Gavin was here. Nothing could hurt her as long as he was by her side. She twined her arms around his neck and kissed him back.

He tasted her surrender and wanted more. His heart was pounding before, but now it was taking flight. He could feel it at the base of his throat, in his ears, in his head, behind his eyes. And it was so wrong because she wasn't herself. She didn't know what she was doing. But she had locked her arms around him, demolishing his control. This was so wrong . . .

It didn't feel wrong. Nothing in his life had felt more right. From their first encounter at Juliet's wedding, he had known this woman was going to be important to him. This went beyond the commission he had been given in his granny's prophecy. This was primitive, mate with his true mate.

Then why was he hesitating?

He was hesitating because he wasn't sure that he could believe what her dream was telling him. Besides, he'd never read anyone's mind before. All he'd ever had from Kate were impressions. Was he reading her correctly now?

He cupped her face with both hands. "Look at me, Kate," he commanded.

Her lashes slowly lifted, and she gazed up at him. Her eyes were dark with grief and pain. It had always puzzled him, but her dream had opened a door to her past, and everything was beginning to add up, all the little hints that he'd been given: Magda's reproaches,

Kate's work at the clinic, her close friendship with Will that went beyond nurse and doctor, and the note she had received from the killer.

"In Scotland, we burn witches."

He tightened his hold on her. He didn't expect her to make things easy for him. She was the most private person he knew. But her dream had given him a wedge into her secret thoughts and, one way or another, he would break down every barrier she kept throwing in his way.

"Make me forget," she whispered, and she raised her head and pressed her lips to his.

No one had ever kissed him like this. Desire was there, and something else: wonder, awe, gentleness, and a million other emotions he could not name. It would take a poet, he thought, to describe how her kisses made him feel, and he was no poet.

"Gavin," she whispered against his lips, "make the ghosts go away."

He speared his fingers through her hair and held her face up as he dropped random kisses on her cheeks, her nose, her throat, her lips. "Always," he murmured past an odd constriction in his throat. "Always, my love."

She could smell the sea through the open window, hear the raucous cries of the gulls and knew that dawn could not be far off. The darkness in her mind began to recede. She was exactly where she wanted to be, with no fears or doubts. On that thought, she gave herself up to the pleasure to be found in her lover's arms.

It was her first time, but she wasn't nervous. As she'd told her mother, her work at the clinic had given her an education that few young women possessed. What she lacked was practice, and she was sure that Gavin would make up for that deficiency. The stray thought made her smile.

No one had told her that her skin would heat like this,

and that her breath would catch, that his kisses would drive her to the edge of reason. She wasn't cowed. She wanted it all, but just when she was voracious with desire and would have allowed him anything, he turned shy on her.

This is her first time. Gavin repeated the litany inside his head. He wasn't going to take her like some ravenous beast of prey. He wanted to make this good for her; he wanted her to know that she came first with him. He murmured soothingly as he unbuttoned her nightgown and slipped it from her shoulders, then, with tantalizing deliberation he kissed her throat, her shoulders, her breasts.

Shuddering with pleasure, she raised herself from the pillows and unbuttoned his shirt. With lips and tongue, she tasted his warm flesh. Gavin stopped breathing, then inhaled sharply as her questing lips dispensed a trail of heat to the waistband of his trousers.

She had registered, absently, the flowery fragrance of the sheets, but it was her lover's scent that inflamed her senses, something dark and primitive that was uniquely his. She sucked on his flesh and then ran her tongue over her lips, savoring his taste.

Her innocent caresses made his blood boil and his hands tremble. "Too many clothes," he whispered and adroitly dispensed with her nightgown. She gave a throaty laugh when he got up and tore out of his own garments with a speed and efficiency that would have alarmed her if he had been anyone but Gavin.

When he joined her on the bed, she welcomed him with open arms. His naked body molded to hers. It came to him, then, that this was the first time for him, also. He had never wanted like this, had never been cherished like this. He gentled his hands and tested every delicate bone in her face, her shoulders, her hands. She was fragile and no match for any man in a test of physical strength, but that did not mean that she was weak. She summoned an ironclad determination when she put her mind to something, as now.

Or had he misread the signs? Was he taking advantage of her at a weak moment?

"Gavin," she whispered, "is this all there is?"

He gave a shaken laugh. "I'm trying to make this easy for you," he said.

She didn't want easy. Her body was so tight, she felt that it would shatter. Why was he so hesitant? What was he waiting for? She, it seemed, would have to have enough courage for both of them.

He groaned when her hands moved from his flanks to his groin. His jutting sex obviously held no fears for her. This was madness. They were going too fast. Where was his restraint? His good intentions?

God, he didn't care. This was glorious. She was glorious. He spread her knees, positioned himself, and thrust through the barrier. When he felt her nails scoring his back and the bite of her teeth on his shoulder, his heart sang. A man wanted his woman to be passionate in bed, and Kate had exceeded his expectations. Then all rational thought slipped away, and he was aware only of the woman in his arms and the driving beat of his body.

Sated, he rolled to his side and anchored her with an arm around her waist. When he heaved a great sigh of contentment, she bolted from the bed and wriggled into her nightgown.

It did not take him long to discover that his wife—he smiled foolishly at his choice of words—that his wife was less than deliriously happy.

He rose to one elbow and surveyed the scowl on her brow. "I'm told," he said, "that the first time may be difficult for a woman."

The scowl became a glare. "I have been grossly misled," she hissed.

"Not by me," he quickly replied.

"By the clinic's female patients. By my own married friends. They should have warned me."

"They could hardly do that. They didn't know you were getting married."

Her lips flattened, but he could hear her breathing, dragonlike, through her nose. He braced himself for her righteous anger, a tongue-lashing that he thought he deserved. He would allow her that much, but she couldn't deny that she'd been a willing participant in what had happened in this bed.

There were no fireworks, no recriminations. When she finally broke the silence, she said in a more controlled tone, "I should get something to put on those scratches."

"Don't forget, you bit me as well." He was trying to coax a smile from her, but his words only earned him a baleful glare.

He watched as she crossed to the table where the ubiquitous bottle of whiskey and glasses were laid out. She returned with a towel and a glass half-filled with his favorite brew.

"What are you going to do with that towel?" he asked suspiciously.

He was reaching for the glass of whiskey when she suddenly exclaimed, "What's wrong with the light?"

He turned his head to look at the gas lamp on the wall, then he sucked in a breath when a fiery liquid splashed into the scratches on his back. "What in blazes, woman?" he roared, turning to face her. That was when she poured the dregs of the whiskey on the bite on his shoulder.

As he sucked in air, she smirked.

"You . . . you . . . you enjoyed doing that! You wanted to pay me back."

"I could hardly call you out. Oh stop fussing. You'll live." She set the empty glass down on the table by the bed, gave him the towel to dry himself off, then proceeded to shake out a quilt in front of the fireplace.

"Kate," he said, "it will soon be dawn. The servants are stirring. What will they think when they see that makeshift bed?"

Her voice was clipped. "I don't care what they think."

She took one of the pillows and crossed to the bed. He watched her pound it into shape, and the thought that passed through his head made him bite down on a laugh. He said carelessly, "I did what you asked me to, didn't I? I chased the ghosts away. There is no murky matron lurking in the shadows . . ."

He knew from the way she froze and her spine straightened that he'd made a colossal blunder. She was motionless for several seconds, then she turned and came toward him with all the grace of a jungle cat ready to spring on her prey.

"How did you know about Matron?" she asked.

His mind worked furiously, but the only answer that made sense to him was the stark truth. "Because," he said, "I'm a seer, and I'm susceptible to your dreams."

Sixteen

It was unbearable. Someone meddling with her mind! And not just anyone, but Gavin, the person she trusted most in the world. She felt as though a nest of squirming worms had invaded her insides. She was going to be sick.

The stricken look on her face had him leaping from the bed. "You're not alone, Kate," he soothed. "It's all right. I'm here."

When he tried to put his arms around her, she shoved him away. Her voice was shaking so hard, she could hardly get the words out. "A seer?" she scoffed. "Yes, I've heard the rumors about you and your crazy granny Valeria, that she was a witch and you inherited her powers, and I don't believe a word of it!"

He was beginning to feel the indignity of reasoning with an angry woman when he was naked. Keeping a wary eye on her, he wriggled into his clothes. He needn't have worried. She looked as though she had turned into a pillar of stone. Only the harsh sound of her breathing indicated that she was in the grip of some violent emotion.

He spread his arms. "Look," he said in his most soothing voice, "how could I have known about Matron if I had not the power to—"

"Meddle in my mind?"

"I don't see it like that. I'm susceptible to your thoughts, that's all."

Her fear converted to a white-hot fury. He would probe and probe until he had learned all her secrets. "A seer you call yourself? A wizard? I'd call you a cheat and a thief! I don't want you to steal my thoughts. If I have something I want to share with you, I'll say it out loud."

He was beginning to lose patience with her. "You don't believe I'm a seer?"

"No," she said emphatically. "I don't believe in witches and wizards. They're charlatans!"

"Then you have nothing to worry about. So, why are you worried, Kate?"

She was worried because she'd sensed that there was something different about her dream tonight. What had been vague before—the hospice, her mother, Matron— was more clearly etched, as though she had looked at them with new eyes. His eyes.

"No!" she said as to herself. "It can't be true." Her eyes narrowed on him. "I have been known to talk in my sleep. That's how you know about Matron."

"And your mother? And your escape from the asylum?"

"It wasn't an asylum!" she fiercely denied. "It was a hospice!"

He said quietly. "It was an asylum, Kate."

Hardly aware of what she was doing, she snatched the empty glass from the table by the bed and threw it against the wall, where it shattered into a stream of sparkling crystals. It wasn't enough for her. She wanted to spring at the man who was causing her so much pain. She wanted to break him, too.

Gavin didn't give her a chance. Before she could move, he had pinioned her arms and forced her into the chair beside the fire.

"Now you listen to me, Kate Cameron! This is important. You're going to sit there, without opening your mouth, until I've had my say. Otherwise, I shall bind and gag you and make you listen to me."

He would do it, too. She could see it in his eyes and the muscle tightening in his jaw. How had it come to this? It was her own fault. She knew better than to let down her guard, but she'd been caught up in something beyond her ken, in sensations she'd never experienced. She hadn't been thinking of consequences. Now they rushed in with an alarming velocity.

She'd made love to him, and her reward was to have her dreams and thoughts stolen by an intruder. There was something else that irked her—the notches on his bedpost.

Disgruntled, angry, she folded her arms across her breasts. "I shall never forgive you for this," she said.

He raised one finger, silencing her. "You're one breath away from being gagged."

She pressed her lips together. She hated him, really hated him.

He stood over her as he began to speak. "There was a time when my brother and cousin believed as I did, that witches and wizards lived on in the minds of the superstitious, and that educated, rational people like us were above such things. Of course, we made allowances for our granny. We thought that her so-called psychic powers were so much theater, a little drama to make her . . . unique. And she was unique. In spite of her little quirks, however, her three grandsons loved her dearly, and she loved us."

He was gazing into space, remembering Drumore Castle, James's domain, and the storm that rattled the tiny windowpanes, and the breakers beating against the rocky promontory on which the castle stood. Somehow or other, he'd thought that his granny would live for many more years. She'd always seemed so youthful and unlike the frail old woman in the bed who made her grandsons promise to take her deathbed prophecies seriously.

He cleared his throat. "But this is not a vindication of my grandmother's character. Suffice it to say that she bequeathed her powers to her grandsons just moments before she died."

She tried not to listen; she tried to pretend that she was completely indifferent to what he was telling her, but that was far from the case. She was interested in spite of herself.

"Each of us," he went on, "was given a cryptic prophesy that meant nothing to us at the time. However, our granny's prophecies caught up with us, James first, then Alex, and now me."

She wanted to hear what the prophecies were, but she was too proud to ask.

"Our powers manifest themselves in different ways," he said, "or they did at first. Cousin James has dreams that foretell of danger. Alex has only to touch an object, and he has visions of its past, present, and future—a valuable asset in his line of work. I was lazy. I didn't want or trust Granny's powers, though I will say that they came in handy in Alex's last case. I discovered I could put thoughts into people's minds, not demonic thoughts, but harmless suggestions to make them happy or feel better. You were an excellent subject, Kate."

Her voice? Gavin Hepburn was the voice who had allayed her fears and made her feel better? It was intolerable! Her mind, her thoughts, her dreams belonged to her and only her. She didn't want him inside her head.

Her eyes began to sting, and she turned her head to look out the window before the sting could turn into tears of self-pity. Dawn, she reflected, trying to divert her thoughts, was not always rosy and golden. Clouds obscured the rising sun, and she could hear the splash of raindrops on something below the window—a canvas awning, perhaps, or something like it. It would be another dreich day in Aberdeen, but that would not deter the spring flowers from pushing through the earth. They were obstinate and sturdy, much like the people of Aberdeen, much like her.

"Kate, look at me." When she looked up at him, he went on softly, "The night you were pursued over the moor, I was asleep in my cottage. What wakened me was a vision I had of you running for your life. I could sense your panic, feel the stitch in your side. But I didn't know where you were. Then Macduff set up his howling and led me to you."

He took a step back and studied her expression. A gamut of emotions flitted across her face—guilt, a grudging gratitude, confusion, and finally a simmering resentment that heated her eyes and flushed her skin.

He rubbed his nose with an index finger. His little wife had a temper, and it was only going to get worse.

"I think we have established," he said, "that I can read your mind when you are agitated or frightened. Strictly speaking, it's not that I try. You're the one who sends out a signal, and I pick it up. But something curious happened recently, and I've been mulling it over."

He crouched down beside her and boxed her in with a hand on each arm of her chair. "That's better," he said.

"Now we are eye to eye. I'm talking about Janet Mayberry. You were there, weren't you, Kate?"

"Was that a question? Am I permitted to speak now?"

He inclined his head. "Please do."

"Where was I supposed to be, exactly?"

"You were inside my head, reading my mind."

She made a face. "I wouldn't enter that sewer if you paid me to."

He sat back on his heels. "It was you I wanted, not Janet. All that aside, you did something no one else has ever done. You read my mind."

It was hard to keep her expression impassive when fear had tied her stomach in knots. She knew where this was going, and she refused to be led along that path. "You are mistaken," she replied, striving to stay calm. "I know about Janet because one of my friends mentioned that she'd seen you leave her room."

He shook his head. "Why are you so afraid? Why won't you admit that you have a talent that few possess?"

She leaned forward slightly, and that brought them nose to nose. "You think you're a seer? A wizard? I won't try to change your mind. But don't confuse me with someone like you. I'm just an ordinary girl with, yes, the gift of intuition, and my intuition is telling me you're talking a lot of rot."

He had come this far. There was no turning back now. This was one battle of wills he could not let her win.

"I should have known," he said, "when you refused to tell me what was in the note from Will's killer. 'We burn witches.'"

"I told you!"

"Only when the other notes came to light. It didn't matter, then. They all said much the same thing." His jaw flexed. "You're a witch. Admit it, Kate."

He had expected a reaction from her, but not the one he got. She pushed out of her chair and launched herself at him. Because he was on his haunches, he didn't have far to fall. He grabbed her, and they both went rolling on the floor.

Shaking with rage, she cried out, "I am not a witch! Now get off me you . . . you lunatic."

She was bucking and kicking, and the only way to restrain her was to roll on top of her. To stay the spate of words, he cupped a hand over her mouth. "I know," he said, "that you were Will's patient." When her eyes widened, he shook his head. "No, he didn't tell me, but he spoke warmly of the work you did at the clinic in Braemar, the clinic for his mentally disturbed patients. Then there were the odd things your sister and your cousins let slip. Oh, your cousins don't know you were a patient, but your parents do."

She said coldly, "My father arranged it, not that it's any of your business."

He exhaled a slow breath. "You're adopted, aren't you, Kate? No one told me. I worked it out for myself." When she was silent, he went on, "I think your mother died in the asylum. I think you're afraid the same thing may happen to you. Kate, you're not mentally disturbed. You're just like my grandmother. You're a witch, Kate."

Great sobs shook her whole body, and she turned her head to the side, as though the sight of him disgusted her.

When the sobs had died away, and he felt her go limp, he rolled to his side, relieving her of his weight. Cupping her face, he said gently, "I think I know how confused you must have felt as a child, but you're a woman now. Accept your gift. Use it."

"You know nothing! Nothing!" Some of the fire returned, but it quickly burned itself out, leaving her more drained than ever. She couldn't think straight. She was in no condition to match wits with him. All she could do was try to shut him out of her mind. Stupid thought! There was no hiding from this man.

He didn't try to stop her when she got up. She snagged her dressing robe, shrugged into it, and crossed, stiff-backed, to the window and stared out. As unobtrusively as possible, he rose, took a step toward her, and halted, unsure what to do for the best.

She spoke over her shoulder in a small, emotion-less voice. "You were, by your own account, a man fully grown when you inherited your gifts." She gave a refined snort, as eloquent as any words to denote what she thought of his gifts. "I was just a child when I realized I was different from other children. I couldn't read minds like you can—"

"Only one mind, yours, Kate, and I don't read it—"

"But I had visions of the future."

"Then you are the true seer."

She turned to face him. "Do you think that made me happy? It was a curse. My visions were frightening. I couldn't control them. I couldn't see what I wanted to see. I couldn't tell what had happened to my mother all those years ago. The visions came to me whether I wanted them to or not. I saw houses burning and people drowning, but no one took me seriously, until, of course, what I predicted came true. The local children called me a freak. By the time I was ten, I didn't have a single friend. That's when I learned to keep my mouth shut."

"And your mother and father? I mean Mr. and Mrs. Cameron?"

"They were worried to death about me." She emitted a strangled laugh. "As for Magda, she was terrified of me, so I don't blame her for her lack of sisterly affection. Normal children tease each other. I would get back at her by inventing a horrible event that would soon overtake her." She shook her head. "Naturally, things couldn't go on the way they were going. My parents knew about Dr. Rankin's work with the mentally disturbed, and he took me on as a patient. He taught me how to block out my visions."

He chuckled. "I've seen the brick wall, and the castle and towers with the moat and drawbridge. What's next, Kate?"

She scowled. "Meddling with my mind again, Hepburn?"

"No," he answered, stretching the truth a little. "I told you, I can't control where my mind takes me. That night on the moor, *you* meddled with *my* mind, oh not deliberately, but you streaked into my dreams like a shooting star. Then, if you'll excuse me for mentioning it, you saved me from a fate worse than death when you smacked me on the fingers in Janet Mayberry's bedchamber."

His little joke didn't win a laugh from her, but she turned to face him, and there was life in her eyes again.

"I'm not admitting anything."

"Of course not," he said.

She eyed him speculatively. "You want me to learn to read your mind?"

"I do."

"How do I do that?"

He tried not to sound too eager. "We practice. We could begin by retracing your dream step by step. I might see something that you overlooked."

"No."

"Why not?"

"That's private."

"At least tell me who was waiting for you outside the hospice. Give me a name."

"I can't," she said wearily. "I don't know who took me away."

Frustration rippled through him. He took a quick step away from her, exhaled a long breath, then swung back to face her. "This isn't a game we are playing. I didn't marry you so that you could live happily ever after. I married you so that you could *live*. We're not out of the woods yet, and we may never get out unless we learn to trust each other."

She could see that he was angry, so she kept her voice low and reasonable. After all, he had saved her life on the moors. They wouldn't be having this conversation if he hadn't come after her.

So much thinking was making her dizzy, but one thing continued to puzzle her. "Why are you so certain that I'm the target? What if our killer kills again? Maybe he's a religious fanatic and . . ." Her voice faded when he shook his head.

"I know," he said, "because it was foretold in my granny's prophecy. She showed me the future but insisted that the future could be changed."

She had trouble finding her breath. "What did the prophecy say?"

"It said . . ." He stopped and shook his head. "Read my mind, Kate. You can do it with a little practice." He lowered his head to whisper in her ear, "Read my mind."

Seventeen

What they needed, he said, was a brisk walk to clear the cobwebs from their minds. "The links are close by. We'll take that road. There's no point in coming to Aberdeen if we don't spend some time at the seashore."

"I thought you came for Dr. Rankin's funeral and to settle his affairs."

"That, too, but a day has twenty-four hours. What is it they say? All work and no play makes Jack a dull boy?"

She'd made him turn his back on her while she dressed, so she couldn't see his grin, but she heard it in his voice. He seemed to find amusement in the oddest things.

"I don't understand," she said. "We've been careful to stay hidden or at least avoid detection when we move about. Now, suddenly, we're going for a stroll to the beach?"

"That's because I've set things up so that if anyone has discovered we're here, they'll follow a false trail. How long does it take you to get dressed?"

"You can turn around now. Who is setting a false trail?"

"Dalziel and Magda, suitably disguised, are pretending to be us. They left five minutes ago by cab for a hotel on Union Street, where they will register in our names. No one will be surprised at our changing hotels. What newly married couple wants to spend their honeymoon with their families? After that, Dalziel is undertaking a number of errands for me."

Her mind barely registered the last part of his account. She was speechless. Magda was pretending to be *her*? Her sister was taking *her* place? The thought was ludicrous. It made her want to laugh. She ground her teeth together.

"When did you arrange this?" she asked abruptly.

"Oh, when you were at your ablutions, you know, washing the scent of me from your skin." His lips were verging on a smile.

She glared. "Have you no delicacy, Hepburn?"

"None whatsoever, not with my wife. Besides, as soon as I walked in the door, I detected the perfume of roses. I like it."

"I don't—" She stopped, waited till she had control of her breathing, and changed direction. "You mentioned errands. What errands?"

"Dalziel is going to the police station to pick up a file for my brother. It's all arranged."

"What's in the file?"

"I'll tell you when Dalziel returns."

He could be maddeningly evasive when he wanted to be. Still, there could be nothing in the file that she need fear.

She gestured to the window. "It's not walking weather. It's raining."

"No, it's threatening to rain. I have an umbrella, see?"

She glanced at the umbrella, frowned up at his grinning face, and marched to the door. Did he always have to have his own way?

"You look very nice," he said and ushered her into the corridor.

She knew she had never looked better, courtesy of Juliet's borrowed garments. His tepid compliment didn't deserve an acknowledgment, so she sailed by him and made for the stairs.

"Where is Macduff?" she asked, whispering now because they seemed to be the only guests in the hotel who were up. "I miss him."

"He's with Dalziel. I told him to make arrangements to send Macduff back to Feughside. He'll be fine."

She made a harrumphing sound. She knew the real source of her irritation. He still hadn't told her what was in his grandmother's prophecy. She knew him well enough to know that he meant what he said, that if she wanted to find out, she would have to read his mind. How was she supposed to do that?

It wasn't raining, though heavy clouds obscured the sun. There was a breeze off the sea with the tang of salt, but it wasn't unpleasant. She held her face up and breathed deeply. The freedom of not looking over her shoulder to see whether someone was following her put her in a better temper.

They were passing the convent of the Sisters of Nazareth. Something hovered at the back of her mind, and she shivered.

"What about your parents?" he asked. "I mean Mr. and Mrs. Cameron. How did they come to adopt you?"

"Must we talk about that now? You said that we were

going to go for a brisk walk to clear the cobwebs from our minds."

He drew her hand through the crook of his arm. "You're right," he said. "We're just a newly married couple in thrall to each other and oblivious of the passing crowd."

His words brought home a truth she had been trying to avoid. Perhaps she was a little enthralled with him, but he would be the last person she'd tell. It would be humiliating to love a man who loved another woman.

As for last night . . . what could she say? She'd forgotten to keep him at a distance. Fortunately, the experience left much to be desired, and she had no wish to repeat it.

"Did you mention a crowd?" she asked. They had left Constitution Street behind and were coming to the links that bordered the beach. "All I can see are seagulls, a ship out at sea, and miles and miles of golden sand."

He patted her hand. "So much the better for our little practice session. No interruptions, just you and me endeavoring to read each other's thoughts."

She stopped and turned to face him. "I don't want you meddling with my mind."

He sighed in exasperation. "You choose what you want me to see. That's not meddling. You're in charge of your own thoughts."

"What's the point? Why don't I tell you what I'm thinking?"

"What are you thinking?" When she hemmed and hawed, he grinned. "You want to know what my grandmother foretold. There's more to it than that, Kate."

There was a wooden rail at this point. He lounged against it, thought for a moment, and began to speak in the most serious tone she had heard him use since they'd spoken their marriage vows.

"I've mentioned my cousin James and his wife, Faith. When he first came into his legacy from our granny, he dreamed about Faith, about her in the future, coming face-to-face with a murderer, and he knew that he was the only one who could save her."

She had questions, but she didn't interrupt, because she didn't want to break his train of thought.

"I don't know how it came about," he went on, "but eventually James was able to read Faith's mind, but only when she was panicked and in grave danger. That was what saved her life. James knew where she was, and he went after her."

He lapsed into a long, reflective silence that she was reluctant to break, but her curiosity finally got the better of her. "Did you dream about me, Gavin? Is that why you came after me out on the moor?"

His grim expression gradually softened, and he smiled. "Yes and no," he replied. "When we met at Juliet's reception, and our eyes held, I was sure you were the one, but the first time I dreamed of you was when I was asleep in my cottage and you were running for your life. Was it a vision? Was it a dream? Or was my mind reading your thoughts? That's what I want to find out."

She gave a choked laugh that held a thread of fear. "I thought I was odd, but you are definitely bizarre."

"Let's find out, shall we?"

She shook her head. "I put all such nonsense behind me when I became Dr. Rankin's patient. As I've told you before, I'm intuitive. I sense things, oh, nothing earthshaking, just feelings and so forth."

"It's the 'so forth' I'm interested in. Do you play cards?" When she simply stared at him, he nodded. "Of course you don't," he said. "It's hard to be impartial when you know everyone else's cards. It takes practice to win a few hands and lose a few." His voice changed, became harder, relentless. "Concentrate! Look into my eyes! Focus! Tell me what I'm thinking."

She stared into his eyes, as relentless as he.

"Well?"

"You're thinking of a woman."

"Very good. Don't stop there. Look closely. Who is she? What is she wearing?"

She put her head to the side. "Oh, now I see her. It's Janet Mayberry, and she isn't wearing a stitch."

She stopped laughing when he clamped his hands on her arms. Neither noticed that the umbrella had rolled to the ground. "I was thinking of you, Kate, thinking that you're as pretty as a picture in your lavender skirt and jacket. I was thinking that you should leave the top buttons undone to show off your beautiful throat."

She almost succumbed to his flattery, but then she remembered that they were playing a game. She pushed out of his arms. "I thought this was to be a serious test?"

"Were you serious when you mentioned Miss Mayberry's name?"

"I was right about the first part," she answered flippantly. "You're always thinking about some woman. I may have gotten the name wrong."

He scowled at her and muttered something she did not catch. "What did you say?"

"I said that if you're going to turn this into a joke, we might as well stop."

She didn't know whether she had offended him or whether he was manipulating her into doing what he wanted. It didn't matter. She was interested in his odd family and especially his grandmother and her prophecies.

"Read my mind, Gavin," she said meekly.

He looked into her eyes. "Focus!" he commanded.

Brow furrowed, she focused. She was thinking of Mrs. Willows, the housekeeper at Craigmyle and the sumptuous clootie dumpling she made every Christmas.

"This won't do," he said. "Something is missing. I can't see a thing."

"Of course something is missing. You told me that your cousin could only read his wife's mind when she was in grave danger."

"What were you thinking of, just now, when I tried to read your thoughts?"

She dimpled. "Mrs. Willow's Christmas pudding. She is our housekeeper, but before that she was our cook. I was just getting to the part of the favors she puts in the batter before she boils it."

He emitted a low growl. "You *are* in grave danger. Why won't you believe it?"

"Ah, but I'm not alarmed or agitated at the moment. I think that would make a difference."

"You're not alarmed?"

"No."

"You would be if you could read my mind."

Her heart skipped a beat. "What?"

"There's no one around. Who would see us if we made love among the sand dunes? I'd begin by unbuttoning every little button on your jacket."

She slapped his hands away when he reached for her. "Will you be serious?"

"I'm perfectly serious."

When she looked into those burning eyes, her throat went dry. She believed him. Her heart wasn't racing; it was sprinting. The danger came from inside herself, not from him. When he reached for her again, she ducked under his arms, picked up her skirts, and began to run.

It was then that the sky opened and the rain came down in torrents. In a matter of moments, she was drenched to the skin. A quick look over her shoulder showed that Gavin fared no better, worse, in fact, because he was trying to control an umbrella that the wind had blown inside out.

She giggled, shook her head, and plowed on. Gavin was shouting for her to stop, but she didn't listen. She knew every nook and cranny on the beach and dashed toward the shelter of a narrow stone tunnel that ran beneath Beach Road. She had almost reached it when she lost her footing on some pebbles and went sprawling into a puddle of brine. It took a moment for her to catch her breath, then she hauled herself up. A few steps took her to the bridge. Now that she was out of the driving rain, she scanned the beach. There was no sign of Gavin, no sign of anyone.

When hands gripped her shoulders from behind, she gave a muffled shriek and spun to face him. "You!" she cried. "You gave me a fright! You were supposed to chase me. You came in the other end. That's cheating!"

He didn't share her mirth. He looked mean and dangerous, his face hard, his eyes leaping with anger. "What in hell's name do you think you were doing, running from me like that? Don't you know that if someone were to kidnap you, or worse, this would be an ideal spot?"

She spoke quietly, softly, as if she were trying to soothe a lion with a thorn in its paw. "No one knew that we were coming to the beach or that I would take shelter under the bridge."

"That's not the point." His voice still bristled with anger. "Don't ever run from me! Don't try to hide from me. How do you think I felt when I turned around, and you were nowhere in sight?"

She put out her hand and touched him briefly. "I'm sorry, Gavin. I wasn't thinking. It won't happen again."

He was breathing hard, his nostrils were flared, but she could tell that he was no longer angry. All the same, she dared not smile or comment on the drenching they'd taken. His hair was plastered to his head, his coat looked to have shrunk a size, and he'd lost his hat and the umbrella.

She looked down at her own outfit and saw that it was glued to her body like a coat of plaster. Raindrops dripped from the brim of her bonnet and ran down her neck in a steady stream. She began to shiver, and her teeth chattered. In a useless attempt to stop the shivering, she hugged herself with her arms.

"Good God!" he exclaimed, "what happened to you? You're as soggy as a wet sponge."

Through chattering teeth, she got out, "I tripped and fell into a puddle."

He shook his head. "You really do need someone to look after you, don't you! No, don't answer. We've got to get you back to the hotel before you come down with pneumonia." He put one arm around her shoulders and clasped her to the shelter of his body. "Hang on tight, and I'll get you back in no time. Then it's a hot bath for you, milady."

She loved his warm smile and the look in his eyes. Though she felt miserable, she managed a wobbly smile of her own.

It did not take them long to return to the hotel. Even so, by the time they entered the back door that led to the kitchens and servants' quarters, Kate's teeth had clamped together in a death grip, and she was shaking uncontrollably. She heard Gavin issue orders, then he whisked her into the servants' staircase, avoiding any guests who might be about, and was soon ushering her into their bridal chamber.

With the precision and indifference of a doctor

caring for a patient, he stripped her of every article of clothing and wrapped her in the quilt from the bed. That done, he added coal to the fire in the grate.

"Feeling warmer?" he asked.

"Yes, thank you."

Since she was the guilty party here, she felt that she ought to make amends. She opened her mouth and quickly shut it. He was stripping out of his own clothes, and she swallowed hard at the vision of male beauty that was revealed. His muscles were hard and tight. There wasn't a vestige of fat on him. He didn't look like the Gavin she knew from last night. Though they'd made love, she hadn't seen him naked. This man looked as though he were an athlete or a mountain climber. When her gaze dropped to his groin, her mouth went dry. She wasn't a complete novice now. He wanted her. Startled, she looked into his eyes.

"You can take that look off your face," he said irritably. He began to towel himself off. "My arousal is nothing more than a reaction to the cold."

She covered her chagrin by fussing with the quilt.

He dragged his shirt on, then his trousers. "I don't need to read your mind," he said. "I can see everything in your face. Rest assured, I am not about to pounce and have my wicked way with you."

He had that backwards but she couldn't tell him that. Nothing brilliant came to mind, so she sat there in misery, clamping her teeth together to stop them from chattering.

Two footmen arrived with a copper tub, then a stream of servants with pails of hot water, which they proceeded to empty into the tub. As soon as the servants left, he locked the door, plucked the quilt off her, and tugged her into his arms. That done, he slowly immersed her in the warm bathwater.

"Tell me if it's too hot," he said.

"It's . . . lovely."

Gradually, her teeth stopped chattering, her breathing evened, and she closed her eyes as the warm water lapped her chin. It was heavenly, like floating in the Gulf Stream that lapped the shores on the west coast. She drifted in a sea of pleasure. She felt the warm brush of his lips against hers. Was she dreaming? She wanted more.

How could anyone, she wondered, put such feeling, such yearning into one feather-soft kiss? Kate tried to make her mind work, but her body was doing its best to make her forget to think. The softest of touches brushed her throat, then dropped to the curve of her breast. She felt herself go moist in response and let out a shivery sigh.

When the touches stopped, she opened her eyes and looked up at him. His eyes, framed by a sweep of dark lashes, studied her intently. His breathing was audible.

And then it came to her. "You're putting thoughts into my mind! That's it, isn't it? You told me that that was your gift! Is this how you make your women compliant, Hepburn? Mmm?"

He began to laugh. "I thought you didn't believe in the transfer of thoughts between people. Isn't that why you wouldn't cooperate when we were practicing on the beach? Make up your mind, Kate. You either believe, or you don't. Which is to be?"

"Tell me your grandmother's prophecy, and I'll tell you whether I believe or not."

"Oh, no. That would be too easy." He cocked his head to the side. "I'd be interested to know what thoughts you think I put into your head."

"Murder and mayhem," she answered sweetly. "Now, if you don't mind, I'd like to dry myself off and get dressed."

He helped her out of the tub, then draped a voluminous towel around her shoulders. She couldn't avoid his probing stare. "What?" she demanded, hoping to sound in command of herself, though her knees felt weak, and her voice was no better.

"I didn't put thoughts in your mind, Kate." He gave her a moment to let his words sink in. "I was reading your mind. You forgot to retreat into your fortified castle, you see. I couldn't help myself. I had to kiss you."

He gave a devilish grin when her jaw dropped. "We'll practice later," he said. "Lock the door behind me, and don't open it to anyone but me."

"You're going to leave me alone?"

"I'm not going far, only to Dalziel's room. This won't take long."

"But . . ."

She was talking to thin air.

Gavin had only five minutes to wait before Dalziel walked through the door. It took him a moment or two to work out what was different about Will's man of business. Dalziel's shoulders no longer drooped, energy radiated from him, and his habitual frown was replaced by a finely drawn look of determination.

There were no greetings or the usual pleasantries. Dalziel pulled up a chair and said at once, "Everything went as planned. I followed your instructions to the letter. No one followed us, but in the event that our villain will be making the rounds of first-class hotels, he'll find your name on the register and the bridal suite booked for several days."

He's enjoying this, thought Gavin. *Maybe Dalziel has missed his calling.* "What happened at the police station?"

An expansive grin spread slowly across Dalziel's face. "I was a little worried about my reception, but they could not have been more helpful. Of course, they'd been instructed by the Home Office to give me whatever they had and answer all my questions."

"We have my brother to thank for that. Go on, what did you discover?"

Dalziel pulled a notebook from his pocket and referred to his notes as he spoke. "There have been three suspicious deaths in Aberdeen that seem linked—"

"They found the notes?"

Dalziel nodded. "The police have had them all this time, but they didn't connect the victims to the clinic, only to the notes. They believe that one man is responsible for all three deaths. They're calling him 'the preacher,' but there is no push, as far as I can tell, to solve the case."

"Because the victims are not people of influence?"

"I'm afraid so."

There was a long silence broken only by the raucous call of gulls. Gavin was thinking that their villain couldn't be very happy at the way things had turned out. He'd want everyone to know that the deaths were connected to the clinic before he attempted to kill Kate. She would be one among many. Yet, he *had* attempted to kill her. That must mean that he didn't know the police in Aberdeen had filed everything away and promptly forgotten it. Or it could mean that he was getting desperate.

Dalziel took up the thread of their conversation. "The communication between the Aberdeen police and the force in Ballater seems nonexistent. The left hand doesn't know what the right is doing."

"It's the same in the secret service. Each agency guards its own patch. How else can they justify their existence?" Gavin stretched his cramped muscles. "I presume that the Aberdeen police know that Will is dead?"

"Yes. He is well-known here, but they believe what they read in the papers, that it was a tragic accident." There was an interval of silence, then Dalziel said, "Have you considered laying all the facts before the police and letting them take it from there?"

"What facts? I only have a theory. They're just as likely to make a note of it and file it away for future reference. I'm not about to take any chances with an incompetent police force. Now tell me what you found out about Mary Macbeth."

Dalziel sighed. "Nothing, I'm afraid. Her name wasn't in any of the police files. There was a census taken a few years back. I may find something there."

They went back and forth, Gavin asking questions as they occurred to him, but Dalziel had very little to add to what he'd already told him.

"You've done well," Gavin said, getting up, and was once again arrested by the change in the other man. Dalziel positively glowed.

After leaving Dalziel, Gavin took a turn around the small courtyard at the back of the hotel. The Regent was not what he was used to—its rooms were cramped, the meals were plain Scottish fare, and the courtyard was too small to allow a man to stretch his legs. With the beach only a short walk away, the small courtyard hardly mattered.

Just thinking about the beach had his muscles bunch in knots. His eyes were only off her for a few moments, and when he looked up, she had disappeared. His reaction was hardly rational. It brought Alice forcefully to mind, when she'd jumped overboard and sunk like a stone. The shock, the fear, the desperate attempt to save her had proved futile. He wasn't going to allow Kate to go the way of Alice.

He winced when he remembered how he'd come at her

like an angry bear. One day, he would explain why he'd been so angry. One day, he would tell her about Alice. Meantime, he had a sacred promise to his granny to keep.

Their practice session had gone as he'd expected. Just getting Kate's compliance was a major undertaking, but she'd finally agreed to participate. Nothing much had happened on the beach, but when she was in the bathtub . . .

Those were her thoughts he'd absorbed. Kate wanted his lips on her, his hands on her, so he had complied, and how like Kate, when she was found out, to put the blame on him.

"My arousal is nothing more than a reaction to the cold." Had he said that? It was a lie, of course. His arousal was a reaction to a woman who was fast becoming an obsession with him. Damned if he knew what her attraction was! Another lie!

One corner of his mouth turned up in a crooked smile. His granny had started something with her prophecy, but now his goal had taken a surprising turn.

Whistling under his breath, he entered the hotel.

When he got to their room, Kate was not there, but her maid, Elsie, was unpacking a trunk of clothes and hanging them in the wardrobe.

"Oh, Mr. Hepburn, sir," she said, dipping him a curtsy, "I was to tell you that Miss Kate has gone downstairs with her cousins for a bite to eat."

"And when did you get here, Elsie? I thought you went home to Braemar." If Kate was with her cousins, he had nothing to worry about.

The maid pointed to the trunk. "I arrived an hour or two ago with Miss . . . I mean, Mrs. Hepburn's things. It was all arranged before the family came up to town. There are a few things I want to press, but I'm finished here. May I go?"

Gavin nodded. "Please do."

It was only idle curiosity that made him open the wardrobe doors and inspect his wife's garments. Though every piece of clothing was perfectly tailored, Kate's choice of colors left him bemused: brown, dark blues, and various shades of gray. These were not the colors he would choose to dress her in. These were not the kind of garments she'd been wearing since the night he'd met her at Juliet's reception. Everything he'd seen her in was borrowed, and she had shown her borrowed finery off to good effect. The clothes in this wardrobe belonged to a dowd.

The thought turned in his mind as he went downstairs to join her.

Eighteen

The funeral service for Dr. Rankin was solemn and comforting but not personal. Kate did not think that the minister could have known the doctor very well. He spoke of Will's dedication to his work and his tireless efforts to improve the lives of the working poor, but he made no mention of his treatment of his mentally disturbed patients, and she wondered if the omission was deliberate. By and large, ministers and priests distrusted psychiaters and all they stood for.

The sanctuary was standing room only, but class distinctions were still in evidence. The working poor had chosen to crowd into the back of the sanctuary, while the well-heeled, fashionable mourners sat at the front, close to the communion table. Internment would take place later that week in Braemar, in the family plot.

As she looked around the mourners who sat in the nearest pews, she realized that she knew most of them from Juliet's wedding reception. Dr. Rankin had no family, and Gavin and Dalziel were his chief mourners, along with Dr. Taggart from the clinic. But Dr. Taggart would not be attending the reception that was to take place at the hotel. His work at the clinic took precedence over everything. As for the working poor, it was the same story. As soon as the service was over, they would go back to work so that their families would not go hungry.

When the mourners left the church and stood outside on the broad stone staircase, waiting for the usual complement of carriages and dark horses with their funeral plumes, Gavin broke the silence that had fallen between them.

"Will wasn't in that building. Will was an outdoors man. When I think of him, I see him fishing for salmon in the river Feugh."

She smiled faintly. "I was thinking along the same lines, only I saw him with his sleeves rolled up, checking on every patient in his clinic. What will happen to it now? Money was always a problem, but Dr. Rankin had backers who believed in him personally. With him gone . . ." She shook her head.

"We'll think of something," he said.

They were interrupted by Sally Anderson, who still managed to look like a Viking, though she was dressed from head to toe in black. "Kate, Gavin, I don't believe you've met my fiancé, Cedric," she said. "He read Dr. Rankin's obituary in the newspapers and came to lend his support."

"Cedric Hayes," said the man at her side. "I'm sorry that we're meeting under such unfortunate circumstances."

"I'm Gavin Hepburn," said Gavin, "and this is my wife, Kate, formerly Kate Cameron."

Kate managed to keep her expression neutral, though she was still shocked when anyone referred to her as

Gavin's wife. Soon, the charade would end, and she wondered what people would call her then.

The conversation had moved to the doctor's work at the clinic, so she had time to study Cedric at leisure. He wasn't what she expected. He was attractive enough if one was partial to Greek statues. He was more than handsome, but there was an air of pride about him that marked him out as a man who knew his own worth.

"Stuffy," was Gavin's verdict when they climbed into the carriage they shared with Magda and Dalziel. "What does your friend see in him?"

"A marriage made in heaven," Kate replied. "That's how Sally describes it. Cedric will bring a title into the family, and she will bring him a fortune. Then they will be free to go their separate ways."

Magda said darkly, "Sally is a fool if she believes that. A woman is never free to go her own way. Even in these enlightened times, there is some man who has her in leading strings."

Kate made no reply, but she guessed that Magda had been warned by their father to be on her best behavior. Their father wouldn't know what to do with leading strings and had certainly never played the heavy-handed role. She slanted a look at Gavin.

He spoke to Magda. "In my experience, it's the other way round. It's women who keep their menfolk in leading strings. What do you say, Dalziel?"

Dalziel, however, was too tactful to contradict a lady, and he answered in such a roundabout way that no one knew what he thought.

The gravity of the occasion soon gave way to a livelier atmosphere and, in Kate's opinion, did not have the feel of a wake at all. There were medical students from Woolmanhill, and their descriptions of Rankin's caustic remarks when some unfortunate student fainted at the sight of blood had everyone laughing.

Kate, naturally, took a great deal of ribbing from her friends.

"I thought," said Lorna Dare, "that you would never marry. Not that any of us believed you. But so soon after you'd met! What came over you, Kate? You know the man's reputation. What were you thinking?"

Kate gave a start when Magda's voice came from over her shoulder. "Who told you that Kate and Gavin had just met?"

Lorna shrugged. "It's common knowledge."

"Then common knowledge is an ass." The haughty tone of Magda's rebuke made Lorna's cheeks burn. Magda went on, "Our family and Gavin's have known each other for ages," and with a dismissive sweep of her lashes, she wandered off.

That was one thing Kate liked about her family. They might bicker in private, but they never criticized each other to outsiders.

For the next little while, she was flanked by Hamish and Rory. They hadn't known Dr. Rankin well, and the gist of their conversation centered on the pretty young women in attendance, those who looked susceptible and those who did not.

"Try to remember," Kate said between her teeth, "that you are gentlemen, and this is a serious affair."

"It doesn't feel serious," said Hamish. "It feels more like a party."

It *did* feel like a party, thought Kate, and just the sort of affair that Will Rankin would want to celebrate his life. She looked over at Gavin. He turned his head, and their eyes met. A slow smile curled his lips. *Yes* was the message that came to her.

She was taken aback. Had he read her mind? Had she read his? If she didn't watch herself, she'd soon be as weird as he.

She was only half aware that her cousins had defected. When she came to herself, she was partnered by Mrs. Cardno. This was intolerable! She wasn't a little girl in need of a nurse. She knew how to take care of herself. And what harm would come to her surrounded by Will's friends and coworkers?

She had, however, misjudged Mrs. Cardno. She hadn't come to watch over her but to invite her to a little séance among friends, who were to meet in Mrs. Cardno's room in about ten minutes.

"A séance," Kate stuttered. She was definitely mixing with the wrong crowd. "I'd love to, except that Gavin wants me to act as his hostess."

Mrs. Cardno patted her hand. "Some other time," she said. "I would ask Magda, but I don't want to spoil her budding romance with Mr. Dalziel," and with that, she collected the ladies from Mrs. Hunter's guesthouse and trooped off.

Dalziel and Magda? Kate almost laughed. Magda had turned down the best in the valley. She wouldn't look twice at a plain sobersides like Dalziel. She wished that old biddies like Mrs. Cardno would mind their own business.

Gavin joined her next. "I'm sorry I had to leave you alone," he said, "but there were so many people who wanted to convey their condolences and talk about Will."

"That's understandable. I'm not complaining, really."

"What did Mrs. Cardno want?"

"She invited me to a séance."

"She *what*?" He lowered his voice. "You're not going to tell me that you believe in that mummery?"

"Certainly not, any more than I believe in sorcerers and witches."

Someone called him by name. "I have to mingle," he said. "Can I trust you to be on your best behavior, or should I manacle you to my wrist?"

"So Magda was right! You men do want to put us in leading strings!"

"It was only a figure of speech, an exaggeration to drive home my point."

She rolled her eyes. "Hepburn," she said, "I'm well able to take care of myself." She gestured with one hand. "What could anyone do with all these witnesses around? Honestly, Gavin, I don't need a bodyguard. Go and mingle."

He relaxed and smiled the smile that never failed to turn her insides to pudding. "Just see that you don't leave this room, and don't talk to strangers."

"Yes, Papa!" she replied. "Now go. You are the chief mourner, after all."

After that exchange, she helped herself to the scrumptious delicacies that were laid out for the guests. This feast, she reflected, could not possibly have come from the hotel's kitchens. Since she knew that Gavin was paying the shot, she deduced that he'd sent in his own caterers to do the job.

She found a quiet nook in a corner and savored each bite. She had finished the crispy ginger shrimps and was beginning on the tiny pork fritters when she was joined by Gordon Massey. She couldn't hide her surprise.

"I had no idea," she said, "that you knew Dr. Rankin."

"We were at school together." He leaned toward her. "Will Rankin spent his early years in Edinburgh, though Aberdonians prefer to forget that fact and claim him as one of their own."

She smiled as she was meant to. "Are your parents here, too?"

"Ah, no. They're settled in a snug little cottage in Braemar and are still trying to trace relatives they have lost touch with over the years." He was gazing down at his plate of appetizers, his fingers hovering over one, then another. He looked up with a smile. "Your father," he said, "certainly knows his history. The debate between him and Miss Anderson's fiancé was becoming too hot for my comfort."

She looked over at her father. "What are they debating?"

"Macbeth. Your father seems to think that he was the best king who ever sat on the throne of Scotland."

Macbeth. The king. She was careful to keep her voice neutral. "And what does Mr. Hayes think?"

"Oh, he's immersed in Shakespeare. Naturally, he thinks the opposite."

The group around her father had grown. Poor Cedric, she thought. No one ever won a debate with her father.

Massey looked on the point of saying more, but Gavin appeared at that moment with a smile that would have done credit to a shark, and after blathering a lot of nonsense, he spirited her away.

His jaw was tight; a muscle pulsed in his cheek. "It's a bit premature for you to set up a flirtation, is it not? We've only been married a few days."

Her jaw went slack. "A flirtation? I wouldn't know how to flirt if my life depended on it."

"Then what did he want?"

"He was just being friendly." There was a challenge in her voice.

He made a scoffing sound.

"Did you say something?" she asked sweetly.

"No. Yes. Just be careful. Men like Massey can't

help themselves. A pretty woman catches their eye, and they're off and running. Every woman under thirty is Massey's best friend."

She gave an involuntary look over her shoulder, and her gaze was caught and held by her friend Sally. Sally didn't look too happy, and Kate wondered if it was because Massey was neglecting her. That last day on Deeside, Sally and Mr. Massey had seemed quite taken with each other.

"What I wanted to tell you," said Gavin, "is that there is trouble in the kitchen. The hotel chef is making things difficult for the caterers. I'm going downstairs to sort them all out. To be on the safe side, I've asked Dalziel to keep an eye on you."

She looked over at Dalziel, who returned her stare with a slight inclination of his head. A little apart from him was Cedric, standing alone now, and looking quite satisfied with his own company. As hostess, it was her duty to say a few words to him. The thought was daunting. How could Sally bear to be married to that stick?

"Did you hear me, Kate?"

"I heard you. Don't forget to put happy, happy thoughts in their heads. You'll have them hugging and kissing you before you know it."

"Very funny!" It was a retort, but he was smiling.

Her mother joined them, and after a moment or two, Gavin gave Kate a look that spoke volumes and then excused himself. Mrs. Cameron did most of the talking, leaving Kate free to let her mind wander. She wasn't thinking of anything in particular when the hair on the back of her neck began to rise. In the next instant, she was transported to the reception at Juliet's wedding. She experienced the same undercurrents of danger that were tempered by confusion. Something or someone was not as it appeared on the surface.

Her pulse started to race. Something was pulling at her mind, something that seemed familiar. Someone who seemed familiar. Who was it? She let her eyes wander over the various knots of people who were standing around. Her gaze passed over a gentleman she did not know, then jerked back and narrowed on him. She'd seen him before. He wasn't handsome, he wasn't plain, but he was smiling, and she knew that she had never seen him smile. He was thirtyish with nothing distinguishing about him. Then where did she know him from? And then it came to her. He was at Juliet's wedding reception, not as a guest but as one of the "invisible" waiters who hovered around tables and generally made themselves useful. He was not a waiter now but masquerading as one of the mourners.

"Mama," she said abruptly cutting off her mother's flow of words, "who is that gentleman over there, the one who is talking to Magda?"

Her mother looked. "I've never seen him before, but there is Mrs. Rees-Jones. I must go and speak to her."

Mrs. Cameron moved away just as the gentleman in question bowed to Magda and turned to go.

The mystery man was leaving. There was no time to find Dalziel or Gavin. If she didn't intercept him, they could lose him altogether. With no clear idea of what she would say, she hurried after him and was stopped in her tracks when her friend Sally stepped in front of her.

"Your mother tells me," Sally said, "that she has sent out invitations to your wedding in Braemar. I believe she called it a 'proper wedding.'"

Kate tried to move around Sally, but Sally thwarted the attempt.

"You know mothers," Kate said, edging to the side so that she could follow the progress of the mystery man, "they want things done right and tight. I hope you and Cedric will be there."

"We'll be there, but . . ."

Sally floundering for words was a new experience for Kate. "But what, Sally, and why the long face?"

She saw her quarry disappear through a side door but was prevented from going after him when Sally grasped her arm. She couldn't shake off her best friend without appearing rude.

Sally's voice was soft and held an appeal. "You mustn't believe everything I say, Kate. I don't believe half of it myself. You're such an innocent. I could never forgive myself if my unguarded tongue influenced you. You could never be happy with a man you did not love and who did not love you."

Kate was all at sea. "Are we talking about Cedric?"

"No," replied Sally succinctly. "I'm talking about Gavin Hepburn. Kate, you know he is not the man for you. All your friends are worried about you. I took it upon myself to speak to you. Listen to me, Kate. It's not too late. Your father is a barrister. It may be possible to annul the marriage."

Kate said, "That's a bit extreme, isn't it? Trust me, Sally, I know what I'm doing." There would be an annulment, but she couldn't tell Sally that, not until their villain was caught. "Besides," she went on, "that's not what you told me at Juliet's wedding. You said that he couldn't take his eyes off me."

"What I said then was meant to bolster your confidence and reduce Lorna's light to a peep."

"Things change," said Kate, wishing people would mind their own business and leave her to take care of her own.

"Has he told you that he loves you?"

Kate's mouth went dry. That was something she

couldn't bring herself to lie about, so she quoted what she'd heard on the subject from Mrs. Cardno. "Love can grow from small beginnings, or so I've heard."

"Piffle! It's obvious that you're in love with him, but Gavin lost his heart a long time ago." Sally opened her mouth, shut it, and shook her head. "I won't say more except that if he hurts you, I'll *kill* him!"

In a swish of skirts, Sally moved away, leaving Kate to ponder her words. One thing she never doubted: though Sally spoke her mind with outrageous frankness, she was a true friend. The allusion to Gavin losing his heart a long time ago naturally referred to Alice. *Alice.* She wondered whether everyone knew about Alice and pitied her. From the speculative glances from the people she passed on her way to the door that the elusive interloper had vanished through, she guessed that Sally was right. Clenching her teeth, she pushed though the door and entered a staircase.

And suddenly it engulfed her, a force so malevolent that she took an involuntary step back. The fine hairs on her neck didn't rise, they stood on end. Goose bumps made her skin prickle. Imminent danger was all around her, if only she had eyes to see it.

Gavin. Where was he? What was keeping him? The list of possibilities was endless, but what gripped her mind was that somehow the villain she was following had gotten to Gavin.

She stood stock-still, taking her bearings. The staircase was at the back of the hotel, overlooking the courtyard and outhouses. There were windows, but the sun's rays barely penetrated the small panes of glass. No one was about, no hotel footmen or maids to be seen. This staircase had no gas lamps on the walls, only the odd candle in a wall sconce to light the way, and seemed derelict, as though the owners of the hotel had forgotten its existence. As she sniffed the air, however, and smelled the stale tobacco smoke, it occurred to her that this out-of-the-way staircase passed for the smoking room for gentlemen who were not allowed to smoke in the reception rooms.

Below her, she heard footsteps. A door banged, then there was silence. Though she was rigid with fear, she didn't lose her head but snatched a heavy brass candlestick from a wobbly table and held it steady as she descended the stairs.

On the half landing, she halted, straining all her senses to find the source of her disquietude. Strangely enough, her intuition had dulled. She no longer knew where the danger was coming from.

An inside door at the foot of the stairs creaked in the draft that came from the outside. Holding the candlestick high above her head, she continued the descent. There was no need to enter the room with the squeaky door. She found him in a grotesque heap at the bottom of the stairs. Her heart leaped to her throat, and she sank to her knees beside him. "Gavin," she cried, but it wasn't Gavin. His eyes were open, staring sightlessly. It was the interloper, the waiter from the Deeside Hotel. It looked as though he'd fallen down the stairs and broken his neck.

She choked back an involuntary sob. It wasn't Gavin! It wasn't Gavin! She couldn't help what she was feeling. All that mattered to her was that Gavin was safe.

How long had she been delayed by Sally? It must have happened then. Wouldn't someone have heard him call out? Shouldn't someone have heard him tumbling down the stairs? A bootboy? A groom? Whoever used this neglected staircase?

"Kate!"

Kate looked up into eyes that blazed with fury: Gavin's eyes. The fire died when he saw what was at her feet. He knelt beside her.

"What happened here?" he asked.

"I think he must have fallen down the stairs."

"And you're here because . . . ?"

She was staring at the pool of blood that was forming on the wooden floor.

Gavin touched her face, bringing her eyes to his. "Kate, what happened here?" he asked gently.

Her brain unfroze. "I thought I recognized him upstairs. I thought I'd seen him at Juliet's wedding. He was one of the waiters."

Gavin studied the interloper's face and nodded. "I think you're right. I think this is the man who waited on Will and me." His brow knit in a frown. "I wonder if he overheard you arranging to meet with Will later? Who would notice him?"

"Yes," she said. "We're not as discreet as we should be around servants."

The door to the outside suddenly opened, and a gust of wind blew it back on its hinges. Her candle went out. In the blink of an eye, Gavin had his revolver in his hand. "Stay down!" he told Kate as he rose to his feet. With his revolver pointing at the open door, he positioned himself in front of her.

A man appeared, stopped, and let out a long breath that reeked of tobacco. He squinted into the dimly lit interior. "Hepburn? Is that you?" The voice belonged to Cedric Hayes. "Come out for a smoke, have you? I'd be happy to keep you . . ." His voice trailed away when Kate rose to stand by Gavin's side. Gavin surreptitiously slipped his revolver into his pocket.

"There's been a terrible accident," he said. "My wife

and I were going out for a breath of fresh air when we came upon this poor sod. I think he must have been coming out for a smoke and fallen down the stairs."

"Who is he?"

Gavin squeezed Kate's hand, a signal for her to keep her mouth shut. "We don't know, but he seems familiar." He lit a candle from one of the wall sconces.

Cedric got down on one knee and examined the dead man's face. "I'll say he looks familiar," he said. "His name is John Liddel, and he was thrown out of Sandhurst for cheating at cards and stealing from other cadets. The Royal Military College, you know? I'd say he was up to no good here." He swore softly. "You'd better ask the guests to check their money and valuables." Then to the corpse, "Didn't anyone tell you, Johnny boy, that the wages of sin are death?"

A startled look passed from Kate to Gavin. Cedric had once been in the military? Incredible!

"What do we do now?" Kate asked.

"We call in the police," said Cedric. "They'll bring in their own doctor if foul play is suspected, but it looks like a case of accidental death to me."

He got to his feet. "Why don't you take your wife to her room and spare her the investigation that is sure to follow?"

"Thank you," said Gavin. "This shouldn't take long. I'll be back as soon as I can.

Kate concealed the candlestick she would have used as a weapon in the folds of her gown and preceded Gavin up the stairs.

Nineteen

The police arrived eventually, made a perfunctory investigation and, after the medical examiner had given his consent, removed the body to the mortuary.

"They found a few expensive trinkets in Liddel's pockets," Gavin told Kate, "as well as a drawstring bag stuffed with a wad of banknotes, and a key to a bedroom in the attic. They also found a rough plan of the hotel. You can imagine what that leads them to believe."

"That he was a thief or a burglar?"

They were in the bridal chamber, with the gas lamps turned up. Gavin was pacing in front of the window, and Kate was sitting close to the fire with a scarlet plaid stole around her shoulders to ward off drafts. They were expected to join Kate's family in the private parlor to talk things over and have a bite to eat.

Gavin nodded. "According to Cedric," he went on, "Liddel was thrown out of Sandhurst for petty theft and cheating at cards. The police have yet to confirm this, but everything leads them to believe that it's a clear case of accidental death."

"Just like the last time," Kate replied reflectively.

Gavin's face was grim when he faced her. "Not quite. In this case, Cedric and I were the only ones to give the police our formal statements. As soon as word got out that the police had been sent for, the hotel emptied of guests *and* mourners."

"Why? What have they to hide?"

Some of the tension went out of him, and he grinned. "It wouldn't be the first time an errant husband had kept an assignation with his light-o'-love in an obscure hotel. He'd hardly want it to get back to his wife, or vice versa if the lady were married, and the police are not known for their discretion in such delicate situations."

She gave him a cool stare. "Had much practice in that quarter, Hepburn?"

"With married women? Never." He waited a breath. "And you? Had much practice with men, Kate?"

She thought of the male patients at the clinic. Suppressing a smile, she said modestly, "A little, but only with married men."

"Careful, Kate, or I'll forget that I'm a husband in name only."

It took a moment for her to grasp his meaning, then hot color flooded her face. "Imbecile," she hissed. "It was a joke."

He gave her a lazy grin. "As I am well aware. Did you know that when your temper is up, your eyes change color? There's a hint of violet in them. It's very attractive."

Voice like ice, she replied, "Can we get back to what is really important—the police investigation?"

He gave a quick chuckle but allowed himself to be diverted. "It's as I told you. They think what they were meant to think, that Liddel was a burglar who came by his just deserts when he tripped and fell down the stairs. Case closed."

"What they were meant to think? It could be true, couldn't it? And if he was the man on the moor, then all our worries are over, and we can stop looking over our shoulders day and night."

He gave her a long, steady look. "You don't really believe that?"

"No. I just wish it were true. I'm speculating. That's all."

"Well, speculate on this. Liddel was at the Deeside Hotel in Ballater. Now he is here in Aberdeen and just happens to show up at our hotel. A thief with his expensive tastes wouldn't waste his time in a second-class establishment like this. He'd try for one of the first-class hotels in Union Street where the pickings would be better. But more important by far, he seems to know where we will be almost before we know it ourselves."

She thought about his words before answering him. "When my family visits Aberdeen, they always put up at this hotel. It's close to the beach and not far from the clinic. It wouldn't be too hard for Liddel to figure out that I'd turn up sooner or later. However . . ."

"What?"

"While you were waiting for the police to arrive, I did a lot of thinking. Liddel wasn't after me. He didn't lure me into that staircase. I followed him."

Another interval of silence went by. "What are you thinking?" Kate asked finally.

"Perhaps he was meeting someone, his partner in crime, I assume. There was a falling-out of thieves, or perhaps it was premeditated, or perhaps his partner decided to cut his losses and act for himself."

"How did Liddel's killer slip away? Cedric was outside smoking a cigar, and I was still upstairs. I would have seen anyone who came through that door."

"Are you sure of that?"

She wasn't sure, because she hadn't kept her eye on the door all the time. She had been waylaid by Sally.

When he extended his hand, she automatically placed her hand in his. He pulled her to her feet. "Something is on your mind," he said. "What is it?"

Her eyes searched his. "What were you doing on the staircase? Were you following me?"

He grinned. "You were emitting a signal that only I can hear. I mentioned that once before. 'Gavin!' you were screaming. 'Come and save me. I'm in mortal danger!' Not that I heard your words clearly, but your message was loud and clear."

"As it was," she replied, not liking his portrait of a woman who needed a man to rescue her at every turn, "I didn't need rescuing at all. The poor man was dead."

He adjusted the stole around her shoulders and examined her critically. "Scarlet becomes you," he said. "You should wear it more often."

"Possibly." Her tone was aloof. "But I wear what is suitable for the occasion." She threw off the stole, folded it neatly, and set it over the back of a chair. "Shall we go?"

They made directly for the private parlor where her family had assembled for a late supper. Everyone was crowded around the table, demolishing, like the frugal Scots they were, the last of the funeral meats the caterers had supplied. Kate was the only one in full mourning.

"Told you so," said Gavin. "You should have worn the scarlet stole."

Kate pretended not to hear. Squaring her shoulders, she made straight for her cousin Hamish. Gavin watched as they became involved in an animated conversation, their two heads bent together like conspirators.

She was up to something, he thought.

Then again, so was he.

Kate lay quietly in bed, breathing evenly, trying to convince her in-name-only husband that she had fallen asleep. She tried to keep her mind blank, but of course, that wasn't possible, so she focused on something irrelevant: the heather-clad moors of home, the broom blazing with its yellow blossoms, and the snow-capped peaks of the Cairngorms.

She liked to think it was a paradise, but it wasn't. Eagles and hawks abounded as did foxes, stoats, and weasels, and birds and beasts of prey were always on the hunt for their next meal. How was it possible that she had become the hunted?

This wasn't the first time she'd been hunted.

The thought exploded through her brain. *This wasn't the first time she had been hunted, she and her mother both.*

Her breathing became erratic. Why? When? How? Who?

She had no answers except that they'd found a temporary shelter with someone. Who? Who had waited for her on the other side of that door in her dream? That's what she had to find out.

She knew where she would find answers. It seemed, now, that she had always known but had suppressed her memories because she was afraid of what they would reveal. But not knowing was far more dangerous than knowing. When she had answers, she would decide how much she would tell Gavin.

"Gavin?" she whispered. Good. He was snoring softly. It was time to join her cousins.

* * *

As soon as he heard the door click, Gavin was off his makeshift bed and grabbing for his clothes. It irked him that she hadn't taken him into her confidence. He couldn't get into her mind for answers because she'd taken good care to wall him off. Hamish was easier to read: adventure, danger and . . . a convent. A convent? What did a convent of nuns have to do with anything? Unless . . . he let the thought revolve in his mind . . . unless that was where Kate and her mother had taken refuge all those years ago.

Refuge? That's not how Kate saw it in her dreams. It was a prison.

What in hell's name was going on?

He dressed in double-quick time and met Dalziel just inside the back door of the hotel. "I'm sorry," said Dalziel, "so sorry. I took my eyes off her for only a moment—"

Gavin held up a hand to silence the other man. "If anyone is to blame, it's me," he said, "and you couldn't have known about the side door. Just tell me where she is now."

"She is with her cousins," Dalziel said. "They're walking toward the beach. And they are armed."

"Armed? Not Kate, surely?"

"I saw Hamish hand her a revolver. I think he showed her how to use it."

"Bloody hell!" He stood there fuming. "Get off to bed, Dalziel," he finally said. "I know where they are going."

He was remembering Kate and he walking along Constitution Street on their way to the beach, and how she had shivered when they passed the old Catholic hospice and school.

He didn't follow her. He aimed to get there before

her. On that thought, he turned into the lane behind the hotel and set off at a sprint.

Hamish became less cocky the nearer they approached the old Catholic hospice. "You never did tell us, Kate, why we had to be armed to face a bevy of nuns. What kind of trouble are you expecting?"

"Keep your eyes peeled," she admonished. "It's not the nuns I'm worried about. It's who we may meet on the way. A woman out alone at this time of night invites the wrong kind of attention."

Rory gave her an awkward pat on the back. "Never fear, Kate. We'll see that no harm comes to you."

She blinked back the sudden sting in her eyes. It was ever thus. Though she was a good five years older than her cousins, even as children, they'd fought her battles for her whenever the local children taunted her with being a freak. And she had fought their battles for them, not with her fists but with her words.

They really were the oddest family, each a little fey in their own way.

"Why isn't Hepburn with us?" Hamish asked.

She knew that tone—censorious, with an edge of belligerence threatening retribution if Gavin failed to live up to what her hotheaded cousins expected of him.

"I didn't invite him," she said simply. "Look, I want answers to what really happened all those years ago. Who was my mother? You know how it has always bothered me. Nobody seems to know. I want to think about it and decide how much I'm going to tell my new husband, that's all."

"And you think you'll find answers at the convent?" asked Rory, disbelief rife in his voice.

"I don't know. I hope so."

"You've left it a wee bit late, haven't you, lass?" Hamish put in.

"I'd forgotten about the convent until we passed it the other day. It may mean nothing at all, but I have to find out."

It was a three-story edifice, and lights shone dimly from various parts of the building. They entered the precincts by an iron gate and approached the lighted porch that overhung the main entrance. Kate used the bellpull to alert the porter to their presence, and after a moment or two, the door swung open. The kindly faced nun did not seem surprised to see them and ushered them inside and shut the heavy door with a bang. Her name, she said, was Sister Anne.

"Sister Dolores is expecting you," said Sister Anne. "The sisters are at Compline, but not Sister Dolores. She cannot manage the stairs, you see."

Kate and her cousins exchanged a quick glance. They were expected? They hadn't even given their names.

The little nun chattered as she led the way. Kate waved her cousins to follow, but she wasn't ready yet, not nearly ready, to leave the corridor where she had last seen her mother. It was all coming back to her, not a dream but a memory. She was in the right place. Matron was a nun, hard-faced and hard of heart. The other nuns went in fear of her as much as the children in the orphanage did. Her mother wasn't housed in the hospice. Few were. Matron believed that illness was sent by God to punish the guilty. Repentance could be won only by prayer and suffering.

Tears dripped slowly down Kate's cheeks as she made her way from the main entrance toward the door that had led to a new life for her. It wasn't the same. Gas sconces were set in the walls where she remembered candles. She'd forgotten about the pervasive scent of incense. Is that why she loved the fresh scents of the Highlands?

She passed the hospice and came to the section where the cells were located, a series of small rooms to house the seriously disturbed. The doors were all open. She entered the first and saw a nun helping a patient to drink from a glass. The nun's words were soft and soothing but inaudible to Kate.

A lump formed in her throat. The bare stone walls were as austere as she remembered them, but she might have been in a different world, a softer, kinder world. There was no Matron here to terrify both nuns and inmates into submission.

If only . . .

She shook herself free of regrets. She wasn't finished yet. She moved on. She was clutching her mother's hand, half dragging her to the door at the end of the corridor. *"Run, Catherine, run, and don't look back."* Her mother struggling with Matron. The door closing. A blanket thrown over her. Her heart beating like a deer's with the hunters closing in for the kill.

She remembered now. She was carried to a waiting carriage, the blanket was removed, and she looked into the face of her rescuer. It was Sister Dolores, the sweetest nun in that house of torture.

Sister Dolores. She was expecting her. Sister Dolores was still here at the convent? Kate picked up her skirts and did an about-turn. Moving swiftly, she made for the staircase that Sister Anne had taken. On the first floor up, a light from one of the rooms spilled into the corridor. She heard someone laughing, a woman's voice. She pushed the door open and froze. Gavin and an elderly nun were seated in chairs flanking the fire, enjoying a quiet tête-à-tête. Of her cousins, Hamish and Rory, there was nary a sign.

The nun looked up. "Ah, Catherine," she said, "you probably don't remember me. I'm Sister—"

Kate ran to the startled nun and went down on her knees in front of her. "Of course I remember you, Sister Dolly. It was you who saved me from Matron all those years . . ." She tried to say more but could not go on. Lowering her head to the sister's lap, she wept all the tears she had stored up since that night she had lost her mother.

"I haven't heard that name in a long time—Sister Dolly. My, how the years fly! Dry your eyes, child, and come and sit by me. Help yourself to the brandy, Mr. Hepburn."

"I'm fine, thank you," Gavin said.

He produced his own voluminous handkerchief and handed it to Kate. He then proceeded to sip from the glass of brandy Sister Dolores had offered him when he'd first introduced himself as Kate's husband. The good sister, at that point, could not place Kate. She'd heard Dr. Rankin mention the name Hepburn a time or two, so she was not surprised by his visit. At that point, he'd told Kate's cousins that their presence was redundant, and he would see his wife safely back to the hotel. Rory would have objected, but Hamish seemed to have a better grasp of the inner workings of the husband-wife relationship.

"I don't know why she didn't go to you in the first place," Hamish had said gruffly. "Come along, Rory. From now on, Kate's husband can fight her battles for her."

There was something about these brothers that appealed to Gavin. They were rough and always ready for a fight, but their devotion to Kate was, in his eyes, their saving grace.

Kate had finished drying her eyes and was now twisting his handkerchief into knots. He wanted to scoop her up in his arms and rock her like a baby. So much for giving her the shaking of her life when he caught up to her!

Kate's voice was rough with emotion. "Sister Dolly, you helped me get away from this place, didn't you? I remember a little, and I want to know how it was done and how you became involved."

Sister Dolores clasped her gnarled hands together and stared at them for a long moment, then looked up with a self-deprecating smile. "I'm afraid that I wasn't a very good nun in those days. I broke my vow of obedience, you see, and I did it with a glad heart. I helped your mother plan your escape, Catherine. She knew that she couldn't go with you. She was prostrate with pneumonia. It took all her strength to get out of her bed and take you from the orphans' wing. She knew you wouldn't leave her if you knew she would stay behind. So she and I both lied to you by omission. You were only an infant. We couldn't tell you that your mother was dying."

Kate swallowed. "When did she die?"

"A few days but no longer than a week after you left. I can tell you this. She was at peace. Her last prayer was for you."

"She was at peace?" Kate repeated. "I thought she was guarded day and night because"—she flicked a glance at Gavin; it seemed pointless now to conceal the truth from him, and she no longer cared what he thought—"because," she went on starkly, "she was insane. Matron said so over and over. My mother was wicked. There was a demon inside her."

"You remember her saying that?"

"It's one of the few things I do remember."

"May God forgive her. Your mother was not insane,

Catherine. Believe it! She saw things others did not. Yes, it's a little strange but not godless. I'm afraid Matron was the wicked one. Our convent was never set up to house the insane. We have children here. The civic authorities would never have allowed such a thing to happen."

In the silence that followed, Gavin reached out and clasped Kate's hand. She looked stunned, as though her world had been turned upside down, and he wondered if this lie about her mother was the obstacle that prevented her from trying to read his thoughts or allowing him to read hers.

"I swear to God," said Sister Dolores, "that your mother was not insane. She came to us, broken in spirit. She would never speak of her misfortunes and accepted Matron's abuse without complaint. As for Matron, she came by her Godly deserts."

"How so?" asked Gavin, trying to give Kate time to come to herself.

Sister Dolores chuckled. "In all innocence, I was the means of bringing about Matron's downfall. You'll notice I find it impossible to call her Mother Superior. Here's how it happened."

Color was coming back to Kate's cheeks, and she was listening intently to what the nun had to say.

"I was prepared to take my punishment for helping you escape this place," said the sister. "You see, I knew I had broken my vow of obedience, but no one suspected me. I had been blessed with an innocent face, you see. Or should I say it was a curse?"

She still had an innocent look about her, though her skin was lined with wrinkles. Gavin couldn't even hazard a guess at how old Sister Dolores might be.

She had slipped into a reflective silence. Heaving a sigh, she looked up at Gavin. "This was a sad, sad place in those days. The mother superior, Matron as we nuns called her, was not fit to have charge of a cat, let alone the sick, the dying, and the orphans who sought refuge with our order. The Sisters of Nazareth are supposed to serve, not rule like temporal despots who love power for the sake of power." She stopped, chuckled again, and went on, "The grace of God never ceases to amaze me. My sin of disobedience weighed heavily on my conscience, so when the priest came to hear the nuns' confessions, I confessed my wrongdoing. Of course, I had to do penance, but the next thing I knew was that Matron was made to answer for how she ruled our hospice and was sent home to Belgium in disgrace."

Belgium, thought Gavin. That would explain the brandy instead of whiskey and the musical lilt to the nun's voice.

"And," said Sister Dolores, "we have been blessed with successors who uphold the principles on which our order was founded: service to the poor and needy."

"Sister," said Kate, "I remember you put me in a carriage. Who was waiting for me in that carriage?"

Sister Dolores shook her head. "All I know is that she was your mother's friend. She never visited, because visitors were not allowed—another of Matron's edicts—but she and your mother passed notes to each other through me. Another sin I had to confess. The priest, Father Francis I believe his name was, absolved me without penance because, he said, it was an act of kindness."

They heard steps coming up the stairs, but no laughter, only voices whispering.

"Ah," said Sister Dolores, "Compline is over. We have a discipline here, Mr. Hepburn: silence from Compline to Matins. You have a few minutes to ask your questions before the bell rings."

Gavin did not waste time. "How did you come to know Dr. Rankin?"

Sister Dolores took a moment to reflect. "You must understand that he knew nothing of Matron. She ruled twenty years ago. Dr. Rankin would not have been allowed to set foot in our convent then. I'm happy to say that things are very different now. He was a man of science, and when he asked if he could visit what we call 'our lost souls,' we were happy to oblige."

"Lost souls?" said Gavin.

"They were deeply troubled patients, but not dangerous. Dr. Rankin could get them to talk, and we were happy to use his gifts, though he was not a Catholic."

Aware of time passing, Gavin moved on. "He made an appointment to see you before he died?"

Sister Dolores shook her head. "No appointment was necessary. He dropped by from time to time, and we were always happy to see him. You should speak to our parish priest at St. Peter's, on Justice Street. Dr. Rankin and Father Paul were good friends."

"What about parish records?" Gavin asked.

"They are kept at St. Peter's. You cannot take them away, but you can examine them if there is a priest in attendance and if you receive permission."

"Thank you, Sister Dolores," Gavin said. He got up. "You have been most helpful."

Kate offered her thanks, too, but at the door, she ran back and kissed the nun on the cheek. "I shall never forget you," she said.

Once outside, Gavin hailed a cab. Kate was surprised. "It's only a short walk from here to the hotel," she said.

"We're not going back to the hotel."

"Then where—"

"We're going where there is a telephone; in short, we're going back to the gatehouse, to Mrs. Hunter's guesthouse."

Twenty

She lay there, tossing and turning, a million threads tangled hopelessly in her mind. She couldn't focus, not when she could hear the muted sound of Gavin's voice next door. He'd finally been connected to his brother at the Home Office and had dropped his voice to a murmur in an effort, she supposed, to keep his conversation private.

She wished that he would close the door, because the snatches of conversation she overheard kept interrupting the flow of what mattered most to her—the questions she had not put to Sister Dolores earlier that night—questions about her father. She wasn't sure that she wanted to hear the answers. What kind of man would desert his wife and child and leave them to fend for themselves? Had she ever known him? Surely, if she had, she would have remembered something.

Sister Dolores's voice seemed to be whispering in her ear. *"Your mother was not insane. She came to us broken in spirit."*

Who broke her mother's spirit? The father she had

never known? Was her mother his legal wife, or was she a simple country girl whom he had seduced and discarded? She'd asked herself these very questions ever since she'd become an adolescent. Her parents claimed not to know. Had they told her the truth?

It didn't matter. She was a grown woman now and was mistress of her own fate. She had a family, a father, mother, and sister; an extended family counting all her cousins, aunts, and uncles. And Sister Dolores had given her something precious—an assurance that her mother wasn't insane.

Too tired to think, she turned on her side and drifted into an exhausted sleep. She wasn't aware when Gavin hung up the telephone and wandered into her room. After his telephone call with Alex, he wasn't going to let her out of his sight. Alex had reached the same conclusion as he, that their villain knew where they would be almost before they knew it themselves. Someone either deliberately or in all innocence had passed the information on to someone else.

Mrs. Cardno came to mind, and he wondered how he could make use of her loose tongue to his advantage. He wasn't willing to accept his brother's next piece of advice, that he should use Kate as bait to lure the killer into the open, but what choice did they have?

Alex's last words drummed inside his head. "She's a Macbeth. She must be. Nothing else makes sense. Don't forget Granny's prophecy. You know what happened to Macbeth."

"Macduff hunted him down."

"Where is your dog now?"

"I sent him back to Feughside."

"If I were you, I'd make sure that he stayed close to your wife."

Macduff, whom he had found as a stray. Or had

Macduff found him? As he remembered, in Shake-speare's play, Macduff slew Macbeth and cut off his head. What insane flight of fancy had made him name his dog Macduff?

She was his wife, Alex said. Damn right she was! It gave him some rights, not to take advantage of her, but at least to keep her close to protect her if some miscreant with murder on his mind were to come through the door.

On that inflexible decision, he placed his revolver on the floor between the bed and a small table and began to shrug out of his outer clothes. He had already closed the shutters, but he left a lamp burning low, just in case he had to rise in a hurry to defend home and hearth. The thought made him grimace. He'd left the lamp on because he didn't want Kate to mistake him for an intruder and maim him with her pocket revolver before he could get a word out of his mouth. And where had she hidden the damned thing?

He'd tried to take the gun away from her, but she wasn't having any of that. She thought that all she had to do was aim and pull the trigger, and the bullet would find its mark. She'd never shot a gun and hoped she never would, but as she sweetly pointed out, their villain didn't know that.

He knew from the clothes that she'd strewn over a couple of chairs that she was sleeping only in her chemise. Before it put ideas in his head, he wrapped himself in the blanket he'd taken from the room he had once shared with Dalziel and lay down beside her. Subduing the picture that came to his mind of Kate in nothing but a chemise, he turned on his side away from her and gave his thoughts a puzzle to solve: who had a motive to want Kate dead? As his focus shifted, bits of the puzzle began to rearrange themselves. Slowly, meticulously, he fitted them into their proper slots. Will, the convent, Kate and her mother, the parish records, the killer who left notes on his victims—notes that the police discounted.

The murderer wouldn't like that. He'd want everyone to know that the deaths were connected. Otherwise, if he got to Kate, her murder would arouse a storm of outrage, and his misdirection would have failed.

At this point, he began to wonder whether he'd been on the wrong track all along, that some sick mind really had a grudge against psychiaters and their patients. What steadied him was his granny's prophecy and her assurance that the future could be changed. He held fast to that thought as his breathing slowed and his lids grew heavy.

She was trapped in a nightmare, and there was no way out. He was after her, the man who wanted to kill her. *Gavin!* The scream echoed inside her mind and faded away. *Gavin!* A sob this time. She was all alone on the moors.

Alone except for the demon who was gaining on her.

She was climbing a steep incline that overlooked a hamlet, but in this ice-cold mist, she could see almost nothing. She was running blindly with no idea of where she was or where she was going. She couldn't stop shivering, and the hairs on the back of her neck quivered in terror.

When the mist began to evaporate, her steps slowed, and she peered through the filmy gauze trying to find cover from her pursuer. On her left was an ancient ruined chapel and burial grounds, and white marble angels stood sentinel by the graves. On her right, horses with black plumes snorted and impatiently pawed the ground with their hooves.

Not funeral horses, she decided as she drew nearer to them, but destriers with a scarlet cross emblazoned on their livery.

As in the way of dreams, the stone angels were stepping down from their pedestals. White cloaks billowed out in the breeze. The emblem on their dark tunics was turning a fiery bloodred. She recognized the symbol. They were warrior knights of the ancient order of the Knights Templar who had settled in Deeside centuries before.

The Knights Templar, her father had told her, were protectors of the weak and helpless. She had nothing to fear from them. Easy to say, but her father was not here. The knights were converging on her, and fear had rooted her to the spot.

She braced herself for she knew not what as they approached. Ice-cold breath drifted over her skin, lingered a moment, then was gone. She let out a long, uneven breath and turned on her heel to watch them. They had formed a line, like a solid wall, between her and the demon who was after her.

Ghosts couldn't make solid walls. Even as she watched, they were disintegrating, but they had given her time to find a place to hide.

Where was Gavin? He wouldn't leave her alone to face the demon. He said that he would save her. Where was his voice? The sense of his presence? Why did she feel so bereft?

Like a flash of light from a dying star, the knowledge that Gavin wouldn't leave her unless something catastrophic had overtaken him burst through her mind. The voice was silent because Gavin was dead. A great void opened before her. That murdering devil had gotten to Gavin and silenced him forever.

In the space of a single heartbeat, despair converted to a white-hot fury. It filled her mouth, her nostrils, her head. She no longer thought of escape. She wanted him to find her. Slowly, she turned to face her enemy. As he emerged from the mist, she let out a shriek like an enraged Fury and flung herself at him. Teeth snapping, fingers like claws, she went for his face.

He was stronger than she, and he dragged her to the ground, but still she fought him. She heaved and bucked to throw him off. She bit his shoulder and took a savage pleasure when he let out a cry. He was shaking her. Her head was bobbing; her teeth were chattering.

Then she heard Gavin's voice and she stilled. Torn between hope and disbelief, she blinked up at him. "Gavin?" she whispered hoarsely.

"I'm here, Kate. Don't struggle. I don't want to hurt you. You were dreaming. That's all it was, a dream." When she continued to stare without saying a word, he gave her another shake. "Do you hear me, Kate? It's Gavin, and I'm right here beside you."

"You're not dead?" she quavered.

"Do I seem like a ghost to you?"

His lighthearted quip did not act on her the way he thought it would. "You bastard," she hissed. "You deserted me when you promised you never would."

"Will you calm down?" He spoke sternly, as if she were a fractious child having a temper tantrum. "It was only a dream."

The effects of the dream still held her in their icy grip. Since she couldn't move, she opened her mouth to yell at him, but what came out was a tearless sob, then another, then a spate of dry, choking sobs she couldn't control. He slipped beneath the covers and gathered her into his arms, wanting only to comfort her.

"You're cold," he said. "Here, let me warm you."

That she allowed him to warm her with his body was an indication of how disturbed she was.

"He's still out there," she whispered against his throat.

He tipped her chin up. "I know. I swear I won't let him touch you. I'll keep you safe."

Her voice rose a notch. "Is that supposed to comfort me? He wants you dead, too! And in my dream, he succeeds. First you, then me."

"It was only a dream."

"Easy for you to say. You weren't there."

He pulled back so that he could see her face. Her unbound hair tumbled over the pillows in a profusion of tangles. Dark circles rimmed her eyes, giving them the appearance of crushed violets. His hands trembled when he cupped her face. It came to him that his life would never be the same again. There was life before Kate and life after she had streaked into his carefree, devil-may-care existence. He'd always had an eye for a pretty face. This difficult woman had changed him irrevocably.

Her fingers snagged his wrists. "Don't you understand anything?" she stuttered, still shaken from a dream that was more real to her than reality. "I thought that he had murdered you."

He understood more than she did. Dreams and visions were the stuff of seers. His hold tightened on her. He had a healthy respect for death, but it wouldn't come to that. He would draw the bastard out and gladly put a bullet in his black heart, no quarter asked or given.

Could it be that easy? He was only a mortal man, after all. He was also a seer of Grampian, but that did not make him invincible. If he were out of the way, how could Kate escape the designs of a cold-blooded killer? She was small-made; her bones were fragile. But she was not helpless, he thought fiercely. She had met this killer on the moors above Ballater, and she had carried the day. She could do it again.

Kate knew that he was in the grip of some powerful emotion, but so was she. She wanted to feel the steady beat of his heart beneath her palm. She wanted to hear the sound of his breathing as he sucked air in and out of his lungs. She wanted to forget the terror of her nightmare and escape to the land of the living. She was wound up so tightly she thought her brain might explode from the pressure.

His fingers shredded her chemise. She tried to unbutton his shirt, failed, and simply tore off the buttons from throat to waist. His body excited her, his moans, his heat. She felt heady with the solid feel of him. He was no dream lover. This was Gavin. Fate had sent him to her, so he said, but she would gladly battle with Fate to keep him safe.

His mind was telling him to slow down and not make this another debacle like the first time they'd made love, but how could he resist her desperate need? And how could he resist his response to her? He felt as though he'd been waiting for her half his life. She was here, now, vibrant and strong and demanding. Time was finite. He wasn't going to waste a minute of it.

She smiled when his lips opened over hers. Through nibbling kisses, she murmured, "I have a lot to learn about passion. Will you teach me, Gavin?"

His lips had moved to her throat. "You're not a novice, Kate. I am. You know more about love—"

She stopped his words with a searing kiss. She didn't want to talk about love, or make undying promises.

Words were misleading. All her life, she had survived by living a lie. She had tried to change to please those she loved and who loved her. And she'd been miserable. This was glorious. A great weight had been lifted from her shoulders. Insanity did not run in her family. Matron would never have the power to hurt her again. At last, here, in Gavin's arms, she could be herself.

Shuddering with sensation, she wound her arms and legs around him. He found her, ready and wet for him. Arms braced to keep his weight from crushing her, he slowly eased into her. She was so tight, he was afraid to move. Kate had other ideas. She arched beneath him, sheathing him deep inside her. Her little cries of arousal drove him over the edge.

"Kate," he said, but it was too late. She was already racing for the crest. Locked together, they went tumbling over the edge.

Kate came awake by degrees. She could hear Gavin's voice next door and assumed that he was talking to his brother in Whitehall. She stretched languidly and turned on her side. A small smile played around her lips. For a lady who thought that her work at the clinic had taught her all that she needed to know about the sexes, she had discovered that she was woefully ignorant.

She knew about sickness and how to bring down a fever by administering a cold bath. She knew about knife wounds and concussions and how to treat them. She knew that she was a competent nurse, more than competent. She'd delivered babies and nursed them until their mothers were ready to take them home. She'd distributed birth control devices, not to the men, who couldn't be trusted to use them, but to their wives who had too many children already. She'd heard jokes about what went on under the covers between a man and a woman, and she'd taken it all in stride. If she had only known the pleasure to be had in a man's arms, she might not have ended up an old maid.

Yes she would.

There was more to her aversion to marriage than ignorance and fear. The taint of insanity ran in her blood, or so she'd thought. She couldn't bring innocent children into the world with that threat hanging over them.

Things were different now. She could marry. She could have children. She could . . . Her thoughts stopped, then started over.

She was married, wasn't she? Sort of. Now why did that thought make her heart beat just a little faster? Her mind drifted to the night just past. How many times had she and Gavin made love after that first sprint to the finishing post? Just thinking about it made her toes curl.

Gavin Hepburn was more than a competent lover. He knew how to play her to prolong their pleasure. He was fascinated by her body, every curve and depression, every pulse point. And she was just as fascinated by his. Bold, lusty, virile. Every woman should be so lucky.

Of course, she thought a little wistfully, he'd had more practice under the covers than she'd had taking care of patients at the clinic, but she was a quick study—

"Bloody hell!"

She bolted upright. Gavin's voice. Gavin in a temper? Another voice answering his. She pushed back the covers, realized she wasn't wearing a stitch, and dragged the covers up to her chin. A quick look around showed that her garments were laid out where she'd left them the night before. Creeping like a cat, she edged her way to a chair. Petticoats first, then she slipped on her frock, and after doing up only enough buttons to make herself respectable, she marched into the next room.

Two startled gentlemen looked up at her entrance, Gavin and Dalziel. They were going through a newspaper that lay on the table between them.

"The *Edinburgh Review*," Gavin said viciously, as though that explained everything.

Dalziel elaborated. "The *Edinburgh Review* takes two days to reach Aberdeen. As soon as I read the lead article, I came right over."

Kate was alarmed by their expressions. "But what does it say?" she asked, her wobbly voice betraying how alarmed she was.

When Gavin stalked to the window and looked out, Dalziel cleared his throat and began. "The lead article is by a contributor, an anonymous contributor, who sent a letter to the editor. All the facts, the editor writes, have been verified by their special correspondent before they published." He paused to marshal his thoughts.

"But what does it say?" Kate repeated.

Gavin answered her. "It says that there is a killer on the loose who appears to have a grudge against anyone who worked at Will's clinics. It gives their names and how they died. It mentions that each victim received a note warning them of their danger. It demands to know why the police are sitting on their fat arses when they should be out shaking trees for clues."

She lowered herself into the nearest hard-backed chair. "How could a . . . what? . . . contributor know so much?"

"He couldn't," Gavin said harshly, "not unless he were a police informant."

"But you don't believe that?"

Gavin hesitated for only a moment. "No."

She looked down at her clasped hands. "Then he is the killer," she said. A longer pause ensued. "And I'm to be his next victim." She was suddenly angry, furious, in fact.

Jumping to her feet, she said, "He has done what you said he would do, he has found a way to bring in those notes to misdirect the police. Well, let him. If it's me he wants, I'll be ready for him."

She marched into the other room. Gavin followed and watched, in some amusement, as she withdrew her revolver from the bottom drawer of the dresser. "You need to keep it closer than that," he said.

"How close do I have to be, before my shot counts?"

"With that toy? I'd say ten paces. Tidy yourself as best you can. We're moving out. There are a few things I want to say to Dalziel first."

She wasn't listening. Her mind was calculating the distance of ten paces between her and her target. *Come on, you murdering devil,* she said in the privacy of her own mind. *I'll be waiting for you and make you sorry that you ever crossed swords with a witch of Braemar.*

She did not expect an answer, nor did she get one, but what she got was just as electrifying. Someone, somewhere, blinked.

"Didn't you hear me?" Gavin demanded roughly. "We're moving out. Tidy yourself, and let's get going. I'll give you five minutes."

When he shut the door, she went through the motions of washing her hands and face, but her mind was preoccupied with the eerie feeling that she had entered the mind of a killer.

Twenty-one

She was becoming dizzy with having to move from one safe house to another at such short notice. So here they were, on the move again, this time in an ancient carriage, with a coachman to match, all of which Mrs. Hunter had loaned them, with hot bricks at her feet and a commodious man's greatcoat to stave off the morning chill.

"I thought," she said, "that you were going to set up an appointment with the priest at St. Peter's to look over the parish records."

"Dalziel will act for me." Gavin folded his copy of the *Edinburgh Review* that he had been reading since they'd left the environs of Aberdeen. "There's not enough light to read by. Is it my imagination, or is it getting dark?"

"It's raining," she replied.

"I wouldn't be surprised if it starts to snow."

"Don't be ridiculous. This is April. All the spring flowers will soon be out."

"It was just a thought." A moment of silence went by. "Why are you so cranky?"

Were all men as dense as he? She was cranky because the only garments she had were the ones she was wearing. She was cranky because they were always on the move. She was cranky because she wanted her family; she wanted her own things; she wanted her life back. But most of all, she was cranky because she sensed that something wasn't right. She could feel it in every breath she inhaled.

And it was these kinds of spurious fancies that got Dr. Rankin to take her on as a patient.

She lifted her chin. "You would be cranky, too, if no one consulted you about where you wished to go or what you wanted to do. I'm not a piece of baggage to be passed from pillar to post. What will my family think when they hear that I'm on my travels again?"

He crossed one booted foot over the opposite knee and smiled expansively. "They'll be deliriously happy. Dalziel will inform them, in the strictest confidence, of course, that we're making for my house on Feughside to fulfill the residency requirements before our marriage can take place."

Her heart jarred. "And what will they think when we don't set a date and go through with the wedding?"

He answered carelessly, "We'll cross that hurdle when we come to it." He spread his hands. "Of course, if you have a better plan, I'd like to hear it."

"Isn't your house the first place our villain will look for us?"

"We can't leave until we meet up with Dalziel." He held up his hand to stop her next protest. "I'm not trying to avoid our villain. On the contrary, I hope he *will* show his face. And I'll be ready for him. Feughside House is isolated," he elaborated when she looked at him dubiously. "We'll know him when we see him, Kate."

"You're setting us both up as bait?"

"As a last resort, but I'm hoping that Dalziel will bring me information that will point right at this egotistical bastard."

She lapsed into silence. In a few days, Dalziel would catch up to them and, all going well, he would have the information Gavin wanted—the name of their killer. Then she and Gavin could go their separate ways.

She felt it again, that whisper of something that made her shiver. She gave Gavin a sideways look. He seemed relaxed, untouched by the doubts that troubled her. If he, a self-confessed wizard, was immune to her fancies, who was she to believe them?

"Why so glum?" he asked, obviously puzzled by her retreat into silence.

She rallied her glum thoughts and answered evenly, "What difference could it have made if I'd had a few words with my parents before we left? And what about my clothes? I've been wearing this frock for two days now."

He wrinkled his nose. "I take your point. You *are* beginning to smell a little rank." When she let out a hiss, he laughed. "That's better," he said. "I thought for a while there that you were sleepwalking. Now you have color in your cheeks and fire in your eyes."

"How can you tell? There isn't enough light in this rickety contraption to see your hand in front of your face."

"Put it down to wizard's eyes," he said.

Her answer was to stare doggedly out the window.

He sighed. "Look," he said, "I'm sorry we had to leave Aberdeen in such a hurry, but I wanted to avoid the detectives who are bound to come calling now that this article"—he twitched the newspaper—"is going the rounds."

His words made awful sense. They'd both been

present when two bodies had turned up. They were bound to be the prime suspects. Now she understood why they were traveling by the less populated South Deeside Road. There were fewer hamlets and almost no risk of meeting anyone they knew.

"We'll break our journey at Maryculter," he said. "There's a little inn there that serves mouthwatering pies and pastries."

"I know it," she said. "The Black Kettle. It stands on what was once Templar land."

When she became absorbed in her own thoughts, he touched her knee, bringing her eyes back to him. "What is it, Kate?" he asked gently.

She hesitated for only a moment. "The Templars were in my dream. At first, I was afraid of them, but I came to see that they wanted to protect me."

"And did they?"

"They were ghosts. What do you think?"

Her tone of voice did not encourage him to pursue the subject, so he closed his eyes and folded his arms across his chest.

The inn at Maryculter was as unpretentious as its proprietor, Colin Sutherland. His customers, Mr. Sutherland told them, were mostly locals, workingmen who would not be showing their faces until their work was done; then they'd drop in for one of his pies and wash it down with the local ale before going home to their wives and children.

Leastways, that was what Kate told Gavin. The landlord's accent was so broad, he could hardly understand a word of it.

"What did you tell him about us?" Gavin asked.

"That we were in service and taking up a position at the hotel in Aboyne."

Gavin was relieved at the change in Kate. He hadn't been exaggerating when he'd told her that she looked and acted like a sleepwalker. So he'd deliberately gotten her dander up. Now he had the pleasure of watching her devour the chicken pie that the landlord had suggested they order.

Between chewing and drinking copious mouthfuls of tea, she explained why she'd forgone the meat pie for the chicken. "You should always take the advice of the proprietor in a small place like this. He can't provide an extensive menu. Only one dish will be fresh, and he knows which one it is."

"Now you tell me," Gavin said, imitating a growl. He shoved his plate aside. "This meat pie is positively revolting. The meat is so stringy I might as well be chewing . . . well . . . string."

Her eyes sparkled, and she gurgled with laughter.

He was loath to say or do anything to spoil the moment, but there were still many questions in his mind that required an answer. They could wait, he decided. They could spare a few minutes just to enjoy themselves.

Under different circumstances, he would have spared a lot more time in planning his strategy for courting Miss Kate Cameron. *How to court your own wife.* Maybe he should write a book about it? The thought almost made him smile—almost but not quite. If he tried to tell her that his misspent youth seemed like a distant memory and best forgotten, would she believe him?

Probably not, but a piece of parchment signifying that they had professed their vows before witnesses was a powerful weapon. He hoped she wouldn't force him to use it.

"What?"

"You looked thoughtful," she said. "What were you thinking a moment ago?"

"I was thinking of writing a book." Before she could probe, he pushed back his chair and got up. "Let's go for a walk to stretch our legs."

"Maryculter," she said, inhaling deeply. "My father regards this spot as holy ground."

"Why is that?"

"Because of the Knights Templar. They owned all this land once, and the lands across the river in Peterculter." She pointed across the river.

"I thought that was a legend."

She looked at him as though he'd used a four letter Anglo-Saxon word. "Don't you know the history of your own backyard?"

"Obviously not, but I'm sure you're going to enlighten me."

She flattened her lips but not for long. "Talk to my father," she said. "He knows everything there is to know about the Templars on Deeside. But don't make the mistake of arguing the point with him. He doesn't suffer fools gladly."

"Is that what he and Sally's fiancé were arguing about at Will's funeral, the Templars?"

She nodded. "For the most part, Cedric thinks he is an expert. Papa thinks he's an ignoramus and said that he could prove that the Templars went as far afield as Braemar."

She seemed to know where she was going, so he allowed her to lead. When they stopped, he looked down on the wide sweep of the river far below them. "What am I looking for?" he asked.

"You're standing on it. The ruins of the Templar chapel. This is all that is left of them in Maryculter, this and their bones where the graveyard once stood."

He looked down at his feet. No moss covered these stones. It was too damn cold. "I thought," he said, "that the Templars were great warriors. Didn't they protect pilgrims on their way to the Holy Land?"

"They were both warriors and monks. Every monk was a soldier, and every soldier was a monk. On Deeside, they farmed great tracts of land. They were also healers and herbalists and brought back many herbs from their travels. The buildings have disappeared, but if you come across a stand of Madonna lilies or betony, you'll know that the Templars were once there."

"Fascinating," he said. The only flowers he knew were the kind that would soften the ire of a tempestuous female. Roses always seemed to work for him. He didn't think roses would work with Kate Cameron.

"How do you know so much?" he asked. He was enjoying the break from plotting and planning for every eventuality in keeping her safe. It felt so . . . domestic. Their villain seemed a million miles away.

She slanted him a quick look. "Some of us on Deeside are more interested in the natural flora and fauna than the artificial variety."

Grinning, he asked, "And what do you consider the artificial variety?"

"Birds of paradise," she retorted succinctly. "You know, ladies who are not precisely ladies."

He drew a finger down her cheek to the corner of her mouth. She gazed up at him with a question in her eyes.

"I married one of the wildflowers," he said. "How do you explain that?"

"Expediency," she retorted. "Don't worry, Gavin. I won't hold you to any promises when the time comes for us to part. I'm just as eager as you to be rid of this bogus marriage."

Sometimes, he wanted to gather her in his arms and soothe all her fears. Other times, he wanted to throttle her. He looked down at her. The shabby greatcoat that he'd purloined from the gatehouse dwarfed her small frame. Her dark hair was caught in the breeze and blew around her face in hopeless disorder. There was a smudge of coal dust on her nose. But it was the oddly vulnerable look in her eyes that told him far more than she knew. Everything inside him softened.

When she inhaled sharply, he looked up. "What is it, Kate? What's troubling you?"

"They can't be Templars' ghosts, can they?" she whispered.

The line of men who appeared above them did seem otherworldly, but as they slowly picked their way down the hillside, what emerged were not Templars. "They're tinkers," he said, "you know, waifs and vagrants. Don't you have tinkers in Braemar?"

"Of course, we do." She burrowed deeper into her coat. "Poor devils. It's usually warmer at this time of year. They must be freezing cold. Well, don't just stand there. Give them a handful of silver. There will be children there, too, hiding with their mothers, not knowing where their next meal is coming from."

He dug in his pocket and came up with a handful of silver. "This goes against my principles," he said darkly. "Tinkers are nothing but rogues and tricksters. They could find something useful to do to feed their families instead of poaching and fishing where they have no business to be."

She took his money from him. "They go where the fancy takes them," she said, "and answer to no one but themselves." She gave him a superior grin. "You should admire them. After all, you have much in common."

He hung back, a bemused smile on his face as she climbed toward the little band of men. In her shabby greatcoat, she could easily have passed for one of them.

When she stomped down the hill to join him, her lips formed a perfect pout. "You fraud!" she said, glowering up at him. "They know you! That nice Mr. Hepburn who allows them to fish on his estate!"

He replied modestly, "I didn't recognize them in this half-light. Is that Wee Alfie, their leader?"

"You know it is!"

When he waved, the tinkers returned the compliment.

She opened her mouth to say something, thought better of it, and blew at the stray tendrils of hair in a vain attempt to blow them from her eyes.

Perfect. *She* was perfect. He knew that he would hold this image of her for a long, long time.

His mood was not so mellow when the lodge he shared with his brother came into view. They'd sent the coach back to Aberdeen when they came to the bridge across the Dee at Ballater. He'd made the walk a million times and thought nothing of it, but it had started to rain, and the walk uphill seemed to have stretched into twice its usual length.

Other things were beginning to occur to him. The lodge was a masculine preserve, unfit for female habitation or, he amended, unfit for someone like Kate. He couldn't remember when the lodge had had a good clearing out or even a dusting. It was too big for his man, Calley, to manage on his own. When company was expected, they hired local people to do the work, but that hadn't happened in an age.

He cast a sideways glance at Kate. She'd hardly said a word on the long trek to the house, and that made him nervous. "I'm sorry for the long walk to the house," he said, "but I had to send the coach back at Ballater. We don't want the police or our villain to know that we're here, not yet anyway."

Between gasps brought on by climbing the steep incline to the house, she got out, "Yes, you already told me. Just get me to a hot bath and a change of clothes, and I'll forgive you."

"My sister-in-law is about your size, and I know she left some of her things in one of the bedchambers."

She nodded absently and looked back over her shoulder. Across the river, she could just make out the village of Ballater. When she turned to look at the house, she shaded her eyes against the setting sun to get a better look. The lodge was a smaller version of the Fife Arms Hotel in Braemar, but there was something about this building that brought a lump to her throat. A safe stronghold for its inhabitants, she thought.

Or was it?

This would never do. She was becoming teary, and she never cried. She didn't have to look far to know what the matter was. The night before, she'd found the sweetest solace in his arms. What was the matter with men? Was making love only an appetite that had to be relieved until they were hungry again? Why didn't he make some reference to what they'd done in their bed?

Aware that he was watching her, she said gaily, "Last time I passed your lodge, there was a wild party in progress. There were scantily clad young women screaming with laughter and equally scantily clad young men weaving among the trees trying to catch them."

"What? When was this?"

She gave a theatrical sigh. "I must have been thirteen or fourteen at the time. A group of us girls from school were celebrating Juliet's birthday and spending the weekend at her house. It's not far from here, is it?"

"No," he replied curtly. "Not far."

"Well," she went on with relish, "Juliet thought it would make a great adventure to creep out of the house when her mother was asleep and spy on the goings-on of the wild Hepburn brothers."

One corner of his mouth began to twitch. "I'm surprised that Mrs. Cardno didn't insist on going with you."

"I think Juliet put something in her tea to make her sleep."

"Yes, Juliet would."

"Too bad she caught you in flagrante delicto, so to speak, or she might have married you instead of Mr. Steele."

A picture of himself chasing half-naked young women ran through his mind. "It never happened," he said. "We rent the place out to hunting parties occasionally. You must have visited the lodge when my brother and I were away." He held up an index finger to prevent her from speaking. "I know for a fact that Juliet's birthday is in September, and I am usually in London then."

"Are you sure?"

"Perfectly sure. That is when the hunting season is in full swing, and I cannot abide hunting poor defenseless creatures who have done me no harm."

"You eat fish, don't you?"

"That's different. I don't put bullets in them or maim them so they can't fend for themselves if they get away. So, how did you hear about the wild party I was supposed to host?"

She lifted her shoulders and let them drop. "It was

only a story going around, a delectable tidbit for us girls to add to our store of legends about Feughside's infamous flirt. You see, you held a sort of fearful fascination for us. You were an older man, too old to notice us, but we noticed you."

"You must have been a precocious brat as an adolescent." He had her by the elbow and was marching her to the front door.

"No. Not really. I was rather shy."

The front door was opened by a well-built gentleman with a hint of the cloister about him. Kate could imagine him on his knees, saying his prayers.

"This is my man, Calley," Gavin said.

Whatever he was going to say next was drowned out by the barking of the dog, who came tearing down the stairs to fling himself against his master's legs. Gavin went down on his haunches and scratched behind his dog's ears. "Yes, I've missed you, too, boy," he said.

Macduff did a little jig and spared Kate a few wet licks on her hands, but it was to Gavin that the dog gave his most tumultuous welcome.

Kate found herself smiling, then yawning, then shivering. Gavin rose. "Come along, Mrs. Hepburn," he said. "I'll show you to our room." To his manservant, he said, "A hot bath for my wife as soon as it can be arranged."

Not a flicker of surprise crossed Calley's stoic face. "Yes, sir," he said.

Kate's fatigue was beginning to tell on her, and she could do no more than follow where she was led. As meek as a child, she allowed Gavin to bathe her and put her to bed. It was only when he tried to turn away that she stirred and latched on to his wrist, so he sat on the edge of the bed and waited for her grip to relax. By degrees, she drifted into sleep.

Odd snatches of conversation came to him. He'd

called her precocious, but that, of course, couldn't have been the case, not when she was tormented by thoughts of her mother's insanity and her own gifts as a witch. She'd said that she was shy. The picture that came to him, however, was of a young girl who had isolated herself because she didn't fit in. She'd learned that the world could be a cold, callous place for misfits.

All his life he'd been petted and pampered and he had taken it for granted. At home, at school, with women, he had both expected and received a warm welcome. Naturally, he made friends easily, unlike Kate, who wouldn't take the chance of getting too close to people in case they hurt her.

Something fierce moved inside him, something fierce and sweet. They had been thrown together by his grandmother's prophecy. Kate had had no choice but to learn to trust him. He had learned something from the experience as well. Easy wasn't always best. Some things were worth a good deal of friction, frustration, and old-fashioned patience. God help him if he did anything to hurt her. Courting Miss Cameron was proving to be one of the hardest tests he had ever set for himself.

"Rule number one," he said under his breath. "No touching without her permission."

Macduff cocked his head as though his master had spoken in a foreign tongue.

"Rule number two," Gavin went on softly. "Always treat her with the utmost respect."

He shut his mouth before he could voice the next rule. To Macduff, he said, "What a dull dog I'm turning out to be." He made a face. "Actions speak louder than words, or so I've heard. Let that be my true test."

She was sleeping soundly, her breathing slow and even. He allowed himself one chaste kiss on her cheek and got up.

"Guard her," he told Macduff. "Guard her with your life."

Macduff was already at the foot of the bed. He shook himself off and placed himself between the bed and the door.

Gavin shut the door soundlessly and went downstairs to have a word with Calley.

Twenty-two

"How long before Dalziel gets here?" Kate asked Gavin on the morning after they arrived.

His sister-in-law's twill gown, he was happy to see, seemed a good fit. "Tomorrow or the next day," he answered easily.

"And after that? What happens then?"

He was silent as he contemplated her.

She answered her own question. "It ends here, doesn't it? You always meant it to end here." Her restless gaze moved around his study before returning to him. "How will you know who he is?"

He indicated that she should take the chair on the other side of his desk. When she was seated, he said carefully, "I'm hoping that Dalziel will give me enough information to reveal the killer, but even if he doesn't, this is an isolated spot. If anyone who was at the Deeside Hotel the night Will was killed shows his face, I think it's safe to say that we'll have our man."

"You mean . . . I'm the bait to lure him out into the open?"

He leaned across his desk and gathered her hands in his. She couldn't remember ever seeing him look so serious. "I never wanted it to come to this," he said, "but no, I'll keep you safe. Have faith, Kate. You know that he will have to kill me to get to you, and that isn't going to happen."

"Because of your grandmother's prophecy," she fairly snapped.

One corner of his mouth quirked. "I'm not letting you out of my sight," was his gentle rejoinder.

She wasn't only afraid for herself. She was afraid for him. She pulled her hands from his and rubbed her arms where goose bumps had broken out.

"What is it, Kate?" he asked.

She didn't know. Shaking her head, she said, "This isn't the first time I've felt like this." Her mind traveled back to the convent. "This isn't the first time I've felt hunted. My mother protected me then. Now you're going to take her place? It doesn't make sense. Twenty years have passed since I left the convent. Who would hate me enough to nurse a grievance for so long? Why not kill me long before now?"

He answered at once, "Because you changed your identity? Because you became Kate Cameron and disappeared from the face of the earth? I'm only speculating, you understand. Something must have happened to make it imperative that he find you."

She was silent for a long time as she considered his words. Finally, she said, "So we wait."

"So we wait."

She jumped to her feet and began to pace. "So what do we do in the meantime? I'm used to being busy. I can't sit around and twiddle my thumbs all day."

"It's not safe for us to show ourselves during the daylight hours," he said. "We don't know who may be watching us, but there's nothing to stop us going for a walk when the sun sets."

Her fingers curled around the back of her chair. "What if he comes for us then? This is a big house. It would need a small army to defend it."

He got up. "Guile," he said, "is often the best defense. There's something I want to show you. Beneath the foundations of the house, in one of the cellars, there is a secret passage that the Hepburns of a bygone age used as an escape route."

At last he had found something to divert her thoughts.

"A secret passage?" she breathed out. "We have one in our house, too. My father says that it was probably used to hide clansmen who found themselves on the wrong side of whatever king or queen came to power. And before that, a Templar monastery was built above it."

"I'm afraid our secret passage may be something of a disappointment. The Hepburns used it to evade the excise men. There was a whiskey still down there at one time."

She was anything but disappointed after he'd taken her through the door to the cellars. "This would have been the stable," she said, her gaze moving slowly over the walls. "Hold the lamp higher so that I can get a better look."

He did as he was bid.

"Of course," she said, "after so much time, there would be little of the Templars left, only a foundation, but it was a good place for your family to build a house."

He shrugged. He didn't know much about the Templars, but Kate was beginning to sound like her father. "Seen enough?" he finally asked.

She nodded.

"I'm showing it to you," he said, "because it's an

escape route, not because it's a relic of some ancient religious order. Pay attention, Kate."

He showed her the secret entrance to the tunnel, a broken-down boiler on concealed tracks. She wasn't impressed and was even less impressed with the holding pen where the smugglers once stored their contraband.

"The Templars didn't build this," she said, as they entered the last tunnel.

"No. I don't suppose they did. Bear with me until you've familiarized yourself with how to get out of here if ever it should come to that."

She balked when the tunnel ended in a crawl space that led to the outside. "No smuggler ever used this black hole," she said. "It's suffocating. And it's too narrow for a smuggler to get his contraband through."

"Calley filled in the tunnel with earth," he said, "after he found a family of badgers had made their home with us. There was a stone at one time blocking the exit, but the elements undermined it. The point is, it's the only way out. If worse comes to worst, use it. Promise me, Kate."

She said the words absently. Her head was turning this way and that, her gaze fixed on the walls and ceiling as they made their way back to the cellars.

"What are you looking for?" he asked.

"Mmm? Oh, there should be a priest's hideout somewhere. Every house in the area has one, or had one until the redcoats found and destroyed it."

"Kate!" He turned to face her. "You haven't been listening to a word I've said. At the first sign of trouble, you are to get yourself down here and use the escape route. It comes out at a stone cairn. We passed it on the way up."

"Where will you be?"

"I won't be far behind you."

"In that case, I promise."

When they entered the kitchen, he said, "I'm sorry the house is in such a mess, but good help is hard to get. I'm afraid it's too much for Calley to manage on his own."

His words had the desired effect. After the ubiquitous breakfast of porridge and cream, Kate rolled up her sleeves and began an all-out assault on her mortal enemy—ground-in dirt, grease, and other stains that could not be identified. To give her her due, she knew her limitations. She could not clean the whole house, she told them. The fewer rooms in use, the better it would be. It made sense to give up the dining room and eat in the kitchen, which would probably be the warmest room in the house anyway. Since it went without saying that she couldn't do it alone, Gavin and his manservant were pressed into service.

The two men exchanged a conspirators' shrug. They had other things they would rather be doing. It could be worse, Gavin reflected. She might have wanted to clear out his study and arrange his books in alphabetical order. As it was, his study was spared and only one reception room and their bedchambers and the kitchen were on her list of things to do.

Anything to keep her mind busy and off their troubles.

It worked, up to a point, but when they had a late supper in Calley's sparkling, pristine kitchen and Kate was strangely quiet, he knew that her thoughts were still occupied with the threat of the unknown. What surprised him was Calley's response to her. His manservant tried to draw her out, but all he got for his pains were polite inanities.

Calley! Who never had two words to say for himself when company was present.

Calley took the first watch and went off with Macduff to relieve Danny so that the boy could have a bite to eat and stretch his legs. Gavin and Kate tidied the kitchen and then trooped upstairs to their chamber.

Kate said, "He's an interesting man, Calley, isn't he?"

"How can you tell? He said very little."

"It's not what he said, it's what he left unsaid. It seems to me he has had his share of misfortunes, but he has pushed them into the deepest reaches of his soul where no one can touch them, not even himself."

He didn't know all the ins and outs of Calley's story, only that when he had found him, Calley was on the run from the law for killing a man. And just like that, Gavin had made up his mind that Calley was worth saving. His granny would have said that it was his gift of discernment that made him decide to trust Calley. At any rate, they'd been together for several years now. In his memory, Kate was the first person to visit the lodge who had managed to get beyond his manservant's wall of reserve. They were two of a kind, she and Calley, lone wolves both.

He crushed the thought. Not if he had anything to do with it.

She turned to him with a little frown on her brow. "Of course, I'm curious, but I don't want you to divulge any secrets. I'm just glad that you found Calley and even more glad that you found me."

Did she know what she was saying? He felt it again, the pull of an emotion that was both fierce and sweet.

He kissed her softly on the mouth and guided her to the bed. "You're sleeping on your feet," he said. "Here, let me help you disrobe."

Kate had other ideas. "Sleep lasts for an eternity. I don't want to waste a moment of the time that remains to us."

His voice was stern. "We have years ahead of us, Kate. Would I lie to you, I, a seer of Grampian?"

She kissed his throat. "You're an untried seer," she murmured, "and I'm an untried witch. Just for tonight, I want to be like the tinkers. I want to live for the moment. Tomorrow, we shall fly our true colors and face our mortal enemy together."

This sounded too much like a prophecy for his comfort. "My mission," he said, "is to keep you safe, and that's what I mean to do."

"You're thinking of your grandmother's prophecy. No. I don't need to hear the words. I've worked it out for myself. Tell me, did she mention that she was sending you to save a witch?" He could hear the whimsy behind her words.

He was more than puzzled. He was all at sea. Kate admitting that she was a full-blown witch was the last thing he expected.

She answered his unspoken question as each was wont to do. "He's coming. I can smell him, taste him, feel him in my pores. The feeling grows stronger with every passing moment. If I were an ordinary girl, I wouldn't admit to any of this. I was ashamed of who and what I was. That doesn't hold true anymore. I have a reason now for wanting to be the best damned witch on Deeside."

"You owe it to your mother," he said.

"Yes," she said, averting her eyes. "I owe it to my mother."

He allowed her to tug him down to the mattress. "We're just tinkers," she whispered, "and when this is over, we'll borrow one of their covered wagons and go where the fancy takes us."

"I'm exactly where I want to be." He was wedged between her legs, with her skirts hiked to her waist. Every part of her anatomy seemed to fascinate him.

Every part of his powerful body fascinated her. He sucked, he licked, he disposed of their garments. Heat from his skin set her own skin on fire. Tears stung her eyes, and she blinked them away. There would be time for weeping later. Just for a little while, she didn't want to think. She wanted this, she wanted him to know that he had been well and truly loved.

She was still shuddering in the aftermath of an earth-shaking climax when he suddenly rolled her onto her belly and brought his hand down on her bare backside with enough force to make her gasp. On the second slap, she rolled and kicked out with her foot. Scrambling to her knees, she glared up at him.

"What was that for?" she demanded angrily. "Don't you know your own strength? That hurt!"

"It was meant to hurt." He was pulling on his clothes. Face tight, eyes narrowed to chips, he loomed over her. "I've been seduced by the best," he said. "Don't you think I know when I'm being played?"

Because her bottom still stung from his unprovoked attack, she tipped up her chin and glared back at him. "You'll have to explain that remark, Hepburn, because I'm sure I don't know what you're talking about."

"I'm a seer, dammit! How many times do I have to tell you? My powers may not work with others, but they work with you, because we're connected."

She put her hands over her ears to let him know that she did not appreciate being shouted at. "I repeat," she said with as much disdain as she could muster, "I don't know what you're talking about."

He brought his face to within inches of hers. "This is my fight, not yours. I don't want you interfering or playing the hero. You're not going to slip away unseen to draw a murderer off. You'll only put us all in danger. Is that what you want?"

Her jaw was slack. He could read her thoughts? How else would he have known that she meant to draw their enemy off. "No," she stuttered. "I don't . . . I won't . . ."

He nodded, seemingly satisfied that she'd gotten the message.

She was still fumbling for words when he scooped up her clothes and stalked to the door. "This is just a precaution," he said, flashing her a devilish grin. "I'll return them in the morning if you promise to be a good girl."

He quit the room, and she heard the key turn in the lock. She wanted to throw a shoe at him, but he'd taken her shoes as well.

The next day at the lodge was almost a repeat of the first. Kate rolled up her sleeves and set to work. The difference was she kept her lips tightly closed and barely said a word when Gavin spoke to her but was as nice as ninepence when Calley addressed her personally.

Macduff also appeared to be in her black books. He'd been set to guard her, of course, and she seemed to take his constant presence as an insult. It came as something of a surprise when she entered Gavin's study after the evening meal and twitched his newspaper aside, the paper he was reading for the umpteenth time since Dalziel had given it to him.

"Here," she said, holding out a leash that was attached to Macduff. "He's your dog, and he needs a bath."

"A bath? Macduff? I thought you liked dogs."

"I do, but Macduff smells as though he has been rolling in a midden."

"That's what dogs are supposed to do," Gavin replied. "They like earthy smells. You wouldn't want him to smell like a rose, would you?"

"I want him to smell like a dog," she retorted, "not like a lump of horse manure."

There was something about the glint in her eyes that made him decide to let her have her way. It was a small thing, and he was relying on her good sense not to provoke his patience. Besides, before handing over her clothes that morning, he had secured her promise to obey him in all things, and he trusted Kate to keep her word.

"Fine," he said, "but I want you to come with us. The fresh air will do you good."

She squared her shoulders as they walked down the hall to the back door. Macduff hesitated, then gamboled after them.

"The only bath Macduff will submit to," Gavin said, "is a frolic in running water. There's a stream just beyond the stable. You can keep Danny company while I see to Macduff. I'll be within earshot at all times."

There was a row of pegs at the back door with old coats hung upon them. He helped her into one, then did the same for himself. When she groped in her jacket and produced her revolver, he was impressed.

"Calley showed me how to use it," she said, and she slipped it into her coat pocket.

"Theory and practice are not the same thing," he replied. "If there is to be any shooting, I'd prefer to be the one to do it."

"As you wish," she answered coolly.

"Look," he said, "you're gifted, but you're a novice. All I'm saying is that what you lack is a little practice."

She wasn't listening. She was sniffing the air.

"What do you smell?" he asked.

"Tinkers," she said. "Or Macduff. It's hard to tell them apart. Shall we go?"

* * *

It wasn't much of a stable, only two sections, one for the horses and one for the harness and tack. Danny came forward, looking curiously from one to the other. He was, by Kate's reckoning, fourteen or fifteen years old, with wild red hair and a liberal sprinkling of freckles across his nose and cheeks. Though he was lame and his gait was awkward, he moved as though he were unaware of his handicap.

Gavin made the introductions and left, promising that he would return in five minutes. A cursory glance around told her that her own father would have been happy to take Danny on as a stableboy. The only lantern was on a stone slab atop the cobblestones. Fire was an ever-present danger if a stable hand got careless.

"Only two horses?" she queried as they moved to the back of the building. As she got a clearer look at them, she was taken aback. She'd expected Gavin to keep great showy beasts, not these sorry looking specimens.

"Don't let their looks fool you, miss," Danny said. "They'll never win any races, but these Highland ponies can see in the dark. They never stumble or balk at hedges or stone dikes."

"Then we have something in common," Kate said. Her mind had taken her back to the wild chase over the desolate moors. If it hadn't been for Gavin—she suppressed a shudder.

They were watching Kate with ears back and nostrils flaring.

"They're not used to strangers," Danny added doubtfully, "so I wouldn't get too close to them if I was you."

"Something else we have in common," Kate said. She noted Danny's puzzled expression and spoke in a more casual tone. "They're no beauties, are they? What made your master buy them?"

Danny chuckled. "He didn't. He found them half-starved to death on the hills. They followed him home. I suppose their owner was afraid to claim them, knowing that Mr. Hepburn would give him the thrashing of his life."

Kate's nimble mind was making connections: Macduff, the Highland ponies, Danny, Calley, herself. They were all strays. Is that how he thought of her and the others? It was a sobering thought. It was more than sobering. It softened the hard knot of resentment that seemed to have lodged in her heart. He was a good man, a caring man, one of the best. What she had to make him understand was that she didn't need mollycoddling. She wasn't helpless.

One of the ponies blew in her ear. The other nuzzled his nose under her arm. She turned to pet them. In the blink of an eye, everything changed. One whinnied softly, the other bared its teeth. They both looked over her shoulder.

She reached in her coat pocket and withdrew her revolver. "Danny, douse the lantern and get behind me."

His jaw went slack. "What?"

"Do it!"

Her imperative had him rushing to obey her. When the light was out, a shadow moved near the open door. Kate cocked the hammer of her revolver.

"Don't shoot! Don't shoot!" It was Dalziel's voice. "Calley told me that Gavin was up at the stable. I came to warn him, came to warn you both. Where is he?"

Gavin's voice answered him. "I'm right here, Dalziel. Calm yourself and tell me what this is about."

"It's not safe here," Dalziel said. "I think I've been followed." He was breathing hard.

"Let's get back to the house," said Gavin. "Danny, you know what to do?"

"Aye, sir. I'm to fetch the tinkers."

"Take Macduff with you, and if there is any sign of trouble, send him to fetch me."

"Aye, sir."

"Hurry," said Dalziel. "Hurry, before they get here."

Twenty-three

"I thought," said Dalziel, "that they were right on my heels. I'm sorry. I panicked."

With the exception of Danny, they were in the kitchen with all the windows and doors locked against the outside world.

"They were waiting for us at Ballater, you see." Looking at Gavin, Dalziel went on. "The police, I mean. They thought you would be on the train. They wanted to know where you were and when I had last seen you. Thank God for Mrs. Cardno. She has known most of them since they were young lads. They were very respectful. She told them that, as far as she knew, you left for Braemar to prepare for your wedding. I'm not sure that they believed her, but they let her go. Eventually they let us go, too, but we are under orders not to leave Ballater."

"Who was on the train with you?" Gavin asked.

Dalziel shook his head. "I don't rightly know. They were spread out through the other coaches. Some, like Mr. and Mrs. Cameron, put up at the hotel, others with

Mrs. Cardno." To Kate he said, "Your parents invited one and all to join them to celebrate your wedding, and most of them accepted."

"Touching," said Gavin dryly.

Kate heaved a sigh. "It's not our wedding reception that is the draw. It's the Knights Templar. You'd be surprised how many visitors to the area seek my father out for the sole purpose of following in the Knights Templars' footsteps. And, of course, he is in his element."

Gavin was staring at his hands. He looked up with a smile. "On this occasion, Kate," he said lightly, "I think that I'm the draw. What else should I know, Dalziel?"

"The police in Aberdeen are sending one of their best with a warrant for your arrest. No one is allowed to leave Ballater until he questions them."

Kate felt the pressure begin to build behind her eyes. The events that Dalziel had related respecting her marriage made perfect sense. When Dalziel had told her parents that she and Gavin had returned to the Highlands to fulfill the residency requirements for a proper marriage to take place, naturally, they had lost no time in making for home.

Her father, in particular, would want to see them well and truly shackled before they could change their minds. She hadn't counted on so many of her friends and people she didn't know making a party of it. This wasn't how it was supposed to be. There were too many suspects. All Gavin wanted was one face to emerge from the crowd, the face of their villain.

"No!" she said with enough force to make everyone fall silent.

"No?" Gavin asked softly.

Her gaze moved from person to person. "My father was once a lawyer," she said. Her voice was hard with determination. "He is still well-connected. He's not going to allow my only offer of marriage to escape so easily. You're stuck with me, Hepburn. Better get used to it."

The laughter died away when Calley opened the door to the broom closet. All Kate could see were brooms and cleaning supplies. Calley put his shoulder to one wall, and the wall slid to the side, revealing an array of firearms. He chose one for Gavin and one for himself.

"Our secret armory," Gavin said.

Kate had never seen anything like these firing pieces. They looked as though they had enough firing power to blow away a building.

Gavin answered her unspoken question. "These sweethearts," he said, caressing the long barrel of his rifle, "are for show. They'll make a lot of noise, but we won't be aiming them at anyone."

"No," said Kate. "We're in enough trouble as it is without killing or maiming policemen."

She placed her own gun on the table, close at hand. Dalziel looked horrified when Calley offered him a revolver, but he accepted it just the same. "I . . . I . . ." he began, and shook his head.

"Dalziel," said Kate severely, "we know that you are a son of the manse, but surely, if someone was about to kill one of us, you would forget your scruples and try to save us?"

He swallowed hard. "Of course, I would." His chin jutted, and he said with more feeling, "Of course, I would!"

"Now that we've got that settled," said Gavin, "would you mind telling us, Dalziel, what you learned from St. Peter's parish records?" A pause followed. "Dalziel! What did you learn from the priest?"

Dalziel seemed to be lost in a daydream. He held the

revolver in his left hand, transferred it to his right and then back again. "It's heavier than it looks," he said.

"Dalziel!" Gavin roared.

"What? Oh, yes. The parish priest. You were right about that." He reached in his pocket and produced a small notebook. "Mary Macbeth," he read, "spinster, lady's companion, married Mr. Geoffrey Gordon of Forres in April of 1856. A year later, their daughter was christened in the same chapel." He looked at Kate. "Her name was Catherine Macbeth Gordon."

A long, pent-up silence ensued. Kate finally remembered to breathe. "My parents were married?"

"Yes," said Dalziel. "It would seem so."

"What happened to my father? Why have I no memories of him?"

Dalziel touched her briefly and then jerked his hand away. "That would be because he died of typhoid fever before you reached your fifth birthday. It's in the parish record."

"I wonder . . ." said Gavin. He looked out the window. "Duck!" he suddenly yelled. "Duck!" he shouted again as a shell blasted the window into a thousand shards.

Kate was frozen in place; Dalziel had thrown himself under the table and came nose to nose with a terrified mouse. "Is this what I am?" he mumbled. "Am I a mouse or a man?"

"What did you say?" Calley shouted.

"I saw myself in a mirror," Dalziel bit out. He got to his feet. "Why have I been given this toy?" He waved his revolver in the air and jumped when a bullet discharged from the muzzle and embedded itself in a rafter.

Gavin laughed, a reckless laugh that made Kate want to box his ears.

Calley smiled, but he kept his eyes trained on the windows. "You're a beginner, Dalziel," he said. "Make sure you point your gun at a real target. When you master that revolver, then we'll let you have one of these Henrys."

More shots followed, but the attackers had evidently backed off a bit.

"Those are not policemen," Dalziel said, mopping at his brow.

"No, indeed," Calley replied. "Policemen don't carry guns. Those must be militia from the barracks at Ballater."

"Or from the castle guard," Gavin added.

"What's the difference?" Dalziel asked.

"The castle guards make up the queen's private army when she resides at Balmoral. Let's test them, shall we?"

He used the butt of his rifle to break one of the windows.

When he pulled the trigger, the report of it going off had the dishes on the table dancing a wild jig. One plate toppled to the floor, lost its momentum, and came to a dizzying halt. The stags' heads were not so fortunate. When the soldiers returned fire, they went flying off the walls in a cloud of dust, and impaled their horns in the cross-beamed ceiling. The floor was littered with plaster, debris, and broken glass.

"They're retreating," Calley shouted, "regrouping."

More shots hit the house, but none entered the kitchen. "They're untried youths by the look of it," Calley said, "but if they call out the castle guard, the hills will be crawling with sharpshooters."

"That's what they want," said Gavin, his face grim, "to pin us down until the elite guard gets here. This calls for a change of tactics. Kate, have you got your revolver?"

"Right here," she said, and she held it up for him to see.

"Get yourself into the cellar, and stay there until we come and get you." He opened the door to the cellar.

She cried out, "I'm not going anywhere without you!"

Black slits of eyes, wizard's eyes, bored into hers, and she felt her own will begin to bend. Then his eyes widened with disbelief.

"Take cover!" he suddenly roared. He reached for Kate.

It was the last thing she remembered before a deafening blast rocked her back on her heels, and she sank into a fiery pit.

Twenty-four

Gavin opened his eyes wide. He was on his back and expected to see stars overhead. What he saw were shadows. As the breeze whistled through his makeshift shelter, he heard the hiss of a gentle rain. Strangely, he was warm and dry, but every bone and muscle in his body felt as though a wall had fallen on him.

As fragments of memory flashed through his mind, he tried to sit up, but stronger arms restrained him, Calley's arms.

"What happened, Calley?" he asked weakly. "Where is Kate? Where am I?"

Calley answered the last question first. "You're in one of the tinkers' wagons. Alfie and his friends chased the soldiers off with hammers and axes. If you look outside, you'll see their torches flickering in the darkness. They seem very attached to you."

"Not to me. To the land. They make their camp here every summer."

"Because you give them permission. At any rate, the militia took one look at them and took to their heels."

"They'll be back," said Gavin, his voice gaining strength, "and with marksmen who shoot to kill."

"That's why we hid you in the tinkers' caravan. It's you they want. You look like a tinker, you smell like a tinker. Your own mother wouldn't know you."

He was getting a bad feeling about Calley's evasiveness. "Where is Kate?" he demanded abruptly.

"How much do you remember?"

This was driving him crazy. He pushed out of the restraining hands and sat up. "Stop fussing! I asked you a simple question. Answer it!"

Calley heaved a sigh. "We think she's in the cellar."

"But that's good, isn't it?" A heartbeat of silence went by. "Calley?"

"We don't know," said Calley somberly. "She may be stunned from the explosion."

An explosion? Gavin remembered it vaguely. He had trouble breathing. He wanted to smash something, but he felt as weak as a kitten. He could hardly hold up his head.

"Why is Kate still in the cellar?" he asked.

"Because a ton of masonry is blocking the entrance. It must have come down in the blast."

The blast. More fragments of memory were coming back to him. "Tell me about the blast," he said. "What caused it?"

Calley shook his head. "The last thing I remember was a small ball, rolling across the kitchen floor. You had just shouted, 'Take cover!' and that's what we did. When we came to, there was no sign of Kate and no sign of whoever tried to kill us."

"A ball?" Gavin said. "A ball caused the explosion?"

"It wasn't a ball," Calley went on savagely. "It was a homemade grenade, concocted by an amateur. That's what saved us. By rights, we should all be dead."

"Amateur?" Gavin tried to get his mind around the blast, but he kept going in circles. "A homemade grenade?"

"In olden days, it was called a petard. Very unsophisticated, just a ball of gunpowder with a fuse."

"I know what a petard is!" One thing Gavin was sure of. "We weren't the target. It was meant for Kate."

When Calley was silent, Gavin scowled up at him. "Kate is not dead, so you can take that look off your face. If she were, I would feel it in my gut."

"How can you tell how I look? It's dark in here."

"I can feel it."

He crawled from under the tarpaulin, climbed out, and held on to the side of the wagon to steady himself. Calley threw a blanket over his shoulders to protect him from the rain. A tinker came running up and thrust a torch into his hand.

"To light the way," he said. "Don't you worry none, Mr. Hepburn. We'll soon have her out of there. And we'll get that bastard who did this, too. Your enemy is our enemy. He made a big mistake when he picked on you."

Gavin was only half listening. He was scouring the shadows. Fingers of light were beginning to filter through the foliage. "It will soon be dawn," he said.

No light would filter into the escape route. That shouldn't matter to Kate. She had cat's eyes, and she had her revolver. She knew how to take care of herself.

He hung on to that thought as they set out for the house at a loping gait. When the incline became steeper, he observed that Calley was in no better shape than he was. They were both panting as though they were at their last gasp.

He subdued his aches and pains by concentrating on

his grandmother's prophecy. Lady Valeria's voice came to him as a frail whisper. *"Look to Macbeth. Fail Macbeth, and you will regret it to your dying day."*

Had he failed her?

As he neared the house, he was blind and deaf to the tinkers who were on guard duty. He was intent only on Lady Valeria and all the wisdom she had tried to impart to her grandsons over the years. They were seers of Grampian. They had great powers if they chose to use them. They had the power to change the future if only they believed.

I believe. He let the words revolve in his mind. *I believe.*

He expected to be enfolded in a warm cocoon of peace. Instead, he felt driven. He was sent to save Kate, and that's what he would do, whatever the cost.

As his mind began to clear, he became convinced that the bastard who had tried to kill Kate was closer than they thought, and that he would continue to try until he succeeded.

I'm coming, Kate. Don't give up. Fight him tooth and nail. If you have to, fight him tooth and nail. No quarter asked, for none will be given.

After entering the house, he pushed into the kitchen and stopped dead at the chaos that met his eyes. Half the ceiling lay in chunks on the floor, kitchen furniture was blackened by fire, and broken glass crunched underfoot. Calley or Dalziel had had the foresight to use the broken shutters to block out the light so that outsiders could not pin down their exact position.

Dalziel was on his knees, directing two swarthy tinkers who were using their hammers to dislodge the masonry. He looked up at Gavin's entrance. "We think we heard something coming from the cellar."

"You *think*?" Gavin's voice grated with sarcasm.

Dalziel's chin lifted, and he squared his shoulders. "What I can tell you is that we've made a small opening that Macduff might manage to squeeze through."

Gavin passed a hand over his eyes. "Forgive me," he said. "I'm not myself. I know that you're doing your best for Kate. So, where is Macduff? And where is Danny?"

Calley answered, "They're together. Danny was first on the scene after the blast. He made sure that we were all right, then went to rally the tinkers who had begun to disperse. We think that Macduff went with him. They're safe, Gavin."

Gavin didn't have the time to reflect on his dog or his stableboy. Wee Alfie's huge frame filled the doorway. He was out of breath. "I'm sorry it took so long," he said, "but I have the information you wanted, Mr. Dalziel, sir."

"That was quick!"

"We ran in relays, same as we do at the games."

By way of explanation, Dalziel said, "I took the liberty of penning a note to Mrs. Cardno. Most of the guests from Aberdeen are staying with her. She would know if anyone slipped away during the night. I thought it was worth a try."

"Good thinking!" Gavin exclaimed, accepting the note Dalziel held out to him. His smile faded when he noticed something among the broken glass, something that didn't belong—Kate's pocket revolver.

Damn and double damn! Couldn't the woman do anything right? If she'd been standing in front of him, he would have given her a good shaking. He picked up her revolver and slipped it into his pocket.

Kate! Fight him! Fight him tooth and nail. Never give in.

Gavin tore the envelope in his haste to read the note.

It was signed by Mrs. Cardno and gave only two words, a man's name.

"Gordon Massey!" he said through clenched teeth. "I thought it would be Cedric Hayes. He, at least, was a military man."

"So was John Liddel," Dalziel pointed out. "I don't think it can be Cedric. He was on the train with us and is, was, settled with Mrs. Cardno when I left. I didn't see Gordon Massey."

Gavin slammed his fist against the wall. "If I'd had access to a telephone . . ." He shook his head. "I used her as bait to entrap a murderer. What colossal conceit on my part!" Pacing, he went on savagely, "Where is he now? How did he escape?"

"Who?" asked Dalziel.

"The man who pitched his grenade at us."

Everyone exchanged glances, but no one said anything. Even the tinkers had stopped their hammering.

"Well? Someone must have seen something."

Calley's tone was gentle. "You were there, too, Gavin. What did you see?"

All the misplaced anger burned away, leaving Gavin drained and sick at heart. "You're right, Calley. All I remember is a flash of brilliant light and a ton of bricks falling on me."

He tried to soften his voice, but everyone heard the strain behind his words. "Can we at least try to go through those final moments?"

Each person told as much as he remembered, which wasn't much.

"I was hallucinating," said Dalziel. "I actually thought that Macduff was playing a cat-and-mouse game with the ball—petard—grenade—thing." He gave an embarrassed laugh that no one shared.

"We were all dazed after the blast," Calley said gravely.

"Yes, but . . ."

"But what, Dalziel?" Gavin's urgency was plain to hear.

Dalziel was beginning to look as though he regretted mentioning Macduff. "It was only a hallucination," he finished lamely.

"No!" said Gavin. "If Macduff scooped up that grenade, he could be injured or dead. He wouldn't get far. He'll be somewhere close to the house. Calley?" he ended, his voice thick with emotion.

"Wait!" said Gavin. "Have you tried to get to Kate through the escape route?"

"What escape route?" Dalziel asked, looking from Calley to Gavin.

Calley used the back of his sleeve to wipe blood that seeped from his nose. "No," he said. "I think the blast must have addled my brain."

"No," said Gavin. "No one could have done as much as you, Calley. We're all still reeling from the force of that blast. Besides, you were not sent to save her. I was. Just find Macduff and Danny. The rest is in my hands now."

On that cryptic note, he turned and left them.

As he stumbled through the door, Calley called out, "Arm yourself, man! You'll need all the help you can get if you come face-to-face with one of those sharp-shooters."

Gavin didn't hear him. He knew that his brain was still fuzzy, but he also knew that he was on the right track. He didn't care about details. His knowledge went deeper than that. The killer and Kate were in the escape route together. If it were not for Macduff, they would all be dead.

Kate! he commanded with all the urgency he could

muster. *Fight him tooth and nail! No quarter asked, for none will be given.*

His feet had never moved faster as he half ran, half slithered down the steep incline to the great stone cairn that stood out starkly against the rising dawn.

Twenty-five

It was the stillness that brought her out of her swoon. Her eyes opened to a complete and profound darkness. As she lay there, stunned, the darkness became less impenetrable. She could see shapes and shadows within shadows, but little else. She was curled up in a ball and had somehow found a sort of shelter beneath the cellar stairs.

She had no idea how long she had been there. She knew that she was in the cellar, and that the blast had brought down a ton of masonry, but there was nothing to indicate whether it was morning or night, no windows to guide her.

As her brain cleared and logical thought began to return, she moved each arm and leg. There were no broken bones, but she could taste blood in her mouth and knew that she would be covered in bruises and abrasions in the next little while.

The dust was settling, and she lifted her head to inhale fresh air. She inhaled the cold air and the musty smell that she expected. What she did not expect was a scent that she hated with a passion, something slimy and malevolent and uniquely his.

She was not alone. *He* was here with her, her cousin Avery. She didn't know what name he was using and wouldn't recognize him after so many years, but she remembered his smell.

Then why hadn't she recognized it before now?

She *had* recognized it, but vaguely. It had become her constant companion in the last little while, the prod that sent her intuitive sense of danger to new heights. It didn't make her want to run. It paralyzed her with fear.

As her thoughts shifted, a shaft of pure terror formed a lump in her breast. Where was Gavin? Calley? Dalziel? She remembered the blast that had sent her reeling down the stairs. She couldn't believe that the others had died in the blast. She had survived. And Gavin was a wizard, a seer of Grampian. He had been sent to save her. Isn't that what he kept telling her? Then where was his voice? Gavin—

She gave a start when she heard a noise from upstairs. It took her a moment to grasp that what she was hearing was the pounding of someone trying to break through to her.

What if they were too late?

Her mind skittered away from the thought and focused on the present. She knew that Cousin Avery was close by, but it appeared that he wasn't aware of her.

Gavin, her mind sobbed. *I never told you that I love you.*

Fight him tooth and nail, Kate. No quarter asked, for none will be given. Fight him!

She waited . . .

That was it? She had bared her soul to this man, and that was all he had to offer? And what did it matter? If Gavin were dead, she wouldn't want to live.

Her archenemy moved, and she turned her head toward the sound. Something odd was going on. With arms outstretched, he was feeling his way around the periphery of the cellar. Comprehension slowly dawned. He was like a blind man, while her cat's eyes had never been keener. She could see him, but he couldn't see her. Then what was he looking for? What did he expect to find in those walls?

It was just out of his reach, the old boiler that concealed the tunnel to the escape route. Is that what he was looking for? She made a small sound, and the next instant, he turned and fired his revolver. It sounded as though he'd fired a hundred shots. The bullet ricocheted from wall to ceiling and God alone knew where. She curled into a ball, and when the noise died away, she chanced another look at him. He was feeling the walls again, but going the other way.

Ask for no quarter, for none will be given.

She looked around for her revolver, but there was no sign of it. She might have lost it in the blast or when she tumbled down the stairs. Even so, she wasn't helpless. She was a witch, if Gavin was to be believed. She had gifts that Cousin Avery could not begin to imagine.

"Stay out of his way," her mother had scolded. *"He is evil through and through."*

Déjà vu. She felt like that little girl again. Her cousin was evil through and through. He liked hurting helpless animals. He liked hurting her. But her mother saw what he was and stepped in to protect her. There was no one he feared more than her mother.

He looked over his shoulder, scanning the shadows, and at last she had a clear view of his face. It was Gordon Massey of the newspaper empire! She could have kicked herself then. What a fool she had been. He'd told her that he was escorting his elderly parents to Braemar to look for long-lost relatives. What a perfect cover for making his inquiries! And all the time, he had been looking for her. He hadn't found her, but he'd found her mother's file in the clinic and put two and two together.

If only she'd confided her secrets to Gavin, they wouldn't all be paying for her stupidity right now.

She swallowed the lump in her throat. It wasn't going to end like this.

She stirred. "Cousin Avery," she said, "I should have known it was you. Still the same, I see. Still the sadistic little bully you were as a boy."

Her voice echoed from every corner of the stone cellar, and though it was dark, her cat's eyes saw him start, then his shadow turned slowly from side to side as he tried to pin her down. She pulled herself to her knees and felt with her fingers, frantically trying to find her revolver. Nothing.

She wanted to keep her cousin talking till she found it, then she'd show no mercy. She'd put a bullet into his black heart. This man had murdered innocent people because they were connected to her, all in an effort to mislead the police. He had murdered Will and his own accomplice, John Liddel. But she was his real target. She may have doubted it once, but no longer, and now that she knew his identity, she knew that he had to be stopped, once and for all.

"So," he said, "you've finally worked it out? Clever, clever Kate."

"You know," she said, "I used to feel sorry for you, the bastard son, left out in the cold. You were barely tolerated by our grandfather. Even as a child I always knew you hated bearing your mother's surname. Smith, wasn't it? Avery Smith. And now you're Gordon Massey. So, Avery, you finally appropriated the family name for yourself. I can't think why you would want to. Our branch of the Gordons isn't exactly illustrious. Their glory days are long over."

She wasn't babbling. She was thinking on two levels. He had a gun. Her revolver seemed determined to hide from her. How could she kill him without a gun? And she knew she had to kill him. It was him or her. A bullet at close range would not ricochet if it hit its target. She could do it, if only she had a gun.

But something else was circling at the back of her mind. He was in no hurry to escape because—

"Tell me about the blast," she said. "What happened there?"

He clicked his tongue and sighed theatrically. "You were *all* supposed to die. I might have guessed that Hepburn's dog would turn up like a bad penny. He saved you in the snowstorm, Kate, but he won't save you this time. He ran at my little grenade as though someone had thrown him a ball to play with. Sad to say, I couldn't stay to watch. Time was of the essence."

Gavin and the others dead? She didn't believe it. Then why didn't they come storming down the stairs and rescue her? There was another exit, the one Calley had filled in with earth. Is that how he meant to rescue her? Then why didn't she hear anything? And why was Avery so confident that he could escape unscathed?

His examining the walls made perfect sense now. Someone had told him about the secret passage. It could well have been her own father. He wouldn't have known the precise details but said enough to point Avery in the right direction. So Avery had entered the house by the secret passage, and that's how he meant to leave it, after he killed her. After all, she was his target, not the others. She smiled grimly. Unfortunately for Avery, he had lost his bearings in the dark.

Advantage to her!

"You were hiding in the priest's cell," she said slowly.

"How clever of you to work it out," he replied. "Yes, I was hiding in that tiny cell behind the fireplace. I thought I would suffocate before the soldiers arrived. I couldn't release my little surprise before the shooting started. The soldiers would be blamed, of course, and I would slip away unseen."

"By way of the escape route."

"Precisely."

A memory slipped into her mind. Avery could never do anything to please their grandfather. She hadn't tried to make a friend of her grandfather either. He hated her, too, both her and her mother. They weren't good enough for his firstborn, Geoffrey Gordon. That was why her father had moved them to Deeside. It was, for so short a time, a golden age. Then her father died, and everything changed.

On a sudden inspiration, she said, "This is about grandfather, isn't it? That's why you kept a grudge for twenty years."

"I should have been his heir," he bit out. "He let me think that I *was* his heir. It wasn't my fault that my father was a wastrel."

As to herself, she said, "It wouldn't have made a difference. My father was the elder. He or his heirs could claim a major share of grandfather's fortune. That's the law."

For once his voice had a lilt in it. "Not if you're dead, and I have a death certificate to prove it. Then everything passes to me. It was in grandfather's will. The old boy had all but given up hope of finding you. He thought that I was the only one left with his blood in my veins."

"Why not let everyone think I was dead?"

"Didn't you hear me? They, the solicitors, wanted proof of death. Only a body and a genuine death certificate would pass their eagle eye. And I thought, why not do this right? They must never suspect that I murdered you."

"So you murdered four innocent people to mislead the police!"

With her cat's eyes, she saw his shoulders lift and drop in an indifferent shrug. "Don't you read the papers, Kate? It was a deranged lunatic with a grievance against psychiaters who was responsible."

Now that he was talking, she wanted answers to things that had always tormented her. "I knew that someone was hunting for my mother and me. After my father died, I mean. Was that you?"

His laugh turned into a cough, reminding her that the air in the cellar was thick with the residue of gunpowder and dust.

"Don't be stupid," he said. "I was only a boy then. Grandfather hired men to track you, but you had disappeared off the face of the earth."

She should be thinking of how to escape. She should be thinking of her psychic powers and how she could use them to disable him. But the last pieces of the puzzle were too riveting to give up.

"I take it our grandfather is dead?"

He almost spat the words. "But still ruling us from the grave. I don't see a penny of my money until I'm the only one left to inherit."

She suppressed a shudder and moved on. "How did you find me?"

He coughed again. "I knew your mother was a Catholic. It took my agents more than a year to examine every parish roll in the north of Scotland. Mary Macbeth. Who could forget a name like that?"

"My name is Cameron."

"Catherine *Macbeth* Cameron. It was in your file. You were adopted by the Camerons."

"What about Dr. Rankin?" she said. "Why did he have to die?"

"Ah, Hepburn's friend." She could hear the shrug in his voice. "I underestimated him. I presented myself as a journalist writing a story about the mentally ill. That was long before Miss Cardno's wedding reception. I hadn't counted on being snowbound with the man. I'd never written that article, you see, and three of his patients had met with suspicious deaths. He was going to make further inquiries, and I couldn't allow that."

She wasn't frightened now; she was enraged. "Your man was the waiter, John Liddel. He overheard Dr. Rankin telling Hepburn he was going to Aberdeen."

"Correct."

He was edging his way to the sound of her voice. "If you come any closer," she said, "I'll fire my revolver at the ceiling." She had no revolver, but he couldn't know that.

She could sense his uncertainty. He was silent for a moment, then said slowly, "Your bullet will ricochet. You're just as likely to hit yourself as me."

"I'll take my chances."

"Kate, Kate, you've misconstrued the situation." His reproach sounded genuine—if you didn't know him.

Her thoughts came thick and fast—how she'd refused to take Gavin seriously; how she'd pooh-poohed his suggestion that she try to read his mind; how she'd kept secrets from him because she was ashamed of who and what she was.

Never again, she promised. *Never again, Gavin. Do you hear me? Please, just let me hear your voice and, as God is my witness, I'll never shut you out of my mind again.*

No voice came to her, only the acrid smell of gunpowder smoke and the tread of a step nearby crushing glass beneath it. He was closing in on her to make the kill.

Then what was she doing, hiding like a child playing hide-and-seek? She was a witch, a novice witch, perhaps, who had yet to test her powers. The trouble was, she had suppressed them for so long they were practically nonexistent. It wasn't so when she was a child. She could read minds. She could see into the future. Isn't that why the local children had thrown stones at her and called her names? All she'd ever wanted was to fit in. And this piece of slime—

Her heart clenched when his voice finally broke the silence. "You won't escape me, Kate."

A veil was torn from her mind. *"You won't escape me, Kate."* She'd come upon him when he was beating his pony mercilessly. She was going to tell on him. He'd come after her then, but she'd hidden herself in the privy, and her mother had rescued her.

There was no one here to rescue her now. Strangely, she didn't want rescuing. She wanted this evil man to come by his just deserts. She had to find a way to raise the alarm.

The entrance to the secret passage was behind the old, broken-down boiler. There was no point in trying to conceal her movements. He might not be able to see her, but he would hear the shrill screech of the boiler as she heaved it out of the way. He wouldn't chance another shot. All the same, he was stronger than she. He could kill her with his bare hands.

It was now or never.

She ran at the boiler with arms crossed over her breasts. The impact knocked her back on her heels, but the boiler wasn't nearly as solid as it looked, and it moved a good two feet, giving her enough space to squeeze through.

He heard the sound and came after her.

If she'd had time, she would have pushed the boiler back on its tracks, but he was only a step behind, and she had to run the race of her life.

He didn't have everything his own way. He thought that she had a gun. It made him cautious, fearing, no doubt, that any bullet fired would bounce off the walls and would hit him and not his intended victim.

Her thoughts raced ahead. When she came to the end of the tunnel, she would come to the holding pen where the smugglers once stored their contraband. She could hide there, but not for long. He *had* to kill her. Without the body, there would be no death certificate and no fortune to claim. She had to outrun him.

One moment she was running like a deer; the next, she was like an arrow shot from a bow. When she came to the holding pen, she flattened herself against the wall and covered her mouth with her hand to stifle the sound of her breathing. Her legs were cramping; there was a stitch in her side.

"Why don't we stop this nonsense and come to terms?" came that hateful voice.

She gulped in air, steeling herself for what she knew she had to do next. The tomblike tunnel was right behind her. She could feel the cold air ruffle her skirts.

The touch of that cool air on her ankles gave her fresh hope. It was like an omen. Where there was a way in, there was a way out.

"Did you hear me, Kate?"

"Oh, I heard you. The trouble is, I don't believe you."

"Why are you bothering?" he asked pleasantly. "They're all dead, you know. I saw to that."

The time for talking was over.

She sank to her knees and entered the tunnel. The thought that all this fiend need do was drag her back by her heels and finish her off with his bare hands was a powerful incentive. The long, narrow passage no longer seemed like a tomb. It was the gateway to her salvation.

Fight him tooth and nail, Kate.

The voice sent a burst of energy to every pulse point in her body. She could feel it burning through her blood, clearing her mind of everything but the one thing that mattered. *She had to kill him.*

She shut her mind to the claustrophobic crawl space, dragged up her skirts, and scurried on her knees down the tunnel toward freedom.

As she advanced, the air began to smell sweeter, cooler. When she dragged herself through to the outside, her brain registered the fingers of dawn reaching up toward the night sky, but she did not savor the beauty of it. She was looking for a weapon, but on that heather-clad slope, there were only small stones that wouldn't put a dent in a pudding.

"So there you are!"

She spun around to see him drag himself out of the tunnel. He was blinking rapidly as his eyes became accustomed to the light. Her night vision was no advantage now.

Fight him, Kate. Fight him tooth and nail.

The old Kate would have been running for her life. The new Kate stood her ground. It was just like her dream. She might die in the attempt, but she had to fight.

When he was still on his knees, she lashed out with her foot. The blow sent his gun in a perfect arc, and it slithered into a clump of heather.

"That won't help you." He had pulled himself to his feet. "Go on, run for the gun or try to run away. I'll be on you in seconds and—"

The element of surprise cut him off in mid-sentence. With head lowered, she charged. The force of the impact drove him back against the wall. Enraged, he drove the air from her lungs with a blow from his fist.

She had the good sense to dodge out of his reach. Keeping a wary eye on him, she gulped in air.

He was so sure that he had crushed her that he sauntered toward her with a smile on his face. "I don't need a gun to finish you off," he said.

She wiped the tears from her eyes and hung her head as though she had no more fight left. "No, please, no," she quavered.

"You won't feel a thing," he crooned.

Nails like talons, she launched herself at him, taking him off guard. He howled as she dug them into the soft flesh of his cheeks and dragged them to his chin.

"Explain those scratches to the police when they come to question you," she panted.

When he came for her again, she brought her knee up and connected solidly with his groin. As he went down, he brought her with him. Air whooshed out of her lungs.

"Gavin," she croaked out. "I knew you would come for me."

It was a ruse to get him to turn his head. Massey was completely taken in. When he turned to follow the direction of her eyes, she wound her arms tight around him and sank her teeth into the softest part of his ear. He screamed, he squirmed, he bucked. She held on for dear life. Blood filled her mouth and ran in a rivulet down her chin, and she exulted in it.

She was tiring. She couldn't hold on much longer. But he wouldn't get away with her murder. She'd left her mark on him for all time.

She heard him before she saw him. Gavin! His face looked drawn and haggard. Breath was rasping in and out of his lungs. His clothes were torn and tattered. But he was *alive*.

She had only moments to register that Gavin was in no condition to help her. When Massey pushed out of her arms, she cried out, "Watch out, Gavin! He's looking for his gun!"

Gavin came to a stumbling halt and sank to his knees in front of her. "I can't help you," he gasped out, "not this time. I can't even hold a gun. Here, you'll need this."

She opened her hand and automatically accepted the gun he had given her, her own pocket revolver. It fit her hand as though it were part of her.

"I don't understand," she said. "Where is your gun?"

"I left it at the house. Shh!" He put his finger to her lips to silence her. "Do your stuff, Kate. We're all depending on you."

Avery had found his gun. He waved it in a show of victory as he hobbled back to them. Kate rose to her feet. "Who wants to go first?" he cried, his gaze moving from Gavin to Kate.

"I will." Kate raised her weapon. Both shots were fired at the same moment. Only one shot found its mark.

Twenty-six

"Everyone is staring at us," Kate whispered in her husband's ear.

"That's because," Gavin responded, "you look as though you've been at the wars. It's most uncommon for the bride to turn up at her wedding with a black eye."

"Or for her groom to be concealing a mass of bruises beneath his fine clothes."

"Ah, but no one knows about that except Calley and you. Must keep up appearances, you know. The ladies expect it."

"*I'm* the only lady you need to impress now, Hepburn."

"*You're* the only lady I have ever wanted to impress, Mrs. Hepburn."

Smiling, arm in arm, they moved among their guests, dispensing little packages of a fruitcake that would still be edible for years to come. Gavin couldn't shudder because it hurt, but he wanted to. Evidently, in the Highlands, that was how the natives preferred their wedding cake. He'd already made up his mind that if there was any cake left over, he would feed it to Macduff for services rendered. Poor Macduff wasn't fit to mix with company. His hair had fallen out, and two legs were in splints, but he was on the mend. He thought he might erect a cairn to his dog. If it were not for Macduff, they would all be dead.

Three days had passed since Kate's bullet had pierced a hole right between her cousin's eyes, three days of hiding out with the tinkers until their names were cleared. After a terse telegram from the Home Office had arrived at Ballater, the police immediately turned their attention on Massey's pseudo parents who were now singing like canaries. They had no idea what their employer was up to, they swore. They needed the money. May God strike them down dead if they told a lie.

That little drama had still to play out. Meantime, Kate's mother and Magda had worked tirelessly to make sure that the reception went off without a hitch, not in Braemar as they originally planned, but in the closest hotel to where most of the guests had assembled, the hotel where Kate's adventure with Gavin had begun.

"You're not superstitious?" he whispered in her ear.

"Why should I be? I'm a witch."

"You're sure of that?"

She stopped dispensing her packages of wedding cake. "Gavin," she said, "the first time in my life I ever fired a gun, I hit my target exactly where I aimed it. Of course I'm sure."

Her eyes wandered over the groups of people, and a little frown hovered on her brow.

"What is it?" Gavin asked.

"Everything is the same as it was at Juliet's reception, yet everything is different."

"Yes, everyone likes a wedding, especially a love match."

Kate's eyes were trained on her sister. She said slowly, "Magda looks like a woman in love. Look, Gavin, she's smiling."

"I've heard that love brings out the best in us."

Magda moved her head, giving Kate a clear view of the gentleman who held her attention. "Dalziel?" Kate said and laughed. "How very appropriate! She *has* changed!"

"And so have we. Love changes us." He made a face. "Did I just use a four letter word?"

"I'm not letting you take it back!"

"Did I ask you to? Enough philosophizing. It's time to fetch a glass of wine for my beautiful wife."

She caught his wrist before he could move away. "And what do you see when you look at me, Gavin? Mmm?"

"Pots of money," he answered at once. "I've snagged myself a rich wife and am the envy of every man here."

She tossed her head. "If you are referring to the money that comes to me from my grandfather, you can forget about that. It's evil money, and I refuse to accept a penny of it."

"Money isn't evil, Kate, it's the *love* of money that is evil. Don't you know your Bible? What if we were to give it away to a worthy cause?"

"What worthy cause?" she asked suspiciously.

"Will's clinics. With enough money to fund them, they could attract young doctors to the area. As it is, the Braemar clinic is on its last legs. The one in Aberdeen can't be far behind. Will's determination to keep them running made all the difference."

She warmed to the idea. "And I'd like to do something

special for the Nazarene nuns as well. They were very kind to my mother."

"They weren't the only ones who were kind to your mother." To the question in her eyes, he answered, "Have you forgotten the lady in the carriage who was waiting at the gates of the convent?"

"No. I shall never forget her. I wish there was some way I could thank her."

"Perhaps you can. She's here."

"She's here?" Kate was astonished.

"She has always been close by, keeping an eye on you."

"Who is she?"

"That's for you to find out."

The aggravating man was gone before she had time to ask her next question. Her gaze came to rest on her parents. After a moment's reflection, she dismissed her mother as the lady in the carriage. Mama couldn't keep secrets, and surely there would have been a hint or two over the years to rouse her suspicions.

The next subject she studied was Mrs. Cardno, but only because Juliet's mother sat down beside her. "Well," said Kate, "you said you wanted an adventure. You should be satisfied."

The habitual twinkle in the old lady's eyes brightened considerably. "I wanted to tell you, but I couldn't. You were safe only as long as I kept my silence. Now that the danger is over, I can freely admit that I've been watching over you. How clever of you to work it out."

"But . . . I haven't worked anything out."

"You haven't? You don't know that I was the lady in the carriage outside the convent?"

Kate's mouth formed a round O.

Mrs. Cardno reached out and patted Kate's hand. "There's much to tell you about your mother and me. We were like sisters, but this isn't the time or place."

"You told my husband, but you couldn't tell me?" Kate couldn't hide the hurt in her tone.

"No. He worked it out without any help from me."

A barrage of questions hovered on Kate's tongue, but her good friend Sally Anderson plopped herself down on the vacant chair on the other side of her, and she was forced to swallow her words.

Mrs. Cardno got up. "We'll talk later," she said, eyeing Sally's mulish expression. "I think you two young things have a lot to say to each other." In a flurry of skirts, she disappeared into the crush.

"What is it, Sally?" Kate asked. "What has put that look on your face?"

Sally ground her teeth. "Cedric," she said, "has broken off our engagement. Seems I'm not good enough for him."

Kate looked over at the group of people who were hanging on her father's words. She was never in any doubt what the topic of conversation would be: the Knights Templar of Deeside. Cedric looked enthralled, animated. He no longer had the look of a bored socialite.

"I thought," she said, "that you and Cedric had it all worked out? He had the title, and you had the money, and after the ceremony you would go your separate ways?"

"Cedric is no longer interested in money," Sally replied acidly. "He has fallen in love."

"What?!"

"And you'll never guess who the lucky girl is."

Kate shook her head.

"Your sister Magda." Glittering green eyes bored into Kate's. "Well, she can't have him. Cedric is mine, and I mean to fight for him."

Kate was shaking with laughter when Gavin returned with her wine.

"What's the joke?" he asked.

She choked out between breaths, " 'Love changes us.' Those were your very words. I think, my dear wizard, that you'll be surprised at what love can do. If I'm not mistaken, a brawl will soon get under way. Yes, yes. Look at Dalziel! If looks could kill, Cedric would be dead."

"Now this is interesting," said her husband, sitting down beside her. "There's nothing I like better than a good brawl. But Dalziel? There's not an angry bone in his—Wow! Dalziel has certainly learned a thing or two in the last little while. He must be taking lessons."

"I wish Calley were here to see the change in him. He would be proud of Dalziel."

"You know that Calley doesn't feel comfortable in a social setting, and Macduff likes them only too well. He'd be right in there, chasing off anyone who laid a hand on Dalziel."

Kate sat back, preparing to enjoy the spectacle. As was usual, it started as a shoving match, on this occasion, between Dalziel and Cedric. Then her cousins got involved. Didn't they always? As more gentlemen joined the fray, the fiddlers played louder and louder. When glasses and other missiles came flying, however, she thought it prudent to leave. Gavin, after all, wasn't fit to fight his way out of bed much less defend himself.

"Time to go," she shouted above the din.

Gavin looked at the tall, walnut cabinet clock that chimed the hour. The witching hour. He nodded. "Time for all good little witches and warlocks to be in their beds."

Arm in arm, they left the reception together.

"Now," said Kate as they made their way to their room, "you have a lot of explaining to do, and you can begin by telling me how you figured out who the lady in the carriage was."

* * *

In the wee hours of the morning, when nothing was stirring, the tinkers struck camp and set out for warmer climes. Before long, they came to a branch in the road and stopped.

"What are they doing?" Kate whispered.

She and Gavin were in one of the tinkers' homes on wheels, as warm as toast, under a blue tarpaulin stretched over a sturdy frame. Their driver jumped down from the box and, after unhitching the horse, bid them a courtly good night, then became one with the shadows as he joined his friends.

"They're trying to decide," said Gavin, "whether they should return to Maryculter or take the route over the peaks that leads to Perthshire and its softer air. And before you ask, no, I didn't read anyone's thoughts. That's not my gift. Yours is the only person's mind I can get into, and only if you're willing. Wee Alfie told me that they'd set up camp here, but we are free to go with them or stay as we please."

He cocked his head to the side. "It's what you wanted, isn't it, footloose and fancy-free? 'We can go where the whim takes us.' Those were your words before we embarked on this unconventional honeymoon."

Her cat's eyes had never been keener as she smiled up at him. He took her breath away, this husband of hers, not because he was handsome, but because beneath the civilized veneer, he was made in the image of a Knight Templar. He was a warrior when he needed to be and a healer when the occasion demanded. There was a time she'd thought that he collected strays, but it was the other way around. They found him.

Her lips, suddenly fierce, covered his. She wound her arms around him and held on tight. Tomorrow, they would decide whether to go or stay. Tonight, in each other's arms, under the stars, was where they were meant to be.

"Read my mind," she said.

"I love you, too," he said, and kissed her.

Discover Romance

berkleyjoveauthors.com

See what's coming up next from your
favorite romance authors and explore all
the latest Berkley, Jove, and Sensation
selections.

See what's new

~

Find author appearances

~

Win fantastic prizes

~

Get reading recommendations

~

Chat with authors and other fans

~

Read interviews with authors you love

*Enter the rich world of
historical romance
with Berkley Books . . .*

Madeline Hunter

Jennifer Ashley

Joanna Bourne

Lynn Kurland

Jodi Thomas

Anne Gracie

Love is timeless.

berkleyjoveauthors.com

Penguin Group (USA) Online

What will you be reading tomorrow?

Patricia Cornwell, Nora Roberts, Catherine Coulter,
Ken Follett, John Sandford, Clive Cussler,
Tom Clancy, Laurell K. Hamilton, Charlaine Harris,
J. R. Ward, W.E.B. Griffin, William Gibson,
Robin Cook, Brian Jacques, Stephen King,
Dean Koontz, Eric Jerome Dickey, Terry McMillan,
Sue Monk Kidd, Amy Tan, Jayne Ann Krentz,
Daniel Silva, Kate Jacobs…

You'll find them all at
penguin.com

Read ex
find tour schedu
an

Subscribe to Peng
and get a
at exciting new t
long befo

PENGU

penguin.com